HELLO DOWN THERE

Michael Parker

Thorndike Press • Thorndike, Maine

Library of Congress Cataloging in Publication Data:

Parker, Michael, 1959-
    Hello down there : a novel / Michael Parker.
        p.   cm.
    ISBN 1-56054-671-9 (alk. paper : lg. print)
    1. Large type books. I. Title.
[PR6066.A66H4   1993b]   92-47099
823'.914—dc20   CIP

Thorndike Large Print® General Series edition published
in 1993 by arrangement with Charles Scribner's Sons.

Cover design by Victor Cormier.

The tree indicium is a trademark of Thorndike Press.

This book is printed on acid-free, high opacity paper. ∞

For Cate

PROLOGUE

Lake Mattamuskeet, North Carolina, October 1950

Midway through the morning prayer, Edwin rubbed a patch in the pinestraw with his boot toe, shredded his cigarette into the sand. He kept his eyes on the men gathered in the yard, tracked the fit of stretch and yawn spreading among them. Yawns signaled asleep, stretches awake; by the time Byron Teague muffled his amen, the tally was tied, convincing Edwin of something he'd suspected before he'd even arrived at Mattamuskeet: that he was the only one not sleepwalking.

Byron Teague launched into a short history of this hunt, which Edwin's mother claimed had become as crucial to Tidewater commerce over the years as many of the more prominent annual gatherings: the Terpsichorean Club ball, the Carolina-State game. This was Edwin's first hunt — he was there only because he was engaged to Byron's daughter Sarah — and so far the weekend had been

7

both loud and bland, like Byron's historical sketch. Edwin had approached it with the scrupulous regard given things put off for years, in this case six, as he'd managed to excuse himself from these hunts since he'd turned sixteen. Driving down the day before through the off-white shades of October coastal plain, he'd imagined his father's friends asking what he planned to do with a degree in European history, guys he'd grown up with ribbing him about his engagement.

Yet so far everyone had ignored him, and he had yet to witness any business negotiations to support his mother's claim. Perhaps Tidewater commerce was settled surreptitiously: timber deals struck in duck blinds, junior loan officers named while crouched in the rustling savannah. Edwin imagined a back room in the lodge where corporations were formed, marriages arranged, road-paving bids rigged.

At the back of the crowd, Edwin noticed Sarah's older brother Skipper and Camp Tremont studying the ground as if Byron were still blessing the hunt. The night before Edwin had eaten a late supper with Skipper and this young lawyer friend of his from Richmond named Cary Tremont, whom everyone called Camp. The rounds of brunswick stew and bourbon had continued well past midnight, when Edwin had wandered off to find his bunk. Skipper and Camp looked to have seen the sun rise. Grimacing to hold back snickers, their face muscles tightened, toning beer-bloated cheeks. Tremont leaned over to whisper just as a flock of geese passed overhead, laughter badly camouflaged as cough drowning out most of the honking which Edwin heard for the first and last time that day.

When the crowd dispersed into the marsh, Edwin followed Skipper and Camp down a side trail. Both walked with their heads down, pushing boots through thick sand.

"This'll do," said Skipper when they came to the edge of the marsh. He and Tremont collapsed beneath some pines.

"Got the big face today," said Tremont.

"Bad," agreed Skipper. He tried to pull his cap off but Tremont snatched it and slid it back on, slanting the bill low like a visor.

"Apply pressure to wounded area," he said.

Tremont grinned at Edwin and picked up the thread of stories he'd begun last night: mock hunting tales in which he was the hero hunter and the heroine-hunted was repetitively buxom and willing.

After an hour of Camp's tales, Edwin gave in and took a drink from the flask of bourbon they passed.

"I dub this spot Camp Tremont," said

Camp Tremont by way of a toast.

"You dub every spot Camp Tremont," said Skipper.

"Wherever I happen to be happens to be Camp Tremont."

A few minutes of half-hearted talk about classes and grades — Skipper and Edwin were in their last year at Chapel Hill — was followed by a long silence during which Skipper nodded off and Tremont caught Edwin staring at him.

"How'd you happen to catch up to the name of Camp?" said Edwin.

Tremont grinned. Edwin sweated, and considered his sentence. *Catch up to the name of Camp?* Suddenly he was self-conscious enough to analyze every word out of his mouth. Talk for him had always been reflexive. He'd never seen the point in weighing words; thoughtful replies were for sluggards. Now the thought of thinking-it-out intimidated him.

He had hoped to prod another hunting tale. He liked Camp Tremont better when he was talking; during the silences Edwin felt as if Tremont had been appointed by the court to represent him for a crime more embarrassing than heinous. Camp was his reluctant counsel, Camp was just doing his job. As Camp's unquestionably guilty client, everything Edwin said was both suspect and humorous, and though Tremont refrained from laughing out-

10

right, the seeds of his smile remained tucked in the corners of his mouth.

"Beats me, Ed," said Camp. "One of those things about which the origins ain't too clear and probably better that way."

"One of the many, many things," said Skipper.

This sent them both into laughter dead-ending in coughs and gasps, which they washed away with slugs of whiskey and water. Camp stretched out in the scant shade of a loblolly.

"Welcome to Camp Tremont," he said.

"Are we going to do any hunting today?" asked Edwin.

"In the very near future," said Camp. "And the very near future is nigh."

Edwin grew aware of his breathing, how wispy it seemed compared to his partners' vigorous puffing.

"I thought you said you weren't all that big on hunting, Edwin," said Skipper. "I believe I remember you saying last night how you just like to walk around in the woods, listen to the birds sing."

Glowing from a shot of bourbon, Edwin had admitted being stirred to an autumnal wistfulness by the sound of geese overhead. Afterwards he'd sipped chaser and hoped it would be forgotten. *Things I say can and will be used against me,* he thought.

"Like going to a whorehouse for the god-damn conversation," said Skipper.

"Nope," said Camp Tremont. "Wrong. Like going to a whorehouse just to watch."

Skipper's laughter interrupted reports drifting across still, blue Mattamuskeet.

"So you think it's wrong to shoot animals?" said Camp.

"Wrong?" said Edwin.

"Immoral."

Edwin had never thought about it. He didn't like to hunt because it bored him. Not the hikes through early morning forests nor the endless waits for quarry to emerge from thickets. Not even the hold-your-breath-and-turn-into-a-tree part. It was the company — the men his father hunted with, his cousins back in Trent — who bored him. A lot of activities were like that for him: he loved to swim, but after he joined the school team and had to compete against Jeffrey Register, he'd hated the smell of chlorine.

"No, I don't think it's immoral."

Tremont smiled and waited, cajoling with his court-appointed patience what Edwin knew to be a pat, if noble, response.

"As long as you eat what you kill."

"And marry what you fuck?" said Skipper.

"Don't think it's quite the same thing," said Edwin.

12

"No, you're right," said Tremont. "It's not the same thing, quite. You can get milk free from a moo-cow, can't you, Edwin?"

More shots sounded. Edwin stared across the lake. Morning sun touched Mattamuskeet, turning the water silver and outlining the lone, lightning-scarred trunk of a tupelo gum. Edwin couldn't think, could not respond. What exactly were they saying here? What exactly were they accusing him of?

"Already started shooting at each other over there," said Skipper.

"Maybe they're shooting at their in-laws," said Camp.

Skipper grinned. "Edwin's going to make a fine brother-in-law. Tell you what, some of them that Sarah's brought home? I wouldn't want to spend the rest of my days sitting across Sunday dinner from them. No, Edwin's the pick of the lot, Camp."

"Already a part of the family, huh?" Camp raised his flask. "To Teaguedom: may it never, ever take a tumble." He passed Edwin the bourbon, and said, "Might as well tell us how Skip's little sister is in reality."

Edwin dragged the back of his hand across his mouth and looked up at Camp.

"In the sack he means," said Skipper.

"The sack's real," said Camp. "Sack's the only really real thing there is."

13

Skipper scooped a handful of sand. "Ain't this real?"

"That's Camp Tremont."

Skipper fanned his fist out, letting the sand drizzle down. He rubbed his palms together and said to Edwin, "Don't just sit there acting uppity. I know goddamn well she's giving it to you."

"Smell it at the dinner table, can't you, Skip?" said Camp Tremont. "I swear: the unmistakable aroma of premarital sex. Can't wash it off until you're dead and married." He reached for the flask. "Tell him the truth, or what you told me anyhow."

"I watched y'all once. At the beach that time, in the boathouse? Saw y'all sneak off and followed you down there."

"And how would you rate that performance?" asked Camp.

"Offhand I'd say he's not a distance man. 'Course what do I know, could've been his first time."

"And how she'd do?" asked Camp.

"None of your business. We're talking about my baby sister."

"You're the one talking," said Camp. "Anyway, to hell with you both. I've seen it all before. In 3-D without the movie glasses."

"You saying my baby sister has been to Camp Tremont?"

"All I'm saying's that your baby sister has tasted reality."

When more shots sounded from the far shore, Edwin turned again toward the lake. The baccharis and juncus shoots surrounding it were thick and waist-high, and from where he sat the marsh looked deceptively solid, as if he could walk out to the water's edge without sinking into the muck. He imagined walking and sinking, saw himself pulling his boots from the bubbly sludge, heard the sucking noise the marsh would make as his footprints filled with water.

He stood and dusted sand from his khakis. "I'm going."

"Edwin says he's going, Skip," said Camp.

"Well, hell, Camp, if Edwin's ready to go, let's go," said Skipper.

The two rose slowly from the ground and shuffled down the path, loosely cradling their guns. Edwin followed behind again, keeping the backs of their heads sighted as the path twisted through the scrub and struggling against the tug of those feelings he hated relishing: self-pity and rectitude, censure and shame. *I don't have to be here,* he thought, *but here I am.* Suddenly his decision to attend this hunt seemed more significant, more pivotal, than the night in August when he'd proposed to Sarah. He heard his mother talking of how important this hunt would be to him in later life, heard in her enunciation of *later* and *life* the fervency with which evangelists spoke of the afterlife. A few feet ahead of him Camp and Skipper snickered. *But I am just as guilty as they are, even more because I promised I'd marry her. Because I continue to sleep with her even though I don't love her.*

He thought of how he always gave in, how readily he succumbed to her ambiguous hints. During these times his lack of resistance was as powerful and as consuming as any obstruction could ever be. *Here I am at the whorehouse, only this time I'm not here just to watch.*

As Edwin fell, dust rose between him and his partners, mixed with a wisp of smoke. Small animals rustled through the scrub as the ringing died down, and from the brush on either side of the trail Camp and Skipper raised their heads. Twisting around to see his boot snared on the root, Edwin pushed himself up off his hands and knees and turned to find them staring up at him, their faces gone thin and quizzical.

Grinning, Edwin reached for his gun. "Sorry," he said. "I tripped."

Three days later, back at school, Edwin met his friend Will Thomasson coming out of the library. They sat down on the steps to talk, facing the teeming quad. Thomasson asked if it were really true.

"What 'it'?" said Edwin.

"You shooting at Skipper Teague and his pal."

"Camp Tremont is his name and I tripped," said Edwin.

"They're claiming it was deliberate. According to Skipper they'd been teasing you about Sarah. So you took a potshot."

"Oh."

"Pretty drastic, but I approve in theory."

"Thanks."

"Yep. Now Skipper's saying he doesn't want you to marry his sister. Swears you're unstable, not to mention 'superior acting.' I'm not sure if he meant you act superior or you think you are. The latter I'd guess. Also he says you've taken advantage of his little sister. Or did he say compromise?"

"What exactly is the difference between the two?"

"Taken advantage of seems the harsher to me, but I think that even if he said compromised, he meant taken advantage of. Compromised suggests some compliance on her part. I don't think that's what he means."

"No, me neither."

"He talks bad about you all the time now."

"Changed his tune. He used to like me."

"True. Last week he liked you. He liked you before you tried to shoot him. All this from a boy who has never, in the time I've known him, changed his mind about anything."

"He's a Teague. His mind was made up for him before he was conceived."

"Still, one would think he could forget your trying to kill him. It was all in a weekend of drink and hunt and fun."

"Wasn't that much fun," said Edwin. "Besides, I'm telling you I tripped. The damn gun went off. Skipper and Tremont were safe by yards. I won't deny that I hate Camp Tremont and I won't say I've never been tempted to kill anyone. But I always curb these tendencies, and not so dramatically in the nick of time. Days before my breaking point. Whole months."

"Quite a time frame you got there," said Thomasson.

"Look," said Edwin. "Me shoot Skipper Teague? Shooting him wouldn't change him. Like you said, he never changes his mind."

"Well, he's changed it," said Thomasson. "It seems shooting *at* him had more effect than shooting him."

"I tripped," said Edwin. "The gun went off. I'm no hunter."

"What'd you go down there for, then?"

18

"For Sarah," said Edwin. "And my mother. She's been bugging me to go since I was sixteen."

"For Sarah and your mother you spend the weekend with drunk judges and traipse around the woods with a guy called Camp whom you hate so much you try to shoot and who by the way, while we're on the subject, is Skipper's choice to replace you as the fiancé of his kid sister, I hear."

"Camp Tremont?"

"Skipper told me they used to go out and that Tremont was all of a sudden interested again and that, since you tried to kill them and all, he doesn't really see why he should go around acting loyal to you anymore."

"Camp Tremont?"

A coed trudging up the library steps looked at Edwin, then quickly down at her shoes. Only when she passed did Edwin realize how he was staring at her, that she was beautiful.

Thomasson laughed and said, "You should see your face right now. God, you hate this Tremont guy."

"Yes. I do. I hate him, but for no damn good reason. I mean I have reasons, but they aren't good reasons especially, or any real different ones. And why do I hate him so much and not my father or my uncle or Skipper? The problem is, I do hate him but I can't

19

say why exactly."

"Maybe you ought to try, instead of pointing a shotgun at him and pulling the trigger."

"I will," said Edwin. "I'll sit down one of these days and do that. Try to put it in words."

1

August 1952

He'd been staring at beige islands left by roof leaks in the ceiling when he spotted the hospital bed rising in the front of the drugstore. Stepping onto the bottom rung of his stool, Roy Green noticed the woman bound by the sheet and the tightly belted straps. Becalmed, basking in the stares of customers, she hovered above the round rack of walking canes hand-carved by the blind while Walter Lehmann, owner of the store, raised and lowered alternate parts of her, forcing her body into long-lost marvels of agility. Lehmann's sales pitch rose as the bed was lowered, the words *comfort* and *versatile* interspersed with the creaking of the hand crank.

This vision arose from that hour which Roy relished, the crack through which the here and now fell daily after his last bite of lunch. As his eyes drifted across the details of this building which after seven years he had come to know as intimately as the body of a lover —

paint peels on the walls had become erotic birthmarks, waterspots above the soda fountain freckles dappling the back of a drowsing woman — Roy ignored his work to daydream.

Today's was a familiar one: his first night here in Trent, North Carolina, which he'd spent at Lehmann's house out on River Road. Five minutes after he arrived, Lehmann had made a fussy presentation of a set of store keys, calling in sweaty children from far backyards to witness this ceremony which, according to Lehmann, represented his "utter trust" in his new pharmacist. They'd had a quick drink on the front porch. Skeleton keys bulged in Roy's pocket, bothering him. He couldn't get used to them; no amount of shifting in the wicker settee could make their presence fade. "I see," said Roy in response to Lehmann's abbreviated history of Trent, and "Is that right?" After five minutes Lehmann stood in the middle of a sentence, shook Roy's hand, and disappeared into a side parlor where his family was waiting. The door sucked shut behind him. For a moment, Roy stood frozen on the porch listening to the focus of radio waves, tuned finally to raucous applause. Above the laughter from a live studio audience rose Lehmann's self-conscious snicker, the hair-triggered titters of a daughter. It was eight-thirty on an August evening, darkness puddling in hedge shadows to seep across lawns. Roy took a long walk around town, through neighborhoods which he did not then realize would never seem the same once they acquired a context, once transformed into shortcuts to the grocery store, streets where coworkers lived, a route taken to avoid the cotton mill at shift change.

He'd not been back to Lehmann's house in the seven years since. The next day he'd left before anyone else was awake, had gone immediately to work, encountering on the back stoop the first thing he'd met this morning: a pallid Benson Fann awaiting his morning Bromo. Because Roy was first-day-on-the-job nervous he had given it to him, just as he'd been giving it to him daily since, excepting his week's vacation and Benson Fann's brief stabs at sobriety. Later, when Lehmann arrived, Roy had suggested that the soda jerk should serve Bromo-Seltzers, had even questioned the ethics of lacing a Bromo with ethyl alcohol. Lehmann had said only that it wasn't worth his worrying over, leaving Roy to discover later that Benson Fann's law office was in a building across the street owned by Lehmann, that for years Lehmann had been performing various pharmaceutical favors to entice him to stay put in the overpriced and undermaintained space.

Down in front Lehmann continued to maneuver the body of the woman into lissome feats.

"What he ought to do is give rides on that thing 'stead of trying to sell it," Ruby McClaurin called to Roy. She'd hiked herself onto the silver curve of the drinkbox to see better. Roy smiled, shook his head in agreement. He'd liked it better when he'd first spotted the woman rising, when she had interrupted his reverie to float upwards through the early afternoon light. He'd liked it better before he'd realized what was happening, before he'd noticed that everyone else was watching, before he understood that this vision was not solely his.

Even after he'd spotted his boss at the hand crank there had remained a hint of the unreal. Lehmann as magician performing two standards at once: levitation and that old crowd-pleasing severance routine. The latter was done without benefit of hand-sawed coffin but just as impressive to Roy since there was a point when the old woman's neck and shoulders rose slowly above the hair-care aisle, sheet taut across collarbones giving her the fade-to-cloudbank look of a beauty queen's yearbook photograph.

Now Lehmann had left the crank and moved in close to a man standing by the headboard. The man crossed his thin arms and stared at Lehmann, then down at the woman Roy had decided was his wife. Hair splayed across the striped and caseless pillow, her stiff body a low ridge of dips and knobs, she seemed to have fallen into a coma. An appropriate reaction to Lehmann's spiel, thought Roy, and he wished he could return to his own post-lunch coma. He longed for that benumbed tingle which he could only compare, poorly, to the slow sensory bubble induced by antihistamines. As Lehmann and the husband haggled over the price of the hospital bed, Roy decided it was time to go back to work.

But after a moment, a few counted pills, he looked up at the ceiling and fell through the crack again, remembered the way the store had seemed to him during his first afternoons there. Almost exactly as it did now: in two years, the building would be sixty years old, but it had not weathered the years well: the chop of ceiling fans shook loose flakes of paint, and sections of the plaster walls were spackled and lumpy.

Still, in warm weather the doors stayed open all day long. Sunlight stretched down the aisles, wavering like light under water, spotting the dusty sundries with a brilliance that seemed to Roy an amazing feat of advertising

Lehmann had worked out with nature to high-light what did not sell. Brand names faded on slow-moving merchandise and the gold-tipped walking canes which filled the display rack were hot to the touch. Even when there was no sun, during storms and the truncated arcs of grey February days, there was comfort in the dankness. In shadowed back aisles Roy imagined hearing products with a short shelf life gasping for breath, struggling to stay put past that date when it was decreed that they would *go bad*. It deepened his connection to the space, this battle for air and light.

There was a flash at the end of his counter. Roy turned to see Speight, the new stockman. Speight propped his pushbroom on the counter edge and stood there as if he'd been summoned for a delivery. Since Jones, the de-livery man, had quit the week before, Speight had been handling both jobs.

"Not got a thing for you yet, Speight," said Roy.

Speight nodded. He rarely acknowledged anything or anyone except with an unreadable nod, so slight that Roy often wondered in ret-rospect if it was not imagined. He moved through the drugstore without making a sound, moved through the world with not much more than the minimum noises, the req-uisite words. Several times he had surprised

Roy behind the drug counter, a grey blur, brief as a squirrel's plunge down a tree trunk. Roy would pivot to find him rounding a corner of one of the short aisles where the drugs were stocked, the pushbroom he dragged an inversion of his profile: he was shoulders and thin limbs, in silhouette a coat hanger dangling a suit of wet clothes.

Speight nodded but did not move, only shifted feet, batted the broom handle between thumb and forefinger, stared at a place just to the left of Roy's right ear. Roy took advantage of this hesitation to study the face of this man who before now had hung about only as long as it took him to nod. He found himself staring at Speight's jaw: a jut of bone, flesh cracked and brittle as sunbaked mudflats. When Speight looked away once, Roy was struck with the idea that someday only that jawbone would remain. He imagined it resting finally in some ravine, beneath an implacable patch of kudzu alongside other severed parts of things — a sprocket from the engine of an abandoned truck, half of a rusty-hinged shed door — to be discovered by a circle of eight-year-olds choking over first cigarettes.

The phone rang. Speight twitched at the noise and scanned the countertop for the phone; Roy ignored the ring, shuddering over the image he'd conjured. What did he care where the stockman's bones ended up? When he looked up Speight was still staring at the phone, as if they would both be fired if Roy didn't pick up immediately.

"Somebody else can get it," said Roy. "Ruby or Miss lipstick counter. What's her name now? They come and go so often I just call them all Miss lipstick counter." When Speight didn't answer — it didn't seem likely after all that he would know her name — Roy hiked himself up on his stool, saw that the girl was still at lunch. Ruby had a customer but only one, a kid, probably wanted a Coke. Ruby could talk on the phone and draw a Coke at the same time, Roy had seen her do it, a patch of her bobbed hair tamped flat by the earpiece, Coke frothing over the rim of the glass.

"Was there something else you wanted, Speight?" Roy wanted what little was left of his doldrum, wanted to fill it with things soothing and familiar, not images of decomposing bone, bugs swarming over a skeleton.

"About Jones quitting?"

"Tired of doing his job and yours, too? Can't blame you."

"Not that so much as I got a boy needs work. Heard you say you was thinking of hiring a boy after school to run deliveries. Say you might? 'Cause my boy needs work bad here."

"How old's this boy?" Ruby had mentioned that Speight's wife had died soon after their youngest son was born, that Speight was father to seven children — five girls unfolding over a decade like a string of paper dolls, sons posted sentry at either end.

"Ten or twelve," said Speight. "Thereabouts."

"And what kind of boy is he?" Speight winced, shifted. The phone rang again and he seemed relieved, sure that these questions would be interrupted now, that the interrogation would be forgotten once Roy hung up. But again Roy made no move toward the phone.

"He's average."

"Average," said Roy. He was beginning to enjoy this, his one and only conversation with Speight, if this scant back and forth could be called conversation. "Don't worry about the phone. If they want what they want bad enough, they'll hang on. And Lehmann can't even hear it, he's too busy spitting into that poor man's face up there, trying to get another dollar out of him. So tell me more about this average boy of yours."

"Smart for his age but undersized."

Roy slipped his stool up and sat. "Tell me

this: does this boy talk any more than you do?"

Speight pretended not to notice the next ring, though there was hope evident in the way his body tensed at the sound of it, still affected by the off-chance it would change things. This is hard for him, thought Roy; he's probably one of those people who hates phones, who equate phone ring with siren. Still, he was interested in hearing from Speight, although he realized that one of the things he found fascinating about him was the fact that he never talked about himself. After nine hours a day of listening to people's problems, many of them imagined and nearly all embellished, a man who never offered anything of himself nor asked anything of others was a welcome, if enigmatic, distraction.

Speight seemed to have sensed that Roy was having fun with all this; the corners of his lips were tucked sullenly into his whiskery cheeks, his eyes had tightened with a passive but concentrated irritation.

"He loves to talk. But people tell me he's got something to say."

"Who tells you that?" When Roy looked away for a minute, out over the store, he noticed Ruby glaring at him. The aisle in front of her fountain was thick with kids jingling loose change in their fists. To hell with her, thought Roy, I didn't go to college to let some counter girl intimidate me into answering the phone, yet when it rang again he threw a hand up, raised an index finger to deflect her, to signal also the importance of this moment. Speight opening up. Newly expansive Speight breaking into monosyllables, sentences.

"His sisters. Some teachers." Roy scrutinized Speight's face for a hint of pride but found nothing, no change. Teachers would not be big in the mute and economical world of Speight, he realized, and for some reason this made him smile, and then laugh. He aimed the laughter toward the ringing phone, as if ignoring it were a joke between the two of them, an amusing act of conspiracy.

"What do *you* think?" he asked Speight.

"I think he can do the job without no trouble."

"About him having something to say, I meant."

Speight sighed. "I don't always listen close as I should. You know how it gets with children talking at you."

But Roy didn't know; he was childless, unmarried, his nearest niece and nephew up in Michigan where he was from. The only children he came into contact with were the older ones he had to sometimes kick out of the back booths when they grew rowdy. The kids of

31

Trent went through a rite-of-passage hatred for him, an institutionalized disrespect also directed at the afternoon usher at the Varsity Theatre and the snarly owner of Little Pep, a drive-in on the outskirts. From his first day on the job, Lehmann had insisted he discipline those who disrupted business, and so seven years' worth of kids, a half generation, held him in active teenage contempt. They had a nickname for him — "Windshield", which had to do with the shiny plate of his forehead, its prominence due to the steady retreat of his thin blond bangs. He knew these kids and he knew the colicky or croupy ones frantic mothers held while waiting for him to fill the dose of paregoric which would bring quiet to their nights.

"Sounds to me like he's *too* smart. Sounds overqualified for any job around here."

Speight took him seriously. That glint of petulance Roy had detected in his eyes faded, he hid his hands in his saggy pockets and stepped foward. "Listen, Mr. Green, he won't be a problem to you with talking too much I mean. He knows when to shut up, he won't sass you, I swear."

Roy was embarrassed. He preferred the peripheral Speight, newsprint blown along by a noiseless drugstore wind, to this desperate one. They hung there, frozen, Speight leaning

32

in a little too closely, like Lehmann wound up by a hard sell. How to get out of this, Roy wondered. When the ring came again he reached for the receiver, cradled it between neck and shoulder.

"Lehmann's Drugs, pharmacist here, can you hold, please?"

He cupped the mouthpiece and said, "I don't know, Speight. Ten-year-old talker might do me a lot of good. All I hear is the talk of people on their way down, or those who want everyone to think they're about to breathe their last. Might be good for me to hear from the opposition."

Speight nodded his characteristic nod.

"I don't see any problems. Lehmann already told me to hire a boy for the job. Bring him in tomorrow."

"He's here already. Out in the alley waiting on me to get off work."

"I'm busy, Speight. Besides, I told you already I've not got anything to go out."

"Might be one on the line there," said Speight.

"Bring him in then," said Roy. As he picked up the phone and spoke he turned to see that Speight was gone already.

"Thanks for waiting," Roy said in his formal phone voice. He continued to speak in routine taking-an-order tones which revealed nothing more than boredom until a minute or so into the conversation when his diction became precise and he slowed down and spoke up, as if talking to someone whose English was marginal. Reaching across the counter for his prescription log, Roy thought of Speight, the jawbone of Speight, this boy of Speight's who loves to talk, who's got something to say, who won't sass me swears his father. He thought of Keane's son on the telephone, thought *To hell with him, let him wait, I won't be a party to it, to hell with Lehmann, too.*

Roy picked the phone up, spoke without force or focus into its mouthpiece — "Excuse me one more moment, please" — then let it dangle against the cabinet.

Lehmann appeared a few seconds later, dabbing sweaty temples.

"Speight's got a bed to load up. Where the hell's he at now? The old man, her tight-assed better half, wanted me to guarantee he could take the bed into the hospital when she got ready. Said he didn't see how they could charge him for a bed if he had one of his own. She looked to me about ready right now. About damn asleep too. Tell Speight be careful not to fold her up in there." Lehmann dug in his back pocket for a wadded handkerchief, stood puffing loudly like an overweight child.

"What's all this?" he said when he spotted

the phone spinning at the end of its kinked cord. A tinny voice floated up to them.

"Keane's son," said Roy. "Edwin Keane again, and I can't listen to him."

Lehmann reached for the receiver. Roy prepared himself, tried to summon indifference, but Lehmann surprised him by stopping the phone from twisting, covering the mouthpiece with a pink hand, dropping his voice to a rasp. "He's called already this week?"

"Three times yesterday, twice this morning. Must really have overdone it this time. Nothing I can do about it."

"The boy is fragile," said Lehmann. "It's his back probably killing him. When's he *supposed* to get it?"

"Friday."

"Well," said Lehmann, and he shook his head hard. "It's his back bothering him that makes him take too much of that mess."

"Seems to me he's getting worse. He's got a prescription, he's supposed to follow the instructions just like anybody else. I don't care whether it's morphine or cod's liver, I'm not going to be a party to it."

Lehmann had uncovered the mouthpiece while Roy was talking, was speaking into it now. "Edwin? Walter Lehmann here, Edwin." A foot away Roy rolled his eyes, imagined Keane doing the same, both of them united briefly against Lehmann's false paternity.

"You understand, son, that your prescription can't be filled until Friday. Today's Wednesday, Edwin. Check the date on your bottle, son. You got your bottle right there beside you?"

While Lehmann spoke, Roy ducked down one of the aisles behind the counter where bottles and boxes of syrups and pills lined dusty shelves. Feeling drained, he breathed deeply and stared at the materials of his trade in the dim light, wondering how much longer he could last. He'd always enjoyed his work, particularly the technical part; he felt that dispensing medicine was about as good a thing as any that he could have done with his life, and he had gained over the years a considerable knowledge of medicine. Still, he was tired. Lehmann's ways had worn him down, and the voice of the Keane boy on the phone always pointed out to him the magnitude of what he had to endure to earn a living, to exist. Work was not something he liked to think about, yet every time he picked up the phone and heard that drowsy voice rise from the pure second of silence he was overwhelmed by all that was wrong with this job, how much he had been ignoring. One word, a hoarse hello, and Roy saw himself not as a pharmacist, a professional trained in the uses of hundreds of medicines and their miraculous healing effects on the body, but as a counter of pills.

Behind him he heard the phone click, then silence. He scanned the shelves, acted as if he was searching for something so that Lehmann would think he was busy and leave him alone. Another lecture about Keane coming up, he thought; but none came, though Lehmann didn't leave, stood studying the prescription log until the phone rang again and Roy heard Lehmann mention Keane's mother's name, heard him ask her how she'd been feeling.

He sighed and braced for the part that would come next, the inevitable next.

"This afternoon by closing," Roy heard his boss say. "My man's got a hospital bed to load up, but soon's he's through I'll send him right on."

When Lehmann appeared at the top of the aisle where Roy was hiding, Roy grabbed a bottle from the shelf and pretended to read its label.

"He's Keane's son is the thing about it," said Lehmann. Roy, dizzy, traded the bottle for another cobalt blue one, held it up to the light and shook it.

"Where the hell's Speight at?"

Roy said nothing.

"You needn't stew, son. I can't goddamn help it if he was born Keane's son, can I?"

Amazing, thought Roy: breaking of the law blamed on an accident of birth. "No," he said. "But then, neither can Keane's son."

Lehmann pointed a finger at Roy, a splotch of sweat unfolding across his armpit, doubling in size as his arm rose. Haggling has given him energy, thought Roy, and he put the bottle up and slumped, prepared to stare at a square of linoleum while Lehmann railed and sweated until his entire shirt sucked tight to his skin.

But a grey cloud appeared to the right of Lehmann's raised arm.

"Here's Speight," said Lehmann, and then, "What do you want, boy, we're busy back here."

Roy lurched forward to bring the three of them into view. Speight had called the boy "undersized," though he didn't seem exactly undersized to Roy. Disproportioned perhaps: squarely in the midst of that sudden pituitary spurt which health texts call puberty. Sunk-gutted, swollen-kneed, his dungarees fell like stovepipe from the bottom of his ribcage to his ankles and were wrenched tight by a too-big belt, the tip of which dangled like the tongue of a tired-out dog. He was assless, hipless, three-quarters leg. Handprints dusted the side of his T-shirt, as if someone had tried to climb him. His hair, buzzed short like his father's, was ash-black and stiff, like a patch of grass which had been set on fire the night before. He had his father's raging facebones, his father's jaw.

"Speight's boy," said Roy, and the three of them turned to him. "What's his name?" Roy asked Speight, but the boy answered — "Randall" — jerking hands from his high-pocketed pants as he spoke.

"I hired him to make deliveries," Roy told Lehmann. "You told me to get a boy this time."

"Starting when?" said Lehmann.

"He's not doing nothing right now," said Speight.

"Show him where we keep the bike. Green's got a delivery's got to go out this minute," said Lehmann. When they were gone he turned to Roy and said, "Good timing, Green. With the boy here we'll get it out quicker and Keane won't call back bugging you."

Roy felt a fumbling for words which he knew would last until Lehmann was out of his sight, would likely last the rest of the day. Much later, at home, the litany of things-he-should-have-said would keep his lips moving for a half hour, until the wordless night noises surrounding him — refrigerator humming off and on in the dark, beating of moth wings against a lamp shade — would grow loud enough for him to hear, exposing his comebacks as spiteful, feeble, hours late.

2

Home from work, Speight stood on the back porch listening to the squawk and cackle of his chickens and staring out over the yard. Desecrated, pecked barren, it reminded Speight of his farmland, of his first glimpse at that soil which he knew nothing about. Dirt was dirt, you put a hoe to it, sprinkled seed and sat back to drink was how he'd always thought of farming. Just looking at the yard made Speight thirsty.

The chickens were one of the few things he'd brought from his farm, that few acres of sunburnt bottomland that he'd left behind like the bones of an animal he'd finally cleaned of meat. It had been a scrawny animal to start. Still, he had managed to keep it going for nine years after his wife died, hiring a neighbor girl to look after the children until Martha grew old enough to take over and working straight through the hours, days, years, farming and cutting cordwood and hiring himself out to the sawmill near Speed. One Tuesday afternoon in late June, a hailstorm took down

41

all but a half acre of his tobacco and it seemed that both he and the farm had converged into a pinched, final thinness. He borrowed a truck from Davenport down at the sawmill and moved back to town the next day.

Though his daughters were ecstatic about the move, they were put out with Speight about the chickens, which among other things denied them the crucial distinction of a Lawn. Trent to them was town, no matter how deficient Trent was as far as towns go. Speight had never been big on Trent. He preferred the openness of the country, or if one had to live so close to others the tight excitement of Norfolk, where he'd worked in the shipyards before he'd married. Yet his kids had spent their formative years in a swamp two miles through a soggy wood to the nearest house. The only lawn they'd known was a bed of mud, sun-baked or flooded, depending on the weather, corrugated always by tractor tread and holes dug by heat-crazed dogs.

On the porch he stepped out of his workboots and beat them against the washer to loosen the wedges of dried mud. As he looked up, Speight saw something move down the long hall that ran from back porch to front. The wide floorboards were warped and the figure, one of his daughters in a dress that hung loosely from her shoulders, bounced where boards sagged. The vision startled Speight: it was like watching a car pass over a distant hill in a haze of heat. He watched the silhouette turn to take the stairs, a hand on the balled post of the banister, a skirt rippling over the landing. When he could no longer hear footfalls it occurred to him to wonder which daughter it had been. He'd seen only vapor, shoulders where hair met loose dress; colors and texture were blurred and, at the height of his mirage, irrelevant.

Randall was suddenly below him, talking in his high-pitched voice about his first day on the job.

"Yes," said Speight thinking of how easy it had been to get Randall hired at the drugstore, how Lehmann had not balked. Lehmann, in fact, had been less of a problem than Green, with all his questions, his drawing it out with all that talk. Randall was so slight and spindly that Speight felt fortunate to have found work for him at all. For the girls he had his eye on the laundry downtown, run by a stern German lady who rustled into the drugstore every afternoon for an ammonia Coke. The hours would be long, both before and after school, and the German lady put him off; she wore clothes starched rigor-mortis stiff and her breath retained the ammonia. But Ruby had told him that she paid well, cash every Thursday afternoon.

For his older son, Hal, he'd figured on a position with the City of Trent, part-time gravedigging. Hal was still saying he'd return for his last year of school, although Speight suspected that if Hal could stand up straight and keep his mouth shut long enough to get on over there, he'd soon be seduced by the silver clinking in his pocket, since to Speight's knowledge the boy had never had a bit of money of his own, and Speight would ration him just enough to want more. The rest Speight would take and he knew that, with Hal, he could take it for quite a while because although his son hated him he was scared of the limitless world away from him and he would stay, cowering and festering, close to home.

Speight sought a way to make the boy even more frightened of the world. He sought a way to keep them all around forever so that they could start paying him back for the years of scrape and pinch. Yet it was more than wanting to be fed in turn, more than wanting their company. He wanted to be thanked a little, liked a bit.

Randall was standing below him, talking, still talking. Speight focused slowly into the middle of the strain, which was the way one had to do it with Randall. Something about

44

a house which had grown whiskers, a bony arm stuck out of a window. Speight wondered if this was something he needed to hear the beginning, middle and end of, then remembered that asking Randall to backtrack was almost always useless, provoking an even more circuitous system of switchback and hairpin.

"But before that, down at the river I come up on that place where you took us once when we had the good tobacco year, remember? A picnic, we swam, Hal went off in the woods with some boys to find some rope you swing out over the river on but got lost, you left him out there, he had to walk back. And those blue church buses stuck up to their floorboards in the quicksand when we were getting ready to go and all those people just been babtized had to get out and push? Had on white sheets still sopping, you could see everything up underneath."

"Hole-up here," said Speight, grabbing Randall to silence him. "You went to the river this afternoon?"

"Down there about an hour."

"When you were supposed to be working?"

"The druggist told me to stop by there on the way to deliver that one package."

"What *one* package."

"The one went out to that man I was telling

45

you about. The one with a face like —"

"Shut up for a minute talking crazy," said Speight, and he swiveled Randall around with one arm and pushed the boy down the hall and out onto the porch, Randall batting open the screen door with his bowed head. It slapped shut behind them and Speight hesitated a half second to make sure none of his daughters had followed, then put both arms on his son's shoulders, bent toward the boy.

"Mess around and lose that job and you get pulled out of school quick as I find out. And I'll send you off."

"To where?" said Randall, and when his father shook him he acted as if all the words had been shaken from him, though there were more, questions about where *off* was, how he'd get out there, what he'd done wrong. He knew he shouldn't say word one, knew he shouldn't try to defend himself.

"Now I know that the druggist didn't tell you to stop by no river on your way to drop off that package. You forget I work there and know what goes on. How come you'd lie to me about something so damn stupid? You go messing around when you're supposed to be working and you might get both of us fired."

Randall nodded. His father's breath passed over his forehead like the roving breeze from a floor fan. He'd want to hold his own breath, clamp his nostrils shut when it came around again.

"Here on out they send you somewhere you go straight there come straight back. Hear? They know about how long it takes and they'll damn well know it when you been dragging ass."

All you got to do is ask the druggist, thought Randall, the druggist will tell you all about how he said I should go down to the river first, said there won't any hurry on this, I should get used to the bike, try to learn the town a little. I told him I knew the town already but he said being it was my first day why didn't I take it easy, wouldn't be long before they have me coming and going. But he knew not to speak, knew not to raise his eyes now. He saw the druggist, his bent head visible about the high counter, bald spot shining pink beneath the lights. I don't know about that man, thought Randall, haven't known him but a few hours and already he's got me into trouble.

"You hear?" said Speight.

"I didn't know."

"You know now." His father unloosened his grip and Randall flew away through the screen door and into the kitchen.

Speight dropped his boots in the hallway and followed, pausing on the threshold of this room he usually avoided, this room which had always reminded him of a church. Begs and pleas lingered in its high-ceilinged hollows, mixing not with ceremonial odors like musty hymnals and well-oiled pews but with secular smells of garbage pail and sidemeat. Here his children congregated when he was away; he knew that here he was denigrated, no doubt damned a time or two. Family business he preferred to conduct in the slope-floored front parlor, since he felt that the kitchen added an incalculable edge against him, and the lack of chairs in the parlor worked in his favor. Yet the kitchen was, to the rest of them, the center of the house. These days he came home intentionally late and took his supper on the back porch with his plate on his lap, his feet propped on the woodpile, alone.

Martha, finishing up the supper dishes, looked up at him as he entered the kitchen but the rest of them, gathered around the table, studied textbooks they'd propped against a wall of pots and pans.

"Ya'll through your lessons?" he asked.

"Yes," said Ellen.

"No," said Marianne.

"How do you think I've even had a chance to sharpen a pencil what with all this to do and no help from a one of them?" said Martha, the oldest, mother to the younger ones and made miserable by this role. Hand towels were thrown over both her shoulders and the way her arms were plunged into the deep of the twin sinks made her look like a double amputee.

"She's worked herself up to her elbows," said Speight, clicking his tongue in an exaggerated *tsk* so that she'd know he was kidding. She didn't turn around, but there were giggles from around the table, Randall and one or two of his daughters, which ones he couldn't tell. They'd gone back to their lessons by the time he looked down. What? thought Speight, what's so important? Pilgrims and hypotenuse and things that come in threes: *Pinta, Niña, Santa Maria.* He'd been good at memorization when he was in school, though he'd finished only seven grades, which then was something but now was just the start. He'd been good at memorizing things from church, too; the Methodist one his mother made him attend until his father died when he was eight and clothes became a problem for them, a symptom actually of a more ignominious problem he'd been dealing with since. Church disappeared from their lives, became a building they passed by on Selden Street. Thank God, Speight's older brother had said when their mother told them they'd no longer have to go, and Speight still remembered the slow-

49

to-fade imprint of his mother's hand across his brother's cheek when she slapped him.

If one of his said the same, he'd laugh. He'd never once taken them to church. Didn't they get enough to memorize in school? Cram a child's head full of the absolutely useless and you don't ever get out what you've put in, as if there was a need in the world he envisioned for his children for names and dates and the number of yards in a mile. It's asking them, begging them to live lazy, to turn out sorry. Daylight porch sitters, people without hands.

And they had this kitchen to congregate in, their own church where they met to speak not so much against sin but against sinking under, giving in.

Encouraged by the little bit of laughter he'd drawn, Speight began to ask them questions. About their teachers, about school, the day they'd had there. Usually he spoke little when he came in late and his questions must have taken them by surprise. Their answers were curt but bordered, just before he ran out of questions, on polite. Sometimes kids forget that they hate a thing, he thought. Not only kids; he did it himself sometimes. There were things he had to will himself, remind himself to hate, which meant of course that he did not hate them at all, since it didn't rise up involuntarily like nausea or desire but was summoned as if by telegram, the lag between sent and received exposing its insincerity.

All this — his questions, their answers, the thought that their desire was trumped-up instead of evoked by his presence — made Speight happy. Even it was only a lapse on their part, it beat the silence of meals interrupted only by cricket chirp and chicken cluck, salt shakers bumping over the unplaned pine. They would all eat together tonight, and he would keep this going as long as he could. Trying to think up more questions, Speight remembered that he was two hours late for supper, that those were the supper dishes Martha was banging about, that he'd purposely stayed late at the drugstore and all of them had finished eating two hours ago. This was why they were being so receptive, he thought, because they know I won't be around for very long.

"Ready for supper," he told Martha, and she moved from sink to stove and spooned sidemeat and simmered vegetables on his plate, which he took to the back porch and ate in silence. Through the open window he heard Randall asking his sisters questions they called stupid, questions about stars, mathematics, the time a circus came to town and someone set the big tent on fire. Speight was listening intently to the questions, to the frothy laughter they elicited, when he spotted two of his hens on the other side of the fence that ran along the right side of his yard. He called Ellen and Martha, told them to get the hens, which by now had wandered up his neighbor's sideyard, out of sight. Both balked, Martha the longest and loudest. Speight kept chewing until they left him, picking gingerly over the fence.

Though there was nothing prim about their return, hens tucked under their arms like textbooks, their faces red and furious. For the first time since he had abandoned his farm, Speight was moved to uncontrolled laughter, long and guttural, heard up and down the block. As he laughed his daughters stomped up the back steps and opened the screen door wide enough to push the chickens onto the porch.

Speight's laughter faded. The chickens flexed beside him, a flurry of wings and noise. Ellen and Martha stood together on the bottom step, glaring up at him.

"Not in here," said Speight. "In the yard."

"Trent people don't keep chickens," said Martha. Speight watched her. She shook. She had her mother's coloring: white in winter, red and white in summer. He remembered the summers when he had taken the children out to the fields with him to play while he worked, how he'd had to cover Martha up so she wouldn't blister. She'd seemed so constricted, so uncomfortable, out of place among the other shirtless barefoot brown ones, but Barbara had insisted, claimed the child got striped if measures weren't taken against the sun. And she did get striped, but beautifully, thought Speight, like a banded serpent amongst colorless scrub.

"Those what can't afford to store-buy them keep them," he said.

Ellen looked away without argument but not Martha. She fumed. He could tell she'd never forget this embarrassment, moving them finally into town, then filling up their yard with nervous hens. He looked hard at her and saw that she'd made up her mind about him, decided on something that he'd rather not know.

He said to Ellen, "Come in and get these."

One hen stood on the table now, stretching its neck and jerking about with its head down, its gullet swiftly pumping. She grabbed it, squeezed it under her arm, nudged the other out with her foot.

Martha did not flinch when the frazzled hens half flew by her. Passing by Speight on the porch she grabbed the plate from his lap and disappeared into the kitchen.

Alone again, Speight bent to the woodpile

to find his bottle of whiskey, then took the long hallway from back porch to front where, on the sawed-off caned chair he'd brought from the farmhouse, he sat down to drink.

Propping his legs on the railing, Speight leaned back to watch the movement down Fontaine: children playing in the street, adults strolling or porch-sitting, their conversations carried across driveways and yards. The sluggish weight of the whiskey warmed and overtook him and he drifted, glaze of the first few drinks spreading unevenly through his body.

He sat, drank, watched, thought, drank. The leaves on the chestnut trees lining the street twitched in the wind which he expected any minute to bring him answers to questions asked silently, by the very act and rhythm of his breath. As the voices of his children echoed in the house behind him, Speight sat still and silent on the front porch in what was to his children a mockery of his role as guardian: he was not keeping evil out so much as keeping them inside.

He heard the screen door slap, followed by footsteps. Randall and Eureka appeared beside him. These were the two with the most prominent and unmistakable Speight features: black eyes and hair, bones straining beneath dark skin, the jut of jaw and the ridge of cheekbone. He stared at Eureka's hair, black like his once was, with only five or so years left before the strands of gray would nickel and dime their way into dominance. While he stared he realized that it was her he'd seen earlier moving like an apparition down the hall.

He knew it even though he'd seen only shape, a wisp of cloth and hair hurrying away.

"Pa," said Randall. "We were wanting to know if we could maybe me and . . ."

"What?" said Speight.

"Go for a walk." Eureka took over. She was good at anticipating her little brother's digressions, good at deciding when they would amuse or annoy. Randall also was a favorite, yet he lacked reserve, he hid nothing, put all into his loose singsong tales. No one else in the family had the time nor the inclination to be so tangential; talk was not encouraged or even much practiced, especially during those years spent in the country, when the daily words of Speight would rarely yield a page. Yet Randall muttered along, answering his own questions without pause, his last words rising half octaves at the end of his sentences.

The two stood before him backlit by grainy light, the air about them busy with clouds of dust and bugs. Speight smelled weeds and the sweet hint of rain moving in from crosstown fields. For a second he wondered if the two of them had not been sent by the others to distract him, but he didn't dwell on it. He was too flattered by the vision before him, of his children in this light that he relished, of these two, shoulders touching like shirts pinned on a clothesline, framed by his favorite time of night. Moments like this he loved them the most, so much more than when they had to be fed or clothed or nursed through the precarious diseases of childhood. It appealed to his vanity to see before him these two in whom his own genes had triumphed over the blander genes of his wife and her family of straw-haired, shoulderless and above all weak-jawed Episcopalians.

"I don't like y'all out so late," he said.

"We won't be gone an hour," said Eureka.

Speight sighed and said hurry then and was left staring at the space so close where they'd stood. For a second the whole street was still until a car chugged up from town, crunching gravel and spitting it out behind. Speight watched as the dust dispersed. Into this moment darkness came. In the houses across the street, line drawn against the fading sky and the thunderheads resting just above the trees, lights winked on, small yellow squares. Someone a block back cranked a car, yelled instructions, idled the car high, let it run awhile before suddenly cutting it off. Speight took

56

a long drink from his bottle, went around to the back porch to stash the backwash in the woodpile.

In the harsh kitchen light — every grease spot showed in those first seconds of illumination, every paint fleck, every blackened hand stain — he sat and stared at a spot on a wall calendar where a bug had been killed in mid-month, a brownish stain crusted on the square of a numbered Thursday. He sat for five minutes before he realized that all his children had gone out, that the house was empty and he was, for the first time in years, home alone.

So intently did he listen for noises of the others that the settling sounds of the house made him change his mind, until he recognized these sounds as what they were. Afterwards, more silence. Speight got up again, began to move through the house. In the room where he slept he opened a closet door and shivered when cool air gusted out. His room was barren, just a bed and the cherry bureau his wife had called the chifforobe, the finish long gone, sides scraped from their careless moves. In an upstairs bedroom shared by three of his daughters, Speight flicked on the overhead light and stood in front of the round mirror.

Room to room to room. Thunderclap and accelerating pelt of rain. In a closet off the sleeping porch he climbed a ladder to the attic, but retreated after poking his head through the trap door and peering into darkness. Back in the kitchen he sat down at the table, wishing his children would return. All of them, and soon.

Later, when he awoke, the house was dark and quiet except for the wheeze of his breath, which shocked him, so ragged and relentless did it sound, like the wind of a desert through which he was straggling, lost. Slowly Speight made his way upstairs. He made it all the way to the end of the hallway, had curled his hand around the cool door knob before he heard the noise — a cough, a creak of bedspring — which let him know that he was no longer alone.

3

"Where is this place?" Eureka asked as she followed Randall through deserted downtown, but Randall didn't answer, didn't slow or turn around. For once he led her through the streets in silence, and she was forced to follow.

Every morning after he fed the chickens Randall would take off on long treks through Trent, a different direction each day. His sisters also took walks after their morning chores, but always the same walk: up Fontaine to Church and left into the five small blocks of business district. "Shopping trips" these strolls were called, although between them there wasn't enough money to buy a stale cracker.

Eureka went with them twice. They saw all the wrong things, stood forever in front of store windows she would never have slowed for.

From then on until she started her after-school job at the laundry, she went with Randall. She let him drag her along a route he'd discovered that morning, some new discovery like this tobacco warehouse he'd been telling her about all afternoon. Randall was so excited that he rambled on about this warehouse and said nothing of his new job.

Her sisters thought it ridiculous that Eureka, at her age, would want to risk tick and snake bite by pushing through a waist-high field of weed to cross a slick sewage pipe over a stagnant creek. But during most of Randall's explorations she never considered what she looked like or who was looking. Usually she was busy listening. Randall talked through everything, he could talk his way into her thickest thoughts, like a bug buzzing into her ear, needling her awake from blackest sleep. His vocabulary was threadbare, his grammar approximate, but he was an original talker, and the only one she knew. Her sisters talked among themselves but rarely to her, and in the presence of her father they were mute, communicating through a code of flicked eyelids, heads dropped to hide smiles. Her older brother Hal gestured rather than talked; his mannerisms were clunky and obvious, and took the place of words.

On their walks she always followed a few steps behind, staring straight ahead unless his monologue alluded to anything peripheral. Trent and its inhabitants held little attraction for her, yet she'd found places to like here, places Randall showed her, places he'd taken her. There was the shed behind the hardware store, roped over with wisteria and filled with abandoned appliances: rusty wringer washers, sooty cookstoves, a dozen clawfoot bathtubs. They went there once, climbing in a window over a crusty oil drum. Randall found another spot near the center of town, a dark lot covered by locust trees and kudzu where some hobos had recently broken camp. Empty wine bottles crowned a litter of half paper, half ash. A creek with a froth of soapsuds cut through the lot. Randall christened it the Cat Tail. They sat in green seclusion for an hour listening to the industrial thrum of Railroad Street, finally to the faint train whistle, muted by the miles it lacked to town.

The warehouse was on a side street down by the river, a wide musty space not long out of use — maybe only a season, as there were still crisp tobacco leaves scattered about the dirt floor. Sheets of tattered burlap were piled in corners and whitewashed beams lined with faint, penciled figures rose to the high tin roof.

As soon as they set foot inside it began to storm. It became so dark that they could only see each other clearly during blinks of lightning. She sent him to the far end to wheel open one of the wooden doors. Rather than return, Randall prowled the edges, humming

61

and poking in the dust. She sat down by a pole in the middle and relished the smells: cured tobacco, damp dust, rain blowing in from the open door. This dark warehouse, here in the middle of this town she detested, comforted her. She was always discovering things to love locked inextricably inside something she could only tolerate. Pure moments buried within tainted hours, buffered by endless bad days. And there was Randall, an inexplicable joy within a family of strangers.

Randall transformed things by surrounding them with words, and he kept them transformed by circulating the words, like currents of air swirling around a kite. Eureka realized that his stories had often kept her afloat as well; they had carried her through the tortuous decline of the farm, right up into their new life in town. Not that the transition was as traumatic for her as it was for her sisters — there were things she liked and already missed about the country, and Trent, with unpaved alleys dead-ending into peanut and tobacco fields, did not require much adjustment.

Eureka realized also that she lacked Randall's originality. He would make do anywhere. He'd find some mystery, deplete it, discover another. She could not rouse herself to the continuous search. She wondered if she'd inherited her father's dogged, doomed complacency. She thought of him in the fields, belted by the plow harness, straddling the wake of thin dirt. Years passed after he realized the value of the furrow underfoot — worthless sand instead of nourishing soil. Years passed after which he knew he should have given up long ago. She could see herself in a similar predicament, in bad debt due to stubbornness.

The rain slackened, drops flurried on the tin. Squinting, she focused on Randall, watched him beat clouds of dust from the piles of discarded burlap with a scraggly broom he'd discovered. It was hard for her to imagine his ever being bothered by the things that would haunt the rest of them — where to go, what to do once there, and the biggest question of all: how to leave this all behind.

She wondered how the rest of them would leave it all behind. There in the still half-darkness she began to imagine the futures of her siblings. Big brother Hal first: Hal years from now in the lush anonymity of a huge city — Atlanta, she thought, or New Orleans maybe. Versions of childhood he would concoct for his lovers would be blandly idyllic: hunting trips with his father, new ponies, trips to the ocean, walks on piers. Hal would have three wives, two of whom would have slight speech impediments; the third would speak with an exaggerated enunciation, superiority over her predecessors upheld by clean bites of consonant. All three would make themselves up for a night on the town, but within moments of leaving the house they would wilt; in the heat, in the overexcitement of a treat too long promised, in the slatternly throb of their first few drinks. By the night's hazy midpoint they would look as if they'd been riding for hours in a convertible, and by the evening's end they would collapse like umbrellas crumpled by a sudden storm into the front seat of Hal's ragged car, where on the way home they would slump and smoke.

Hal would not answer when they threw their voices from screenless windows, calling him inside. He would switch jobs. He would end up part owner of a juke joint on the outskirts of some Texas town, still going strong way past sixty, kept alive by beer and ill will. Late in life he would cohabit with a Mexican woman whom he'd grow to love, a keen-witted woman who would cuss him in a language which he would imitate poorly, with a thick-tongued gringo roll of the *r*. He would have two false semi-retirements, would eventually sell his part of the bar and buy a cab to drive nights when he couldn't sleep. He'd wear a crimped hat held together by dried sweat and the dust of Texas. He would smoke continuously without enjoyment.

The lives of her sisters would be spent right here in Trent. The town would grow unchecked through the shadeless fields and her sisters would grow fatter and older in sync with this place that was once to propel them into society. Their fate would be the fate of Trent. They might move, marry their boyfriends whose hairstyles rose from scalps like buttes from the floor of a desert, might marry and move into a new part of town, a dead-end road out past the river, tight with new duplexes and rectangular yards of crabgrass reclaimed from fields of sand and cocklespur, but it would be only an extension of Fontaine Street, the part of town that they had landed in when they moved in from the country, the Trent of drafty clapboard houses and backyard chickens. Their neighbors might be Edna Rivenbark, who took men into the cemetery two at a time before it was even dusk, or Jay Jay Drawhorn, who walked the Sunday downtown streets shirtless and incoherent, swinging arms as short and clubbed as cordwood and picking fights with passersby.

Her sisters, too, would dream up an idealized family life for future reference, for posterity, for the children who would fill their houses and who might someday ask what their mother's childhood was like. Her sisters would answer with anecdotes in which the word "family" misrepresented what it had been — people with the same last name crowding a succession of too-small houses — in which "family" stood for an intangible yet loyal connection. When in the future her father would succumb to old age and illness and end up in the hospital her sisters would crowd the waiting rooms and cast doleful looks at each other through the cigarette smoke. At the height of this listless vigil they would talk in creaks and moans while beside them their aging husbands would doze, their names lassoed in red above workshirt pockets, their butte haircuts eroded to flat tops the color of cinderblock from which dandruff flew loose like brick dust.

The clarity of this reverie unnerved Eureka, yet she couldn't dislodge it even when she tried. Staring down to the far end of the warehouse, searching for Randall, she saw instead friends of her sisters from Fontaine strolling over to the Speight corner of the waiting room. A nurse would deliver the news at ten o'clock one morning and her sisters would hoist each other out of their chairs and fall, squinting, into the day outside, reconvene at a neighbor's house where they would work through a dozen Pyrex rectangles of casserole and talk bad about those siblings who were absent — Hal,

Randall, Eureka.

For Randall, like Hal, would be long gone. After he left he would not keep up with any of them. His neglect would not spring from anger or disgust from his origins, nor some aloof desire to appear rootless or unencumbered, but out of forgetfulness. He forgot his past, raced longlegged and breathless through *now*, toward *what's next*. The moment he leaves here he'll forget, thought Eureka — at least for a while, at least until middle age when, out on the road, memories of the slow, harsh bake of his childhood would heat up during nights of patchy sleep.

He'll make his discoveries and take his trips. Eureka pictured him years from now in some place like England, grown up and good-looking in an angled, jerky-gestured way. A man who spent his days rooting around: in libraries, in books; in paragraphs, sentences, words, syllables. In foreign train stations, in towns where ancient cities lay buried beneath the soles of his sandals; in people's minds; in the mind of some foreign girl with whetstone eyes.

She might not see him again, ever. She would miss him but his flight would not bother her so much because he was so pure and so obviously destined to become untethered and float away. She'd prepared for it, had been preparing for it since he was small.

Now he was standing under a leak in the warehouse roof, which had dwindled to a sparse hypnotic drip. His hair was matted with rainwater. His cheeks were wet.

"Don't go get sopping, he'll blame me," she called, but he didn't seem to hear and besides she didn't really care. They needed to get back — she'd said an hour, he'd be worried, what with the lightning — but she was comfortable here, in the midst of those summer moments she remembered from the country, when the sun comes out after a storm and everything seems too bright, too vital. Outside the back door in the black wet wood she heard the bushes drying out in the sun, branches snapping skyward once dry. A new room of daylight had opened, and its reclaimed light seemed to Eureka a physical grace, a gift of air and light during which she could continue to dream.

It begged the question, this magical time: how will *you* leave? She thought about where she'd go first: Probably another Trent. Her future husband's Trent, identical almost to this Trent she sat in the middle of but not her own, not filled with relatives which might make it tolerable for a while. She wished for a man like Randall but expected someone like her father: a gruff and tight-lipped man who would storm home grungy, whiskery and disagreeable one night and the next take her out for fish. From the first he would be tightly wound and short-fused, but he would be in love with her in his limited way, in awe of her flashes of independence.

She closed her eyes and pictured the car that would take her away: a black Buick, shiny and modern. Nothing else about him would be so modern. A new car smelling of crisp upholstery, cigar smoke, sweat. Brassy voices on the radio, the windows rolled up tight so that she could hear how good the music sounded. A few miles outside of town the new smell of the car would make her feel nauseated. He would not let her touch the window. He would turn up the radio. He would not talk to her. His new smell, too, would turn acrid, as outside the flat familiar miles passed.

Darkness was spreading outward from the warehouse corners. She called Randall over, and this time he came.

"We got to go now," she said, offering him her hand.

"I didn't get to tell you about work. About what happened on my first day and all."

"Tell me on the way home," she said. But for a block he said nothing and she, waiting, eyed the dark corners of town, windswept damp after the storm. Past the padlocked storefronts, their doors set back from plate glass in deep shadow. She switched places with Randall on the sidewalk so that he bounced between her and the stores, but soon she no longer felt nervous because he started talking and his words turned the periphery bland, then invisible.

"Wasn't like I thought it was going to be," he said, and he told her exactly how he'd imagined his first day, how he'd pictured being sent to deliver pills to old ladies in houses downtown, women whose hot rooms smelled of chicken broth. They'd be waiting for him in front parlors where the air was thick and yellow, pacing past drapes so stiff they seemed shellacked. They'd tip him a penny or two, coins moistened clammy by arthritic fists. Widows who'd want to show him pictures or have him walk a piece of oak furniture across a lumpy rug for another penny but he'd have to say no ma'am I'm in a hurry, he would have to move ahead, keep an eye out always for time. It was a big something to shoulder, this working at the same place as his father.

"What was it like instead?"

He told her how he'd been hired. How he'd been playing in the alley with some boys he knew, colored boys he liked because he often came upon them on his afternoon treks, passed them in strange and different-every-day places and they seemed kindred in their wanderlust, explorers who did not limit themselves to the safety of sunken, sad-mud parts of town where they lived and did not acknowledge the hated stares of those whose neighborhoods they passed through. Stares he drew, too, because he was not known, though he wasn't colored and didn't have to worry as much. He'd struck up a friendship with these boys based on this shared desire to roam and discover while in the rectangles of block and vacant lot, white kids chose the same unbalanced teams for games of lethargic baseball.

One of these colored boys was called Dogate by the others and for the longest time while they sneaked around the warehouse behind the feed and seed trying to find a low-limbed tree to climb so that they could get up on the roof and see all town from above, Randall wondered how he could have been named or even nicknamed something so odd. Finally he asked and another boy, Mac Koy he was called, said we call him that cause he told the teacher Dog Ate My Homework even when he knew everydamnbody said that, said Mac Koy, it won't even a good lie, it was a tired-ass lie. "This boy Dog Ate tells tiredass lies and that's why they call him Dog Ate for short," Randall told Eureka. "It's not Eight like in seven-eight, it's ate like he . . ."

"I get it," she said. "Go on."

"Anyway Pa come out in the alleyway and called me down out of a tree I'd found. He didn't say nothing, just grabbed me by the shoulder and marched me inside and back behind the drug counter. That half-bald druggist staring at me. He looked mad, I swear, though I hadn't done nothing to him, I never even met the man before. Then Mr. Lehmann, Pa's boss, he didn't even hardly look at me, just told Pa to show me the bike and send me on out."

"So where did they send you?"

But he ignored her question because he sensed she was listening now.

"There was this man stuck his hand out of a house that had the face of Pa. At first I didn't even know where the street was so I went by the post office and asked a mailman behind the counter. It was getting late because I'd already been down to the river. I walked around down there looking for letters lovebirds carved into tree trunks and remember that time we went down there for a picnic?"

"Wait a minute," she said. "How come you went to the river?"

"Druggist told me to," he said.

She stopped in front of Melton's Grill and put a hand out on a parking meter to steady herself. She took her shoe off and shook it until a pebble bounced on the sidewalk. "Randall?" As if calling him, as if he'd kept going. "He did not either tell you on your first day of work to go down to the river."

"Did so, said take your time, son, it wasn't any huge hurry on this one here so I rode out by that big grass." He paused, remembering the way cropped lawns of River Road estates curved neatly into the ditches like tucked bedsheets, how the expansive acreage made even the mansions look small. Yards were what this town held, his older sisters were right, although he didn't usually agree with them or share their taste. When he'd slowed to stare cars came up from nowhere, blowing horns, goading him onto the river where he'd located the place they'd gone once for a picnic. People gathered there late afternoons to fish and drink, on weekends to be baptized. Randall didn't like to swim here; tannic from cypress knees had tinted the water Co'-Cola colored. He waded for a while, then sat on the bank thinking of water words, of one in particular he'd learned that day in school — tributary. And of the ocean.

He'd never seen the ocean, though he had heard it. His teacher had told him it was only fifty miles away, and on summer nights, his neck craned toward the open window of the sleeping porch he shared with Hal, head lifted above his pillow, he sometimes heard the sea.

It didn't sound a bit like the faint, wispy static inside the conch shell his teacher had passed around at school — that was a trick, an insult. What Randall heard was wild, a sibilant call which shook houses and trees, a trill in the wind taxied up the slight grade of the coastal plain to a backyard tree whose branches swept the clapboard outside the sleeping porch. Tousled by waves blown in from past Hatteras, the tree bent closer to shake its leaves in Randall's offered ear, rattling the sounds of the sea.

Randall felt privileged to live so close to the ocean — only fifty miles in this country his teachers had used words like vast and immense to describe. If he ever met anyone from someplace unfortunately inland — Indiana, Minnesota, Utah — he would be more than happy to describe in detail, complete with sound effects, the ocean as it sounded outside his window at night.

"What did you do down there at the river?" she asked when she saw that he was stuck there.

"Took my shoes off and snuck my toes up under the sand. Went wading. But then I said it's late so I got on the bike and pedaled fast on back to town."

Traffic had grown thick on the river road, farm trucks from the last day's sale at the produce market headed back into the country. Alongside the river it was cool, woods crowding the bank filtered the sun, but when the road veered and the trees gave way to the line of mill shacks on the outskirts, Randall had felt flushed and sluggish. Old people sat scarecrow on unpainted porches, watching his passage moving only their eyes. Randall had pedaled faster, toward town.

"When I come up on the house I got spooked because it looked like Pa."

"You keep saying. What do you mean it looked like him?"

"Had whiskers. You know how sometimes seems like his eyes are drains on the bottom of sinks where something black's been washed? And the porch was like lips from out in the middle of the street where I stopped at first."

She laughed. He shot her a "you-laugh" look she couldn't see, remembered the house: set off at the dead end of the street, backed up to woods on two sides. Windows like eye sockets blackened and sunken, mildew staining the shingles resembling the shadow of whisker which crept hourly, perceptibly almost, across his father's chin and cheeks.

"So what happened when you knocked on the door of this house that favored your Pa?"

"He's yours, too. Anyway he don't use the door."

Leaning his bike against a front yard tree he'd crossed the porch, knocked. Inside he'd heard a shuffling, then quick foot-steps. He stood back from the door but was surprised by the sound of a window being forced open. The frame sliding up the tin run-ner echoed and a hand appeared, followed by a voice.

"This man was sick as the house he lived in and he acted mad as hell at me. When you want him you don't go to his door, you tap on the glass of this one window. That's how you call him outside. It'll confuse you at first."

"Over here," the voice had said, "over here quick."

"He must of been bad sick because his hand was only bone. It was red and shaky. He grabbed the bag and cussed me, talking about how long I took, talking about come quicker, quicker, always quicker."

When he'd gotten within a foot of the win-dow the curtains shivered enough for him to see dim outlines — a man's head, furniture. Air escaped from the house in a whoosh.

"His house had bad bad breath. Like it had been shut up for three hundred years. Base-ment breath, attic breath, closet breath, breath out an old innertube."

76

Randall had jumped back as the hand snatched the package; because of the darkness inside it seemed the arm belonged to the house itself, seemed the house was talking to him when the voice came again, "Where have you goddamn been boy, where have you been all this time, you've got to come quickly when I call."

"When the man shut the window it made a noise would not die down."

Curtains pulled to, window slamming into its sill and leaving that echo again, rattle of sill, runner and glass distracting him from the thin arm retreating into the blackness. He'd lingered until a car came down the street, the sudden chug of its engine absorbing the tinny reverberation and jarring him back to his bicycle, back to work.

"I didn't move for a while, just stood there wondering if this was going to be what work was like."

"I still don't get why the druggist sent you to the river first," said Eureka. They were picking through the high grass of the backyard, moving quietly since their sundown curfew had long since passed.

"Maybe I looked tired to him," said Randall. "Maybe he's lazy and don't like for people to work harder than him. Maybe . . ."

He fell quiet then as they approached their

father slumped asleep at the kitchen table, his presence in this room that he hated as much a mystery as Randall's trip to the river.

4

Sometime after the new boy finally arrived with his medicine, Edwin Keane's telephone rang.

He had to turn on the overhead light to locate the phone, hidden beneath a stack of laundered shirts his father had brought him. He kept the bungalow dark always, dark in the daytime. Drew the shades and pulled the curtains, shuttered the windows in winter, except for one: the kitchen window closest to Johnsontown, that part of Trent which never slept.

Though a thick wood separated the bungalow from Johnsontown, noises pushed constant and unmuted through the pine maze. Edwin saw by the kitchen window often, always on Saturday nights, Johnsontown tuned in like radio.

He heard very few voices besides those floating through the pines. There was the druggist's voice, which disembodied by telephone and pitched in bland midwestern tones meant to convey both pressured grace and piety, didn't seem sincere enough to count; the voice of his father, who stopped by Tuesday and Thursday afternoons for a short bourbon and soda and asked the same questions in a voice which, though only a coffee table's width away, seemed to travel twice the five blocks it took for the druggist's to reach him.

Briefly there had been the voice of the cook Jenny, whom Edwin's mother had hired to housekeep. Edwin had fired her after a week. He'd heard enough of her voice in the first hour of her first day, though he'd fired her not because she was an inveterate gossip but because everything she cooked smelled and tasted the same. Morphine took care of his appetite and since he had little to do all day but sit, read, smoke and wait for his medicine to arrive, he could handle the cleaning. He enjoyed roving through the bungalow armed with a broom to swipe at corner cobwebs, but he let go the dusting and floor-scrubbing — who cared, no one except his father came by anyway and his father's idea of cozy was the dirt-floored shack down in East Lake he fled to during duck hunting season.

Occasionally there was another voice — his mother's bourbon rocks and filtered cigarette rasp — though not lately and not at all in person. On the telephone, lying in silent wait, ready to pounce without warning.

"Jones came by already?" she said before Edwin could slur his hello.

"Somebody new. A boy. Not Jones."

"Whomever they sent," his mother said, humming thick and smooth on the whom, as if to make clear that the turnover down at the drugstore was of no interest to her, though Jones had delivered for Lehmann since before Edwin was born.

"Someone came, at any rate."

"At any pace, you mean," said Edwin. "He just left."

"Just now?"

"Five minutes."

"It was over an hour ago that I talked to Walter Lehmann."

"Two." When she was about to speak he added, "And a half."

"Well, you say he's new, maybe the boy got lost."

"Lost for two hours in this town? He'd have to not speak English, be blind or both."

"Seems futile for you to be putting Trent down all the time."

"In my position you mean? You mean I'm lucky to have a hellhole to come home to?"

Slowly she filled the pause with an exaggerated sigh. "Better me hearing this than your father I suppose." He knew that she didn't actually mind him criticizing Trent, that she welcomed the switch from his usual narcotic complacency. Both knew that Edwin would never say such a thing to his father, that conversations between Edwin and his father were parodies of outrageous politeness. Saying he hated Trent would not ripple his father's stalwart sense of place; Trent was where his father had been born, schooled, where he'd inherited a law practice, where his brother and sister lived, where he owned real estate: a half block of businesses downtown, this very bungalow and others identical but less kept-up through the woods in Johnsontown.

"I'm stopping by on my way downtown," his mother said.

"Now?"

"Give me ten minutes."

"Why?"

"Why? Why am I dropping in? Because I want to see how you're getting along. That's why."

He could hear it in the mock surprise and repetition of her why; feigned shock in response to his why, guilt she felt for sending him to live in the bungalow. The same guilt which had led her to hire Jenny, that had caused her to pick up the phone and call. But his father had been out of town Thursday and hadn't come by for his bourbon soda, which meant that in four days Edwin had spoken to no one except that stick-figured boy who showed up on his porch. There had been only those few words with the boy and now he couldn't remember if the boy had even said anything. He just remembered him standing there dangling his arms toward his knees as if frozen in the middle of some grade-school calisthenics.

Maybe he didn't speak. Maybe it's time I have a conversation, he thought.

And his mother did know how to listen. They had a history. Sometimes after his shot, his mother listened as if leaning over his crib, craning to hear the sound of his breathing during his first night home from the hospital.

He learned to listen to her, too, but that came later.

"I'm not going anywhere within the next hour," he told her.

A pause on her part he decided was held-back laughter: he had meant for her to laugh, and because she was irreverent in the gracefully pungent manner of a fifty-year-old coastal plain woman, because she was a poke-fun-at-everything-especially-your-own-misfortune type, her stifled laughter made him nervous.

"Can I bring you anything?"

Medicine, he almost said. But they'd been

through that, an hour ago, though soon he'd need more, need her help to get it.

"Everything I could ever desire is right here in this kitchen."

"I can't believe that. But let's us talk about it when I get there."

Driving into town, Edith Keane thought of how her son had sounded on the phone, slurred words reminding her of the six months they'd endured at home together after his return from the hospital. B.B., she thought as she followed the road hugging the river's last curve, Before Bungalow. She pulled down the sun visor as if to hide her smile; she felt horrible for finding it funny, worse for dividing her days in such a way — Before Bungalow, After Bungalow.

Yet those six months had been even more horrible. After the first few weeks she'd mostly avoided him and when she'd forced herself to check on him had found him propped up on pillows with a forlorn lag to his features, smoking cigarettes lit one from another, staring out the window, awaiting his next shot.

At first he had adhered to the dosage prescribed by his doctor — Edwin's uncle, her husband's brother, Arthur — and he seemed to her sufficiently anesthetized, never lucid yet never looped as she'd often seen him since. But after a month he began to complain. Pain in his back, he said. It had been broken in the accident and was the reason for the morphine in the first place; he'd spent six months in traction under heavy sedation. The plan, according to Arthur, was for Edwin to taper off at home.

Yet Arthur was not a good doctor for several reasons, the most pathetic of which was that he hated to hear people complain. Rather than listen to patients whine about insomnia or short breath, he'd as soon scribble out something to shut them up.

When Edwin began to complain to her, he had already been complaining to others for some time: especially to Tillett, their driver and handyman. Twice a day Tillett spent a half hour sitting by Edwin's bed telling him stories of Johnsontown, where Tillett had caroused for going on forty years. Tillett's tales always seemed to soothe Edwin, but after Edwin had been home for six weeks or so, Tillett came to her in the kitchen one morning.

"He ain't listened to me all week."

"What are you talking about, Tillett?" She was pouring coffee and had her back to him though she felt him come up behind her, knew who it was because of his deferential silence when entering a room where she was eating.

"Eddie keep saying his back hurting him bad."

"Well, maybe he sprained it somehow. Getting up to go to the bathroom. I'm sure he'll feel better, long as he stays put."

"He's been complaining about it all week. Won't let me talk. Don't want to hear it."

"It doesn't hurt to listen, Tillett. You don't have to entertain him all the time."

Tillett smiled at her. He had this way of staying put until she told him things she'd rather not. He was impossible to lie to or even mislead, he wanted whole stories and was willing to wait for them. He made her nervous. He was smarter than either of them would care to admit and his sense of time — that he could always put life off until he found out what he wanted to know — startled her. And she was jealous of his way with Edwin and had taken it out on him, subtly she felt, for years.

"I see exactly what you trying to say," said Tillett. "But it ain't like he want me just to sit there nod up a storm while he talk. He want somebody to do something. Keeps asking me ask you call Doctor Keane."

"I'll talk to him," she'd said.

She'd called Arthur, who'd driven over during his lunch hour, eaten with her on the gazebo and lectured the whole time about the danger of addiction. They'd gone in afterwards to see Edwin, and after he recounted his nights of no sleep and persistent pain, Arthur had upped the dosage by a half grain.

Within a day or so, things between her and Edwin began to change. She noticed that after his shot there were moments of clarity for him, whole hours sometimes during which normal emotional patterns returned. He came physically into focus; the looseness about his eyes disappeared, his face grew sharper, and he looked to her like he did when he was very young — six or seven — and was excited by a new and mysterious discovery.

His body was a body again instead of baggage dragged wearily about. After his shot he slumped — for some reason this was impossible when he was in pain. As a result she began to associate good posture with pain. Overnight she became stoop-shouldered, sway-backed.

His limbs sprang to life, he had reflexes, sometimes he even talked with his hands, dramatic chops and slices reminding her of guest speakers at her husband's annual Rotary Club spouse dinner. Though his speech was thickly slurred he was more articulate, more expansive. Curious, too: he asked her questions about her life, a gesture which she realized would disappear with the dwindling effects of the drug.

The longer he stayed upstairs the more she would hear him on the hallway phone begging the pharmacist for an early delivery. Even though his desperate tone annoyed and embarrassed her, she hated listening to his pleas and was enraged at the obstinance of that insolent young druggist. He'd been working down there for years, yet who knew the first thing about him? She would listen until she couldn't listen and then she'd lift the receiver from his shaky hands and demand to speak directly to Lehmann.

Lehmann always listened to her. The Keane family had owned that building since before Lehmann had come to Trent. Within a half hour of hanging up, old wizened Jones would weave up the drive, sack bouncing in the rusty handlebar basket. Within an hour she'd be settled in the wingback, her feet on Edwin's bed, basking in the attention he paid her.

Yet she couldn't keep it up for long, living for that half hour when she was treated with ephemeral interest because of some chemical coursing through his bloodstream. Since the accident, everything in her life had changed. What should have been six months of depression had lasted twice that long and showed no signs of lifting. She'd always been bored by self-pity, but now she spent whole weeks in bed and did not tire of the pillow-hugging, sheet-thrashing indulgence of these days.

Her friends treated her differently, gingerly. They wanted to give her time to work it out, but after a few months *she* began to feel like the victim. She imagined herself crumpled along a sidewalk surrounded by a circle of her closest friends, the order to stand back, give her room obeyed with an alacrity which made her suspect that none of them wanted to get involved. When she and Thomas were invited out, Thomas unconditionally refused. She didn't talk to Thomas about Edwin much these days, couldn't without arguing. He worked all the time now, had sold the cottage at Nags Head a few months after the accident, put the money into a trust for Edwin. As if Edwin needed another trust.

As she neared the end of Edgecombe Street, the sight of the bungalow reminded her of the day she'd thought of sending Edwin there to live. She'd been lunching in the gazebo, having forced herself outside to avoid the misery of another meal eaten alone in the kitchen, but things were as bad in the full noon light until she happened to think of the bungalow. How had she remembered? Thomas took care of the rental properties, this place he'd inherited from his mother's maiden sister, it had nothing to do with her family. What caused her to think of it during that tasteless meal of tomato soup and chicken salad which she picked at self-consciously after Tillett showed in the sideyard armed with hedge clippers and a ladder? Some random linkage she could not reconstruct. She could only remember the way the soup tasted after the idea came to her, of tomato instead of tin can. The house is empty, the house is perfect, she'd told herself. I will set him up over there to rebuild.

Rebuild replaced in Later Life as her favorite phrase.

She tried the front door and found it locked; the windows were shut, curtains pulled tightly to. It took him two minutes to answer. He led her through the front unlived-in rooms, filled with furniture Thomas had ordered brand-new from the store. A crisp shade still shrouded in plastic sat atop the ribbed stem of a floor lamp, and from the arm of a rocking chair a price tag dangled. She flipped the switch on an overhead light but there was no bulb. In the kitchen a caved-in cot was pushed beneath the only open window in the house, looking out on the wood which bordered Johnsontown. She knew these woods and what went on there. Who in Trent did not, who from the West End had not grown up warned away from them and wanting to slip just once into their lusty shadows for an hour or two?

She hadn't realized the wood was so close.

Voices carried through its thickness, though not much sunlight pierced the tangle of branch and vine. She thought of light along the river, how textured and brilliant the surfaces it grazed. Even cheap plywood appeared richly grained, regal mahogany when river light found it. For the first time since she'd called him a half hour ago she felt guilty for sending him here, wondered how he could begin to rebuild in this — what was the word the psychiatrist who'd come round to talk to her while Edwin was in traction favored? *Environment.* At the time she'd thought of science experiments, of volunteers paid to receive electric shocks in sterile cubicles.

Edwin sat down on the edge of the cot and coughed. He didn't seem to have changed clothes since she'd seen him last. His white shirt was sweat-soaked, faintly sallow like jaundiced skin. Clothes were strewn about the kitchen. At the foot of the cot the bedclothes had been kicked into a thick ridge. Books covered counters, piles lined the kitchen table. In the corner next to the pantry he'd set his phonograph atop a night stand.

He lives in the kitchen, she thought, the rest of this house a waste.

He'd pulled her wingback in from the parlor and she scooted it up to the cot, sat down and slumped. Small talk followed, tiny talk compared to what-comes-next, she thought. Five minutes of current events: Edwin didn't read the papers anymore, his father had both the *Trentonian* and the *Raleigh News and Observer* delivered to the bungalow but Edwin let them wither where they landed, and Thomas finally canceled them when a bumper crop of yellowed tubes littered the front and side yards. Five minutes about Thomas's business trip to Raleigh and Greensboro. Two to give him a message from Tillett. When all the banalities were out of the way she waited, scrutinizing his movements for hints that *her* part was about to begin.

But he acted oblivious. His speech matched the slow-motioned troll of fingers through his hair, consonants so softened by morphine that his words emerged deboned, invertebrate.

Maybe he needs more medicine, she thought, and she considered calling Lehmann until she remembered what her brother-in-law had told her over lunch a few days ago — that since he'd been back from the hospital Edwin had tripled his daily intake, that he was up to fifteen grains a day, that recent X-rays revealed that the bones in his back were healing quickly. Of course Arthur knew nothing of the early deliveries, she didn't dare tell him of her calls to Lehmann, and she trusted Lehmann never to tell. Arthur, after all, was her brother-in-law, any medical request would carry his implicit sanction, she had been able to insinuate his approval without actually incriminating herself, and all for that half hour following Edwin's shot.

That half hour which so far had not started. She glanced down at her watch, saw that she had been marking time for thirty minutes. What she would not give then to be coddled by the very person whose situation had created this need, new to her, to be coddled. He was the only person who could coddle; the lemon meringues and shopping trips to Raleigh and hastily assembled bridge games of her friends were transparent gestures in comparison. Only Edwin could open things up again. The perversity of her need was outweighed by the symmetry. She had convinced herself that this was only a more intensified version of what all parents went through eventually, *I am only honest about wanting something back for the miserable void his misfortune has created and I am blaming him only as much as we all blame our children for making us give up so much so that they can feel well-adjusted.* She'd have picked up the phone and called Lehmann then and there, if she had not reached out to run her hand distractedly over the kitchen wall and recoiled at the touch of the pocked plaster, clammy as a corpse's skin.

93

Environment, that crisp and clinical term, back to haunt her again. She could blame it on the bungalow instead of his medicine; after all, their talks had always been illuminated by river light. She stared around the room again, lowered her eyes from the sagging lines of the ceiling to her son.

"You have to be somewhere?"

She could not look at him for long. "Errands to run but I've got some time. Why?"

He looked to the ceiling in answer. She felt accused by this, her disappointment in their "talk" so obvious. *I'm boring you,* his rising eyes said, *you hate it here, go away, go.*

"What time is it getting to be?" She rose and stood by the sink, surveying the wreckage of the counter: forks with tines so crusted that the slits between them were joined like webbed feet. Pots triple-stacked, a cookie bisected by a serrated crescent of teeth marks.

"Looking for a clock?" he said.

"In the wrong place I guess."

"You're doing remarkably well, not mentioning the mess."

"Not me has to live with it," she said.

"And not mentioning the cook I fired."

"If she bothered you she bothered you. Some people work on your nerves."

"You're appalled."

"It looks a tad depressing right now."

"Not your favorite time of day, though."

True. She hated it: interminable afternoon, Goddamned afternoon she called it to herself. Morning was fresh-breathed and expansive, a many-cornered stretch of sun and shade through which she was content to roam; evening a decrescendo of an excuse during which everything — extra helpings, more wine, staying out late or going to bed earlier — was justification for frustrations accrued by day. But afternoon was morning and night meeting in a seam five hours long and unevenly cobbled, a threshold impossible not to trip over.

"You should come over some other time." He said this lightly, with the extractable sincerity of a child inviting another home from school.

It seemed comic, his asking her to come back, as if the hour was responsible for the thwarted conversation. But she remembered how she'd felt after those half hours by his side at home, how the chance that she would uncover something had seemed dangerous and vital.

"Of course I will," she said. "I don't hate the place at all, Edwin, and I still say it's good for you to get out on your own. Though I tell you, lots of folks in this town don't see it that way."

"Seems futile for us to complain about this town."

She said, "I'm talking about the people in it."

"Same thing."

"Only difference is they can talk."

"I like it here, actually," he said. He turned back toward the window; she slumped against the counter. He began to mumble, how Trent had everything he required, everything he needed was right here in this room. She quit listening when she realized that her moment would not come, there was no way she could steer the conversation away short of slapping him and saying shut up, ask me questions, what about me don't let's talk about Trent or this nasty kitchen let's talk about me, me.

"I have to go."

He twitched once and went quiet, pivoted around to face her.

"You just got here," he said.

She looked at her watch. "An hour almost."

"Come back tomorrow then," he said.

"Your father will be coming by for his drink."

"You're busy?"

"All week. Work to do in the courtyard."

"Lobster Women?"

She nodded. It was one of the few activities she'd kept since the accident, her work with the church courtyard committee. Seventy-five years ago a group of parishioners had transformed the courtyard into a garden now known throughout the South for its mix of plants rare to the area. Keeping it up was hard work but satisfying in a way that gardening at home could never be: there were write-ups in the magazines and guided tours, an annual party the parish held for them. Edwin called them the Lobster Women because every year they raised money for supplies by importing several dozen lobsters from Maine and holding a lobster sale. They had held the sale for two decades and it had become a local holiday of sorts, a social event with its own ritualized system and pace: people stood around the courtyard for hours watching children poke lobsters with twigs from the pecan tree the tubs circled; the lobsters raised their blue claws sluggishly, as if stunned by the trip down from Maine and the lingering humidity of eastern North Carolina October.

Edwin thought the courtyard project a worthless pursuit for a church and said so often; it was the one object of his ridicule which she felt she didn't have to tolerate. She'd rather he'd have made fun of the Eucharist, since she held her courtyard work higher, thought of it as infinitely more spiritual.

"We're working on a new section. Lots to do."

"What time tomorrow?"

"Oh," she said and she shook her head, mock weary at the thought of the work to be done. "I imagine I'll be there on and off past supper."

"I'll come by," said Edwin.

She matched his smile and said what she had to say to get out: okay, fine, 'bye.

5

Eureka took a canopied path along the walls of the courtyard to a marble bench where she could see but not be seen, though since she'd been going there she'd seen hardly anyone, only a group of ladies who sometimes came late in the day and never stayed long. They wore kerchiefs and gloves, carried clippers and bamboo rakes, and as she passed by them they lowered their voices or quit talking altogether.

A leaf collection: she felt it was busy work, an assignment for someone Randall's age, yet it was her homework and she always did her homework, so she had come to the Episcopal church to steal exotic leaves from the courtyard. That morning she'd told Randall about the assignment and he'd wanted to come along so much he claimed he was going to fake a stomach ache to get sent home from the drugstore. Since school had started and they'd both begun afternoon jobs, Randall talked often of how much he missed his explorations. It had taken her all of the half mile to his school to talk him out of his scheme; she'd promised to take him back after supper and he'd leaned against the flagpole until the late bell sounded, lecturing her about the silver plaques identifying genus and species in Latin which she would have to take care to copy correctly.

She'd missed him this week. Since he'd started work she'd come every afternoon to the courtyard where she'd spent the hours until supper doing her homework or reading biographies she'd checked out from the school library. She was unloading the paper bag of supplies she'd brought along for her leaf collection — scissors and paste, a dime store photo album with silver stick-on triangles — when the women filed in. They spread out in a corner near the gate and went to work. For a half hour Eureka watched from her inlet of green and sunlit silence. She dug her feet in the gravel of the path and sat undetected until an old woman pushing a wheelbarrow spotted her and stopped to stare.

Eureka stared back through the willow tendrils. The wheelbarrow driver stopped to talk to another woman who looked Eureka's way briefly before going back to work. When the load was full, the woman pushed the wheelbarrow along her way. The woman wore lime-green gloves rolled up to her wrists; a wind blew her hair back in wild strands, twisting it into curls tight as phone cord.

The woman put down the wheelbarrow and stood, panting, in front of the bench. Eureka thought she was hyperventilating; she thought she was asking if Eureka was a parishioner though she couldn't be sure because she was too busy looking at the woman's thick green fingers, especially the little one of her left hand which was moving, clawing at the air like an inchworm desperate for traction. When she finished her sentence Eureka swallowed hard and held her breath, her cure for hiccup and inappropriate laughter both, and exhaled a "Pardon?"

The woman raked her bangs and said, "I said this really is reserved for our parishioners." Up close she appeared to be held together by disdain and a paste of pancaked rouge; the longer Eureka looked at her the more scornful the woman seemed. By the time she finishes blessing me out for not being a parishioner she'll be hard as the statue of St. Francis in the center of the courtyard, thought Eureka. Looking back to the statue, she noticed the other woman prop her rake on one of St. Francis's green shoulders and start toward them. Pretty soon they will have me surrounded, she thought, blanched women bearing rakes chasing me through downtown streets, pointing toward me with fingers lime and lemon and fuchsia even and wait — just wait — until I tell Randall.

"I just come here to read." Eureka held up her botany book. She felt her shoulders twitch and she stifled the beginnings of a shrug which she knew was of all gestures offensive to ladies of this ilk the most slatternly and unpardonable. Yet the desire built with the sensual intensity of itch or sneeze and again she breathed big to stifle a laugh as she imagined giving herself over to it, chasing Wheelbarrow Woman through the courtyard with shoulders flexed wild and rapid as a hen's wings.

The image made her sassy. "This is a church, isn't it? I thought they let anyone in a church."

"If we let anyone in here we would have to work a whole lot harder to keep our courtyard clean." The woman stretched her lips out in what could have possibly been mistaken at a distance for a smile.

How to answer that? Did this mean she didn't want dirt tracked through her courtyard on the way to the sanctuary? Was the garden, with its botanical specimens, the real sanctuary?

But she didn't have to answer because by then the other woman had reached them, pointed to the botany text Eureka still held, and said, "Leaf collection?"

"Yes," said Eureka.

"You must have Jerry Strickland for botany."

"That's right," said Eureka.

The younger woman stood shoulder to shoulder with her friend, who clutched the rubber grips of the barrow, deflated by her arrival. "Edwin had to do one, too. 'Leventh grade I believe. Hated it. Put it off so long he had Thomas out picking leaves off the trees by flashlight."

To Eureka she said, "This is the place to come, though. Children have been coming here for their collections since Strickland's been teaching here. Better stay away from the plain ones. He'll know right away where you went when he sees some of these rare leaves, might mark you down if you stick a loblolly needle in there."

Wheelbarrow Woman had begun to tremor again. "I have never understood why we work so hard just to let these children tear through here pulling leaves off our trees," she said. But she calmed down as soon as the other draped an arm around her and said, "She's being careful, Julia. She's picking them up off the ground. We're all going out to Sally's now, put our feet up for a while. I'll help you dump this last load, then you can ride with me out there."

Obviously this woman had come to rescue

her, though when she left Eureka she felt worse than before she'd arrived. She left Eureka feeling no enthusiasm for a task she'd thought of from the start as obligatory, left her feeling like a dim figure in a ghostly parade of Mr. Strickland's botany students, as flat and plain as a loblolly needle.

An hour later Edwin stood behind a row of azaleas by the gate and watched the girl at work. He'd stopped by to see if his mother was around, wasn't surprised to find that the Lobster Women had cleared out early, regrouped no doubt at one of their houses to drink bourbon tinted grainy by late afternoon river light. He had no intention of leaving the house when he'd told her the day before that he'd drop by the courtyard: both knew he was testing her, needling her for not coming to see him and blaming her for the lackluster tone of yesterday's talk.

He'd been both drawn out and forced out: seduced by the day itself, which flashed outside his kitchen window, alternately sunlit white then brooding with purplish shadow, and repelled by an image of himself crawling past the wrecked Packard and the body of Sarah mired facedown in Serenitowinity Swamp. It had been with him all day, coming into sharper focus as the effects of his shot waned; when more shots failed to make it fade, he'd decided for the first time in months to get out of the house.

From his hiding place Edwin watched the bike shoot past, its driver's long legs pumping so swiftly that black shoe merged with pedal. Past green-tinted St. Francis and the algae-gummed birdbaths, down the center path until he braked in a wide-arced fishtail which spewed gravel amongst the morning labors of the Lobster Women.

The girl let the scrapbook fall to the ground. Though Edwin had been sequestered for a year and had no idea who lived in Trent now, he was immediately curious about this girl, wondered who she was and what she was doing in this courtyard. She was thin and dark and her coal-colored hair was wind-thickened, wild. When she bent to copy the Latin from the plaque he knew exactly why she was there. *Why* stifled the *who*, at least for a moment while he was reminded of the thousand worthless tasks one is assigned in this world.

But the *who* returned as he watched her cross the courtyard to where the boy struggled to catch the kickstand in gravel. She spoke to the boy in a tone familiar and filled with soft fury, and as Edwin moved closer to hear better he recognized the boy.

"I *am* at work," the boy was saying. His

voice was high and hoarse and lilting and Edwin knew at once he had not heard it before, that the boy had not spoken at all when he'd found him frozen on the front porch. "Official drugstore business."

"Don't dare try and tell me the druggist sent you off to the river again." She was leaning into him now, her chin an inch from his forehead. Edwin stared at the pieces of leaves caught in the weave of her knee socks.

"Nope," said the boy, and he began to chant: "Nope, nope, nopester, nosirreester the druggist did not send me to no river nor to see no man whose house has the face of our father who art in hey now nope nopester."

"Hush up and listen," said the girl. "If you get fired you know what'll come."

"Free trip down the basement to see the cave crickets and the wharf rats and the snake-skins tangled in the cobwebster corners . . ."

"And the belt attached one end to his hand the other to you," said the girl.

"And the opossums and the o'raccoons and the old moldy-ass rotten windows and doorsters . . ."

"Shut up," she said, clamping his shoulder blades, but this strange kid — Edwin couldn't believe he was the same quiet gawky one, but those were the same arms stretching toward his knees, the same stubby hair and even the same handed-down dungarees — continued to tick and chant like an auctioneer, backing odd suffixes up to his words and spraying his sister's chin with exuberant syllables.

"Okay," the boy said finally. "I'm between deliveries, see, but the druggist, he gave me a whole list of places to go, about two hours' worth for not even a slowpokester but a normal-moving person which I busted my butt and dropped them off all in a hour so I could stop by over here and help you before I have to —"

"What if someone from the drugstore sees you here in the courtyard?"

"I'll hide the bike. Besides I'll be in the trees. No one can see me up there."

"You're not about to climb any tree. They already tried to kick me out of here once today, no way I'm going to let you break a limb off one of their wonderful trees."

"You mean you're picking 'em up off the ground?"

The girl nodded. The boy gave her a disgusted look, exaggerated his disgust by spitting into the coiffed boxwoods, and said, "Leaves anybody could get? Ant leaves? Baby crawled-all-over-leaves, slug-slimed leaves? And the good stuff going to waste up there, A-plus ones left alone while you fill your book up with those scrawny D-minus speciments?"

"Speci*mens*. I suppose you were born to collect leaves," she said, but the boy didn't answer, acted as if irony were beneath him and this girl — his sister — was beneath him, too, with her pedestrian taste in foliage. What is this I'm watching, thought Edwin, who exactly are these people? He let himself fantasize about who they were and how they came to be there, and when he came back to the moment they had quit talking and the boy was shimmying up a nearby trunk.

They worked for a half hour without stopping, the boy talking all the time about leaves, trees, asking the girl to call up the Latin names to him, which he would repeat — *Pinus tæda, Diospyros virginiana, Ulmus americana* — while he shook limbs, sending down thick green storms. She selected one leaf to stick between the pages of her botany text with the Latin written on a scrap and tucked alongside like a bookmark. The boy talked about chlorophone, which the girl corrected to chlorophyll, and once he called down a name — Eureka — which the girl answered with a "what?"

Edwin said the name to himself, thinking of the unflinching sobriety of his own, so obviously chosen for him long before he arrived in the world.

He watched her copy names from plaques. Every few seconds a tree would shake, touching off another shower. After a long and vigorous quake the high voice from above called out "Helloooo downnn therrrre." Each word drawn out and trilled, as if echoing through some place hollow and dark: the bottom of a well from which the sky was a distant and formidable seal. "Hello down there" — the call came again, slower this time with a thin but passionate vibrato. Edwin felt his eyes drawn to the treetops as those words floated down. In the long silence following he looked to her again, and when the call came he watched her for as long as he could, feeling as if they'd been found together in this moment, found and isolated in the purity of the present. Leaves would spiral down but they were in no hurry and did not look forward or skyward; no answer was expected from them when the call came again.

He was no longer bothered that she was here for a silly homework assignment. In this moment all reason and purpose dissolved, as did the image of Serenitowinity which had hovered all day in the back of his mind and the corner of his vision. He couldn't remember why he'd left the house when he tried to; he couldn't remember why she wanted leaves. He stood in the courtyard washed clean, hidden from her but no longer hiding anything.

Above them the branches rustled and he

watched the boy drop to the ground beside her, roll in the grass. Edwin couldn't tell how old she was. Beside the boy she looked younger, but alone — when he was in the trees and she was sitting cross-legged in the grass pasting leaves in her textbook — she seemed of a vague age.

When the two of them stood to leave he crouched farther behind the bushes. The boy mounted the bike but pushed it along with his feet instead of pedaling, to keep up with the girl. Walking, she seemed older; not because of any easy twist or strut but because of the way she held herself, arms still and draped close to her sides. And because of the way her skirt fit, of the shape of her back, its perfect gradual curve into hips, because of her hips and the backs of her tanned legs disappearing into socks studded with pieces of leaves. Because of her ankles even though he could not see them, even though they were hidden from behind blue-ribbed socks pulled high. But when she stopped at the corner while her little brother stood on his bike pedals to peek over the Collinses' brick wall, she grabbed him by the belt and yanked in a brash way that made Edwin rethink her age once again. Once again her age shifted with circumstance, she reinvented herself into the moment, climbed aboard without baggage or destination, empty-handed but well-equipped. The longer he looked the less sure he was and he liked that: he wanted to know even less.

Two o'clock in the afternoon and the only sounds in the drugstore came from the steady swoosh of ceiling fan and the radio, turned so low that it seemed as if the announcer's voice was also affected by the doldrums which had fallen over Lehmann's. Ruby McClaurin, withered feather duster in hand, stood at the top of an aisle with one foot raised and resting on the window stage, peering across the street. Occasional customers wandered the aisles as if they'd forgotten what they'd come to buy. They smoked cigarettes until they tired of them, then dropped them to the black-and-white diamond-tiled floor, crushed them with heel twists, without looking down. From the drug counter Roy stared at the butts smoldering on the floor, ash dusting the diamonds. His day had been interminable and was only a bit more than half over. There were no scripts to fill and he'd had to busy himself with inventory, but at least Lehmann had not returned from lunch to lord over him while he counted.

That morning they'd had words about Edwin Keane.

"You realize, don't you, that you could lose your business because of him?" Roy had said to Lehmann. Keane had just called for the fourth time, Lehmann intercepting finally and instructing Roy to send over half the amount the script called for before the boy's mother started calling.

"I don't want them tying up my phone lines all day. Just send over enough to tide him, just enough to knock him out 'til tomorrow when it's due."

"We're not doctors, you know. You're not even a druggist. Neither of us can prescribe drugs."

Lehmann feigned weariness. He sat down on a stool, rose his left leg slowly, lifted his haunch high above the stool, pulled his handkerchief out. "No, son, we ain't doctors. We don't make doctor money, but we are in this business for a small profit at least and if I don't go along with this thing that boy's mother might jerk this building right out from under me and we can't sell drugs on the goddamn sidewalk, and we'll both be out a living."

Roy was quiet, watching Lehmann refold his handkerchief with the dramatic precision color guards give a flag at the end of the day. There was something particularly Trentian in this gesture to Roy; Trent men had a way of intimidating by applying their hands to trivial tasks. Simple, irrelevant movements were given priority over your comments. Lehmann was not a native — he'd been born in Norfolk, had bought this drugstore when he was in his mid-twenties — yet he was a tireless mimic, and he aped every masculine quirk he could identify.

"That's something they don't teach you boys about up there in Chapel Hill, people that can put your ass out on the sidewalk without moving a muscle. Don't teach you that, just how to package laxatives, how to count goddamn pills."

Why *should* they teach that? thought Roy. And what would the course be called: Phar 45: People Who Can Put Your Ass Out on the Sidewalk? He'd have registered without even looking up the workload, given a title like that. Or Phar 90: Social, Political and Economic Pressures in Backwater Drugstores Run by Sycophantic Businessmen. A master's degree in such courses could not have prepared him for Lehmann, Trent either for that matter.

"That's my job, Mr. Lehmann, counting pills. If I don't count right, they'll put me out on the street anyway, a hell of a lot quicker than Edwin's father can."

"Not his father I worry about," said Lehmann. He was smoothing his handkerchief, rubbing hard as if he could erase the mucus stains.

"But his father's family holds the lease, I thought."

"Won't ask where you learned to think," said Lehmann. "Seems like you'd have learned something from hands-on. You've been here for what now, five years?"

"Seven."

"Mother's one holds the reins in that carriage."

Desperately Roy tried to think of something smart-assed to say, something caustic to come back on the cracker quaintness of Lehmann's euphemism. But sarcasm bounced off Lehmann; it was one of the things he'd failed to master from the natives, who were literal-minded only when signing contracts or bone-lessly drunk.

"But still," said Roy, "you know the law. Both the state and the local boards check how much morphine goes out of here every week. Of course his uncle would be in bigger trouble than we would, but still, we're supplying it early, and now you're telling me to fill it without a script."

"There's all kinda holes in that law, son," said Lehmann. "First of all, the law says a doctor and I quote 'in attendance' unquote can prescribe without keeping a record. And small amounts is exempt. Arthur'll just say he was attending and felt a small amount was in order and we won't stand to gain by crossing him on that.

"But there's another hole, even bigger. A lot of people — doctors and druggists both — were indicted for what the court called maintenance — keeping a dope addict doped up just because he's a dope addict. But I did some checking. Every time a prosecution come down it was in the case of some poor saps feeding the habit of what the court calls a nonmedical addict. Other words, one who got started on that mess because he liked it, not because he needed it. As far as I know, there never has been a verdict against somebody keeping up a fellow like Keane's son, who has good reason to get it. Plus, most of these other type addicts is pure white trash. And trash hadn't ever done well in court around here."

"You've done your homework, I see."

"That's my job. Wasn't going to wait around for you to do it."

"Don't wait around for me to send him any more medicine either. Not without a script."

"You do what I say or you're going to be out of a job quicker than Keane or the State Board can get to you. You've got to where you like to talk back to me a little too much."

"After seven years you'd think I'd be able to have a say in things around here."

As he rose and turned to leave, Lehmann said, "Seven more and maybe we'll talk."

Seven years: Roy had felt groggy at the thought, and he'd had a hard time concentrating since, had messed up every count he'd taken.

When the phone rang, slicing the afternoon quiet, rousing Ruby from her perch and sending her down the aisle to dust, Roy knew already who it was.

"May I please speak with the pharmacist today," said Edwin. The connection sounded long-distance, Keane's voice sedated into a near whisper.

"Hope you're fine," Edwin said after Roy identified himself. "I'm in need of medicine myself."

"I'm afraid I'm going to have to call your doctor about this, Mr. Keane. You'll kill yourself if you keep this up, and I don't really want to be responsible for that."

"Afraid?" said Keane. "You're afraid? I know, figure of speech, colloquialism, all that. Don't take it literally. But afraid? You're not really afraid. Think about it."

Roy held the mouthpiece away from his ear and stared quizzically at the circle of tiny black holes, though no one was around to see. "Think about what?"

Keane snorted faintly — the only time Roy had heard him laugh — and said, "Call him. Call the doctor. He's my uncle, and along with my father he holds the title to the building you're standing in." A pause, then: "A few months ago I would never have been able to say it like that, but you certainly know, given your line of work, how desperate pain can make a person."

"Morphine is a serious narcotic, Mr. Keane. There are strict laws concerning its dispensation. I've done some checking up on this subject with you in mind, and I learned that quite a few years ago — during the First World War I think — the government passed a bill called the Harrison Act which required doctors and pharmacists to keep accurate records of certain substances."

"Research," said Edwin. "I'm impressed."

"I didn't do it to impress you, but I did find out something that might help. There's a hospital in Lexington, Kentucky, which specializes in curing addicts. It's run by the government, and in the event you can't be cured after a significant stay, there's a chance of getting something called a government prescription, which in my opinion would be a much more regulated, not to mention safer road to take than the one we're on."

"This is a road we're on?"

"If you went there and they couldn't cure you and they gave you a government script, at least what we're doing here would be legal."

"You amaze me, Green. Goddamn amazing that you'd spend all that time looking out for me. But listen: I don't want to go to Kentucky. I have no curiosity about Kentucky and I am geographically speaking a curious person. So many aren't. They don't give a damn for landscape, it can be blank as a page for all they care but anyway, Kentucky. Mammoth Cave, maybe, but not another hospital, especially not one run by the government. How can the government make the pain in my back disappear?"

"With a government script, I could legally dispense your medicine. Now I just send it over at your whim, which is not only wrong but illegal."

"Tell the new boy to hurry," said Edwin. "Last time he was late."

"I'm afraid I can't send anything until Friday. That's when the refill date is."

"Afraid again when you're not really afraid. I like how you try to stand up for yourself."

"I'm busy."

"You know what comes next. I'll have my mother call Lehmann."

"Mr. Lehmann is not a pharmacist."

"No, he's no pharmacist, but he doesn't need to be. He's an old ass-kisser who knows what will happen if he doesn't do it."

In all the calls that Keane had made, Roy had never heard him talk like this; he'd never once been rude. Usually he insisted for a few minutes, then turned it over to his mother, who was always rude. She talked to Roy as if he didn't understand English, interrupted him to ask for Lehmann, was nasty if Lehmann couldn't come to the phone immediately. Edwin had even apologized for her in the past. She got like that, he'd explained, because she hated to see him in pain.

"Do what you have to do," said Roy. "I can't help but say that it seems you've resorted to a new low. In the past you've always had some respect for my position. You've never tried to pressure me like this before. Seems like a turn for the worse to me."

"I guess I took that worse turn before I ever met you, Mr. Green. Now I've got to live with it, and the best way for me to live with it is with my medicine, so if you'll send it over now."

"You'll have to go above me, I guess."

"Easily done," said Edwin. And what bothered Roy more than the fact that he would do it was the fact that it was so easily done.

★ ★ ★

This time Randall was not so spooked. He picked through the knee-high grass, crossed the porch to tap twice on the window. A quick step back and he was ready: for the blind to jerk and the window to rise, the bad basement breath to roll out. Ready even for the arm to pluck the bag out of his hand. He held the package out in offering, cocked one foot behind so that when the time came he could pivot and run.

While he waited the door opened and a figure appeared behind the screen.

"Over here," said the silhouette. Randall inched over, close enough to stare. Worn screen bagging between them made the man's skin rust-colored, rough looking. Creeping from measly sideburns was the strangest beard Randall had ever seen — not a semi-defiant, halfhearted, three-week college-boy beard nor a bushy avuncular one but a patchy growth, dark brown and red, which seemed to have grown against the will of the body.

He wore a plaid shirt so faded it seemed stenciled across his chest, sloppily tucked into stained chinos. Socks with holes at the big-toe mark, no shoes.

"Come to the door from now on," he said.

"I don't care," said Randall, but only because he was nervous did he say something

120

so ridiculous and uncalled for and besides he did care; he would rather go to the window so that the whole thing would be over with quick and the transaction would be less personal. He thought of other places where business was done through windows, post office and bus station and the state stores they were opening up now where his father went to buy whiskey.

"Thing is, before . . ." The man started but he paused to stare away with such pure focus that Randall swiveled his head around expecting to see an army advancing but saw only the ragged grass, the houses across the street shut tight and marooned by midafternoon stillness. "Before you were late."

Randall looked away from his eyes which seemed too wet and red to work.

"From now on you can't be late, ever."

Randall said nothing, though it was hard not to take up for himself since he'd been *ordered* to be late. Why is it, he wondered, that the druggist likes to keep this man waiting when it seems to upset him so?

"Come on in, then." Randall followed him through a dark room which smelled like the showroom of Dusselbach's Furniture downtown, of vinyl and the stiff wool of new rugs. As his eyes adjusted he saw furniture brand-new and, in the kitchen the man led him to, furniture even his father would have taken to the dump: a saggy cot; a table piled high with books, magazines and dishes. In one corner, hunkered like a farmhand awaiting an early morning ride, an easy chair draped with bedspreads of stained chenille; in another on a chipped chest a phonograph upon which a record revolved, its dusty arm cocked in mid-air above the spinning black disc.

"I'll take that," the man said, and Randall handed him the package. "Sit down, I'll be back."

Randall took the easy chair by the only open window. Outside a breeze raked branches across the shingles, bringing in voices from the trees, stray phrases Randall sifted and tried to make sense of. "Get down off there," he heard someone say; and then a child's cry followed by a faint but curt "I tolt you."

Five minutes later the man returned. He shuffled his socks along the warped linoleum, sat down on the cot and smiled right through Randall. He made Randall want to hold his shoulders up.

"All I've got to offer is tapwater."

"That's okay," said Randall. He looked away, out the window, wished for the tree voices again, anything to deflect the sear of this man's smile. He held it like a high note and it was too pure, thought Randall. Maybe he should have taken off out the back when left alone, maybe he shouldn't have come inside. He could get up and leave now, say he had another delivery, due back at the drugstore, late for work.

"I won't keep you but a minute," the man said, and Randall sat straight up in the chair with his hands palm down under his legs, his arms locked tight. "I want to ask you something, okay?"

"Ask me what?"

"Let's start with your name."

"It's Randall. Speight."

"Just moved to Trent?"

"From out in the country, near Speed's store. My daddy had a farm."

"So you have a sister?"

"Five," said Randall.

The man slumped farther into the cot. He'd begun to sweat, had grown pastier by the minute, yet now he was smiling *at* Randall instead of through him. "Five sisters?"

Randall nodded. "And Hal. But he don't count, he stays gone."

"Okay," the man said, and the way he pitched conspiratorially forward suggested that they'd reached their true subject, were through with the mundane who-what-when. "Okay," he said, "I was out walking, it was one day last week, let's see . . . doesn't matter when but in the afternoon, and I happened to stop by the courtyard of thc Episcopal church. You were there with a girl."

"Eureka. She had a project in botany, a leaf collection, she was just going to pick up any old leaf off the ground until I came by there and —"

"Eureka's your sister?"

"No one knows where the name came from. She don't. Martha Know-It-All don't."

"Eureka," the man said, and then he repeated it.

"Think it's Indian?"

"I couldn't say. Maybe. How old is Eureka?"

"I'm not for sure but I think, um, seventeen?"

"And do you two spend a lot of time at the courtyard?"

"Did before. Now we both got jobs in the afternoon, she's over at the laundry and I work at . . . well, you ought to know where I work."

The man seemed to float in and out, sometimes listening, sometimes glazing over with that X-ray smile like before. "Can you get her to go there on Saturday? Can you get her over to the courtyard?"

Randall shook his head no. "She's at the laundry all day on Saturdays."

"Some night after dark then? Can you get

her to go there?"

"My daddy likes us home before dark."

The man leaned back on the cot. Suddenly it became even hotter in the low-ceilinged kitchen, harder to breathe.

"I'm going to tell you something serious, even though we just met. I know I can trust you. I'm very sick, Randall. I was in a bad accident, I was in the hospital for a long time, and now I'm in a lot of pain. It's rare that I even get out of this kitchen. Took me months to build up to that walk I took the other day. So I'm going to ask you to do this kind of as a favor to me. Can you do this one thing for me and not tell anyone?"

"But I don't even know who you are."

The man stared at him for a long time, as if this statement stumped him, as if he was trying to remember his name. Randall watched the man hoist himself up slowly, walk across the room, wrench out a drawer, start piling things on a counter: a hammer, two tiny lightbulbs, kitchen matches, a picture frame. Randall studied the phonograph. The record was warped, and he kept time by watching the ripple come around, as if each minute he spent in this kitchen was slightly imperfect, warped also.

The man held two ten-dollar bills in front of Randall's face.

"Here," the man said. "Take it and get her there. As a favor. I'll let you know later what time, when you come to bring my medicine."

In his life Randall had never been given money to save or play with and he didn't care enough about money in general either to reach for it or turn it down. There were things he wanted to buy but what interested him more was where those bills had been. He could tell by their limpness that they were well-traveled and had stories to tell. Tucked in his hip pocket they would talk to him while he pedaled around town, telling him of things they'd paid for in places far away and exotic.

"I've got to go," he said, and he stood and pushed the bills in his pocket and turned to leave, but the man put a bony hand on his collarbone, leaned in close to him. Randall could smell him, a slept-in-his-clothes smell, yesterday's stench dried and gone beneath the skin.

"Wait a minute. Do you think you can do it? Will she go with you?"

"Sure, she'll go," said Randall, and he tried to wrench away but the man held him still.

"That's good you're so sure. How can you be so sure?"

"She always does," said Randall. "Anywhere I go she'll go, too."

"I envy you then." The man's face glazed

over with that moony smile again, and it seemed to Randall that it was not envy he felt at all. And if it was envy it could not be for him.

6

She drew him out. Summoned by the chance he'd see her, Edwin took long walks daily through the middle of town, drawing tired similes from passersby: *Skinny as a rail, like a sick pup, white as a sheet, like death warmed over.*

"To think I'm responsible for this," his mother told his father after another of her friends called to say they'd seen him pass by Melton's Cafeteria. A breathlessness to each caller's tone suggested their wish to reach her first with the news. "Like when people call up here during the day to tell Tillett his chickens are trying to cross South Boulevard."

"Fixing to cross South Boulevard they say whenever I answer," said Thomas.

"You're not taking this very seriously," she said. She remembered how Edwin had looked when she'd stopped by, eyes like water glinting back at the bottom of a well, that crabgrassy growth covering his chin. Maybe the bungalow was a mistake. At least if he was home and wanted to take a walk, he'd have their ten acres and no one would have to see him besides Tillett.

"I believe you ought to talk to him, Thomas." They were sitting at the dinner table, though they'd finished their coffee a half hour before. The candles were molten stubs now, and trapped moths beat against the lampshades, faintly filling their silences.

"Why?"

"He shouldn't be wandering around town in the shape he's in."

"You don't think it's good for him to get out?"

"You see him twice a week. Don't you even look at him when you're over there?"

"Everyone knows what happened, Edith. People realize he's in too much pain to worry about a good shave. No one is going to think bad about him because his trousers aren't pressed. People here feel sorry for Edwin."

Thomas Keane felt sorry for Edwin, and he saw no reason why anyone else in town should feel differently. Awful things happened to people and then they were taken care of, by families and friends first, sure, but also by entire towns. Here in Trent were several examples: Jeffrey McCallister, who'd been paralyzed in a boating accident a week after he'd been awarded a Morehead Scholarship to study at Chapel Hill. Mr. Kenan, the blind linotype operator at the *Trentonian,* who had lost his sight during the war when his regiment had stumbled into heavy shelling. Everyone knew these two, everyone knew their stories, everyone helped them out. There were other, more pathetically disabled like Edna Rivenbark, whose family and belongings had gone up in a house fire and who now had trouble keeping her pants pulled up in the presence of the masculine gender, and Jay Jay Drawhorn, born raving, who regularly exposed himself to anyone unlucky enough to be sharing his stretch of sidewalk when the urge struck. These two were a little harder to take but still they were tolerated, allowed a freedom to roam as complete as a campus dog's. Thomas Keane thought that there was an inherent quota which every town took care of unconditionally, a quota built in and naturally balanced, and as far as Trent was concerned, far from filled. Edwin was no burden. Let him walk the streets if he wanted. There was room.

"I don't see a thing wrong with him taking a walk," he said. "He's not bothering anybody, and he's been cooped up all winter, only person he spoke to besides me was old Jones brings his medicine. I don't think he even uses his telephone."

"That's not exactly true," she said. "He talks to the druggist all the time and he sees your dear doctor brother every other week, remember?"

"What do you mean he talks to the druggist all the time? What do you mean, 'my dear doctor brother'?"

"Term of endearment," she said in a tone that made his question seem defensive. Thomas knew nothing of her calls to Lehmann, nothing about how much medicine Edwin took, and she thought it should stay that way. "I guess he and the druggist have become friends."

Thomas looked up at her, confused. "That young guy? Green?"

"I wonder why he doesn't keep in touch with his friends from school," she said. "I know some of his friends still write, that Thomasson boy from Asheville. I don't think Edwin answers his letters, though."

"I imagine that part of his life seems like school recess now. What all he's been through, no wonder he wants to be alone. He still feels a fair amount of guilt about Sarah, though there's no reason on this earth he should."

"Hard on himself," she said. "I don't wonder where that comes from."

"I've decided to hire a driver for him," said Thomas. It took a second for her to understand him; she was only aware that he'd changed the subject, ignored her comment which he

131

probably thought maudlin, a statement which if graced with a reply would lead to a half-hour's argument about her *getting over it.*

"A driver? There's a difference between a walk around the block and an excursion."

"What's the difference? You said he should see his friends more often. If I hired a driver, part-time of course, he could get out of town some without us having to chauffeur."

"I don't really think he's ready. I mean, he can hardly take care of himself. He's in horrible pain still."

"He feels good enough to take a walk. Besides, I'm not talking about cross-continental treks here. I just want him to have the option. You know he'll never get behind a wheel again, he'll stay right here in Trent rest of his life. No reason why he shouldn't, of course, everyone here understands and he'll have as good a life here as anywhere else. Better. But say he should want to go up to Chapel Hill for the weekend or down to Nags Head, well he won't have to come begging now."

"Well, what about his walks? Will you talk to him?"

"And tell him what? To put on a clean shirt?"

"To begin," she said.

"I'm telling you, Edith, people understand."

People *seemed* to understand. They smiled and spoke when he passed down the sidewalks, his slight smirk as unflinching as Ruby McClaurin's afternoon smile. Twice during his courthouse loop he passed through her field of vision and not even his odd image — bones and bad skin, sallow shirt beneath ratty seersucker, ruptured canvas track shoes salvaged from a closet bottom — could rouse Ruby from her catatonia.

Morphine made Edwin feel as if it were always early afternoon, a time of day that had been for years both transcendent and unnerving to him. He'd first fallen under its spell when he was home sick from grade school. His mother always went out for lunch, leaving him alone in the huge house which came alive as soon as she left: bangs and creaks of shutter and floorboard replaced by silence as soon as he crept from his sickbed to investigate. In the severe weekday quiet, moments between one and four seemed indistinguishable. Drifts into half-sleep upset by sudden noises: trucks gear-grinding out on the bypass, chainsaws ripping through the backwoods.

During these early afternoons Edwin first considered God, death, the intricacies of consciousness, whether a tree falling in uninhabited woods makes noise. And sex. He masturbated for the first time while his mother was out and forever afterwards he thought of early afternoons when masturbating, as if that time was as much the object of fantasy as the erotic images he conjured.

It gave him erections, it was fertile time for thought and dream, yet there was often an inimical edge to the stretch which made Edwin want to do something destructive, which made him at the very least want to gargle up a great strange yell.

His early afternoon walk took him down both sides of Main, once around the court square, out Sycamore to the high school. The grounds were quiet in between the hourly havoc touched off by bells. Each day he stood beneath the pines lining the playing fields and waited for classes to change. Finally the bell would ring, the din would rise above the grounds like a cloud, the yard would fill with streams of girls who looked nothing at all like *her*. After the schoolyard had cleared of smokers and stragglers Edwin would start the last leg of his walk, down side streets toward the Episcopal church.

In the courtyard he would sit in the shade and wait until he heard the revved engines of the bus fleet, signal that school was out. For the next hour he would frame his gaze on the front gate and watch for movement with the tingly sensitivity of a sniper. For two days there were no visitors; on the third, near the end of the hour, a stripped-down crew of Lobster Women strolled in, his mother leading the way.

When she saw him she laid her clippers in the grass, said something to the Lobster Women that he couldn't hear, came straight over. Her friends pretended to weed a pristine flower bed, bending stiffly, talking to each other in whispers that carried.

"You've gotten some sun looks like," she said. Her own face was wind-whipped into a handsome darkness, her forearms newly freckled. "What brings you to church on a weekday?"

"Fresh air," said Edwin. Was this church or churchyard, he almost asked, but she knew how he felt about the Lobster Women and their botanical diversions, knew not to bring it up in front of them.

She stood straight before him, posture-perfect.

"Speaking of sun," he said.

"Nancy and I ran down to Nags Head for the day yesterday," she said. "Needed a break from all this yardwork. Wasn't long enough of course, spent most of the day in the car so we decided to take the train to New York for a long weekend."

"How long?" asked Edwin. They both laughed, Edwin remembering those times they'd co-conspired against Thomas concerning these long weekends of hers, helped her concoct excuses for excursions up and down the Eastern Seaboard, provided dinner table defense of her wanderlust.

"Six days maybe?" she said.

"A weekend so long it grazes another," he said.

"But I haven't been away in forever," she said. She talked awhile about her travel plans, checked on her friends who were squatting in a line now, conspicuously avoiding looking their way, then sat beside him on the bench.

"How've you been?"

"Pretty well. Pain's steady but getting out's been sort of good."

"I don't see a thing wrong with you taking a walk now and then, but I'm surprised by how active you've been. Last time we talked you said you felt like hiding out for the rest of your life."

"That wasn't the last time I don't think."

"Well, one time."

"There haven't been that many times."

She looked to her friends again, then said, "I know, and I'm sorry. There was a period when I had to stay away, to try to put my life back together. And it was good for me

136

I think. I believe it might be good for your father to do the same."

"Stay away from me for six months?"

"Put his life back together. You know what I mean."

"He has his work."

"And little else these days," she said. "Since he sold the cottage he never leaves town except to go to East Lake."

"He sold the cottage?"

She scooted toward him, shook her head slowly. "What in the world do you two talk about?"

"We talk about attitude."

She sighed, scooted an inch closer, and said, "Well that doesn't much surprise me. But let's not talk about your daddy now. Let's talk about Edwin. You know I've always been wary of sudden changes in people, ever since Helen Butler."

Edwin wondered what this had to do with attitude.

"Because of what happened to Helen Butler, I mean."

He gave up. "So what happened to Helen Butler?"

"She died before you were born. She was someone I wanted for a friend. Helen was without a doubt — and I shouldn't say this now because she's dead, but on the other hand that's when — oh, anyway I'll just say it: she was the iciest person I've ever met. Best I've seen at putting you in your place with a look. She had ways of complimenting furniture that let you know exactly how pitiful your existence on earth was to her."

"Why did you want her for your friend then?" His tone revealed his annoyance, his shame at not holding out longer, for giving in.

"She was, well, in a word, undeniable. She was who I wanted to be, all except for her disposition, which no one could envy. She had the same kind of upbringing, same schooling, same advantages I had but she seemed to have made it all into something so permanent. Everything with her was so secure. Oh, I'm being vague. There's really no way to explain Helen Butler, the way I saw her at least. I'd have to explain me." She inclined her head toward the statue in the center of the courtyard. "If I started on that we'd be sitting here as long as St. Francis has been standing over there."

"St. Edith of Rivershore," said Edwin.

"St. Edwin of Edgecombe," his mother said.

"More like the patron saint of Johnsontown," he said.

"Quit now. It's probably blasphemy."

"Oh, we're blast-pheming now? Sacrilege in the sacred garden of the Lobster Women?"

"You're trying to shock me to get me off the subject, but it won't work. Helen Butler was just one of those people whom you are instinctively, irrationally jealous of."

"Even though you really sort of hate them," said Edwin. It was meant to be a question but came out a statement, similar feelings of his own supplying the last syllable's lilt.

"Even though you don't get invited to their bridge club, aren't included in the trips they organize to Saint Simons. She was head of Tour of Homes that one year that our house, which had been in your father's family since . . . oh, but you know that. Anyway, Helen, she . . . oh I'll never get this story told." She slumped on the bench. "Helen Butler," she said.

"Sudden change of," said Edwin.

"Her husband, Ches, was a doctor, agreeable man but a little bland to me. Arthur knew him in medical school, they'd roomed together at Charlottesville, that's how he happened to end up here, he was in practice with your uncle for a while, so it was not as if I could avoid Helen, with all our connections. Plus you know how this town is, like all towns this size if you're in a certain segment. . . ."

"Milieu you mean."

"If you're in a certain set you're . . ."

"Sunk?"

"I know it's been awhile since you've had a conversation, but you need to not interrupt so much. I can finish my sentences, might take me 'til supper but I can find the words for Helen Butler, what happened to her. Where was I?"

"You couldn't avoid her."

"Right. And couldn't avoid knowing that she wasn't happy in Trent. She broadcasted it, see? She was raised in Richmond, up on Church Hill and she thought any structure not semi-detached might just as well be a tobacco barn. She told me once that the country made her nervous. Too wide open, said Helen, said the flatness 'round here made it feel like outer space. She'd bring this up every time she'd have a couple of drinks, on and on about how there wasn't any gravity here and gravity I believe she meant in some special secret-code way, something to do with tradition and culture. Though now I'm about around to feeling like there's too much gravity, too much to hold you down. Anyway it was Helen who started the push for a public park. In a town the size of this one. We all agreed to help. Too scared not to, even though those of us who grew up here knew that public parks, well, it wasn't top priority. It was a pipe dream was what it was. 'Course your father was furious at me for going along with it. Women

140

didn't get involved in civic affairs so much back then, not that they do now, and Thomas said she browbeat me into it which she did, intimidated all of us by treating us like bumpkins.

"I was obsessed with her. She was always so cold to me, and all of us were sure she made fun of us when she went back to Richmond to visit. One day I'm sitting at home when Helen calls me up and asks me over for tea. Of course I went, and she was as charming that day as anyone I've ever met. Amazing. The friend I've always wanted. Friendship is like — don't you dare laugh at your old sentimental mama now — it's like a special potion, everything's got to be mixed just right, confidences and mysteries, or it'll all blow up. With Helen I felt the perfect proportions that in all other friendship before or since I've never been able to get right.

"We saw each other a lot over the next three weeks. It was a wonderful time, too: Helen was like someone visiting from England whom all the ladies in town wanted to have over. During those few days it seemed she was right about this place being like outer space — we all gravitated toward her and I tell you after five years of putting up with her attitude we really ravaged her good side. We didn't give her any rest, kept her going night and day.

"One evening Betsy Graham called me up, said Helen had collapsed and was up at Duke Hospital. A brain tumor. Whatever part of your brain makes you a good person, that makes you do the right thing? That's the part that had been affected. This tumor nudged that unknown part of her, turned her into a pure delight for the last three weeks of her life."

My getting out of the house, taking walks around town, was analogous to Helen Butler's abrupt shift from bitch to saint, Edwin thought.

"That part of the brain which makes you do the right thing," Edwin said.

"Don't know what it's called, but it's up there. 'Course I wouldn't want anyone else to be affected like Helen. I mean, you know I'd rather her have stayed hateful and lived than what happened. But I didn't think I'd ever told you about her and being in the court-yard here reminds me of her."

"She was a Lobster Woman?"

"Lord, no. I mean that public park mess."

"I thought it was sudden changes made you think of her, your distrust of."

"I'm going to change the subject suddenly and ask how you are."

He remembered those days at home, when she would grab the phone out of his hand and

142

harangue Lehmann into sending his medicine over so that he would invite her into his room and, as soon as the morphine lifted him away into some far corner of early afternoon, be nice to her. Ask her questions. He remembered how she'd slumped in the wingback, her bare feet splayed across the covers, tangent after tangent, monologues which made "Helen Butler" seem concise.

"I'm on my way back up."

"That's good to hear. Don't you think you should clean yourself up a bit before you go traipsing through town?"

"Sorry."

"*I'm sorry* if I sound stuffy. You know I don't really care how you look as long as you're feeling better. But two things come to mind. First you've heard before: 'when you look good you generally feel good.' "

"So you really think a change of clothes will do the trick?"

She held her hand up to silence him.

"And the other is that people may respond differently if you're more presentable. Already you're an item for curiosity about town because of all you've been through. People, even those here at home, have a tendency to be rather tactless with their sympathy. They don't mean anything by it, of course."

"Don't mean anything by their sympathy?"

"That's the second time today you've twisted my words around. I know that deep down you want to make things easier for yourself."

"That doesn't seem to always be the case," he said.

"Listen to me, Edwin. Will you try to make yourself a little more presentable?"

"Certainly."

"Your father's going to start sending someone from the laundry by each week, so he won't have to pick it up and drop it off."

"Sounds like a conspiracy to me. Clean clothes as ticket to spiritual and physical rejuvenation?"

She ignored this. "I never will understand why you let that Jenny go."

"She specialized in cooked-to-death okra. No diet for the sick and tired."

"I can get her back easy enough when you come down off your high horse."

"Don't need her. She got in my way."

"Any more problems with that druggist?"

"That druggist is a problem. Thinks he's a social reformer or something. A druggist Carrie Nation, only his ax is dull. He's gotten even more sanctimonious lately."

"Let me give Walter Lehmann a call."

"Let me handle it," he said, though he knew there would come a time, sooner rather than later, when he would ask for her help.

"Just remember you don't have to put up with anything from that druggist. He's not the one in pain."

"Speaking of medicine," he said.

As they rose from the bench his mother slipped an arm around his waist and drew him close to her. "I'll come by when I get back, promise," she said as they walked toward the gate. The Lobster Women bent to work in their wake, swiveled to watch them away as they passed. "I would have come more often but I really did get the idea that you valued your privacy these days."

"I'm tired of privacy," said Edwin. "It's like you've been saying for months now. Time for me to rebuild."

Next morning the driver showed up at the bungalow. He was tall, rawboned, bowlegged, blue-jeaned, broganed, two-toned: forehead and cheeks tinted hangover red, his neck tractor-tanned dull copper. Edwin could not help but stare at his hands, so huge they seemed snakebit-swollen.

"Mr. Tom Keane's son Ed?" Edwin heard as soon as he'd cracked the door a half-inch. "Been hired to drive you, name's Deems."

"Drive me where, Deems?"

"Wherever you'll be wanting to go, don't

145

matter to me one iota."

"Did my mother send you over here?"

"It was your daddy called. I work for my grandaddy, he's got a body shop out on number nine? Here's my phone out there and you just call anytime and I'll be by here to carry you like I said wherever you want, it's up to-ya."

"I don't need a driver," said Edwin, staring at the slip of paper Deems pushed against the screen. "I'm just to the point where I can take walks again."

"Don't need to be able to walk to ride around," said Deems.

"Yes, well. That's true, Deems. You've got me there."

"Think maybe you can talk your daddy into something a little more our age to drive? I didn't know, I meant I don't mind his big Dodge if that's all y'all got, thought maybe you had a Thunderbird tucked away in some garage maybe from before."

"From before?"

"Before you was in that bad wreck back here. 'Course I'll drive whatever he gives me to, I just love to drive is all."

"I imagine you're getting paid for it, aren't you, Deems?"

" 'Magine," said Deems. His beery grin, the way he smacked his lips over the two syllables,

146

prodded Edwin to imagine how much it was costing to retain Deems to drive him nowhere. Of course it was his father's money, he could spend it however he wanted, but still: it seemed part of a grand plan, these snowballing schemes. First his mother entices him out of the bungalow, then his father decides to send around the laundry folks to make sure he's properly attired. Now this driver.

"I can't see that I'll need a driver."

"Well maybe you ought talk to Mr. Tom."

"Right. I'll do that. I'll call Mr. Tom up on the telephone right now. I appreciate it, Deems."

"Take my number so you'll have it handy." Edwin opened the door for it, crushed it between two fingers and held it up for Deems to see.

"Call anytime."

"Thanks again, Deems."

"I'm not hard to catch up to. Somebody always knows where I'm at." Through the sliver of screen door Edwin watched Deems drive a half block in reverse down the sidewalk, the car listing toward the street. When he reached a driveway ramp he dropped into the street, braked, blew the horn and scratched off, the family Dodge fishtailing down Edgecombe and finally out of sight.

★ ★ ★

147

In the corner of the store the Keane boy loitered by the spinning display of eyeglass frames. Spotting him on his way up the aisle, Roy kept walking, squeezed past Ruby behind the soda fountain. Drawing himself a Coke, he maneuvered a view of Edwin from the cover of the lemon squeezer.

"What in the world," whispered Ruby between customers. She slid down to lean beside Roy on the drinkbox, suctioned her shoulder to his and whispered. "I will be," she said, and "That's just about the saddest thing."

Fortunately she was interrupted by a spurt of grade-schoolers lining up for vanilla Cokes. Edwin had stopped spinning the eyeglass rack; he stood in the middle of the aisle, staring off toward the drug counter. Though it was warm out he wore a gabardine suit coat and seemed oblivious to the sweat soaking his shirt, glued to his chest like a second skin.

Roy hadn't seen him since a few months before the accident and had to concentrate hard to find the slightest hint of what he'd looked like a year and a half ago: another handsome, healthy college kid. He'd seemed scrubbed always, as if his skin repelled dirt the way it now appeared to resist soap and water. Roy leaned back against the icebox and drank his Coke, watching this boy who had come to remind him of all he'd had to put up with in this world. True that he's only a symptom, thought Roy, yet when I hear his voice broken and wheezy through the telephone I know that within minutes I'll be kowtowing again, sucking up to Lehmann who sucks up to Keane's mother who sucks up to no one, doesn't have to, who the hell is she to lord over all of us. . . . The boy may be a symptom but there will come a day when I'll have to treat him as a cause.

And after having seen him, that day seemed close at hand. Clearly Keane was out of control, anything Roy could do to help, even delay his deliveries for an hour or two, would buy the boy a little more life, even freeing him for an hour or two from the manipulation of those around him which seemed to Roy as insidious and as constricting as the morphine, would help Roy, too, help him take back some of the power that had been. . . .

Dumping the dregs of his Coke into a sink, Roy started toward Keane, knowing that as long as he slumped there unseen his hate-cadence would continue. It would intensify and he would grow more and more bitter until the day was lost, and so he crossed the three aisles to save what was left of the afternoon.

"Interest you in a pair of glasses?"

Edwin lowered his gaze from the fan blades.

"Afternoon, Mr. Keane," said Roy.

Edwin smiled. "Sorry, after all this time and I don't even know your name."

"Green. Roy Green."

"Do I look like I sound on the telephone?"

"You look closer."

Edwin's eyes rose to the fan again. "I'm feeling good today, Roy Green," he said.

Two feet seemed inadequate to hold him erect and tethered to earth. "I guess you're here to see Mr. Lehmann."

"You'll do," said Edwin. Up close there were vestiges of the way he'd looked before his accident, a phosphorescence in his eyes, a squareness in the shoulders, things hidden by distance, buried by saggy wardrobe and ruined posture. Something here to save, thought Roy, *more here to save than I thought.*

"I don't have anything to say to Lehmann," said Edwin.

"I was under the impression Mr. Lehmann was a close friend of the family."

Edwin laughed, wobbling closer. "Once I came in here to buy a rubber," he said. Not a whisper but a rasp, loud enough for a woman bent by the nail files to straighten and move up the aisle.

Roy waited without reaction while Edwin seemed to consider what he'd just said, as if deciding if it were true.

"Not from Lehmann though. Not from you.

A woman sold it to me. Soda jerkess."

"That so?" said Roy.

"And I used it on a girl I didn't really love."

"I'm sure that's a first." He said it to discourage him, to cut him off before he grew maudlin and confessional in the middle of the drugstore in the middle of the afternoon. But sarcasm did not phase him, nor callousness, nor blank looks of boredom.

"Used it on her that very night in fact. But wait. You don't use it on a girl, do you? Do you, Roy Green? Wouldn't use a rubber on a girl. Would it be *with* a girl?"

"I'm not really sure which preposition is called for," said Roy.

"In a girl?"

"I was a pharmacy major," said Roy, flushing as he spoke, aware that this was less a question of grammar than something far more crucial. It gave him the creeps until he remembered how far gone the boy was, decided with relief that it could be morphine talk.

"Of course you majored in pharmacy," Keane said, smiling. "And it's a fine business to be in, exciting line of work I'm sure. Let me ask you something, Mr. Green. While I've got you here in the absolute flesh."

"What's that?"

"Why do you call me all the time?"

I won't speak again, I'll will him out of here

with silence. *Don't laugh, you'll encourage him,* his father used to say when he was being a smartass. Yet despite all at stake there *was* something funny about it, Keane's delivery perhaps. Once he saw the humor he found the laughter hard to squelch. A small smile spread, a lopsided moony smile blooming from Keane in return which made Roy feel defeated.

"I don't dislike you, Roy Green. I understand you're trying to help me. But I'm beyond all that."

Might as well take him back in the stockroom and inject him myself now, thought Roy.

"Although some things are changing for me. Like, for instance, I've started making public appearances. This being one."

"And does this one have a purpose or is it purely social?"

"Its purpose is twofold. Number one, I came to tell you that I didn't tell Lehmann about how you've been treating me lately. Your little sermons. I just went over your head like I said I'd do, but I didn't drag you into it."

"By going over my head you drag me into it. You know that anyway, and I've told you how I feel about this. I'm not going to be a party to it any longer. From now on I send over what your uncle prescribes — which by the way is way more than you need — when and only when the refill date comes up. I don't really care what you tell Lehmann."

"Lehmann *is* pitiful, isn't he?"

Another trick, another test. He wouldn't fall for it this time. "You might want to wait until you get out of this store to voice your opinion about him."

"You're pretty much of a tight-ass yourself aren't you, Roy?"

"I'm pretty much busy. And I've wasted pretty much time listening to you already."

"Okay, but one more thing. Number two of two. I want to see the boy."

"What boy?"

"The delivery boy. You know, the new kid."

"What would you want with him?"

"Yardwork. I need him to mow my yard, okay?"

"He works here after school. I doubt if he has time for your yardwork."

"You're his manager?"

"No, but I'm responsible for him while he's at work, and I don't think he's quite old enough to take on two jobs and attend school, too."

"So he's not here?"

"Out on a delivery right now." Roy had no idea where the boy was, hadn't seen him since he'd sent him out an hour or so ago. What would Keane want with him but to berate him for being late with his medicine, which he had been consistently since he'd started and as long as Roy was in charge would continue to be. Randall was working out fine. He was sharp and quick, independent but loyal like his father — Roy trusted him to do what he was told and to do it without questions. "Let me get his father for you. He works here, too, he's down in the basement right now, you can ask him about the yardwork."

"No need," said Edwin, already turning and starting toward the show window where Randall appeared holding the handle of a pushbroom high and two-handed above his head. Keane followed him down the next aisle and caught up with him in front of the razor blades. Roy stood on tiptoes to spy but couldn't hear a word, saw only Keane bend to whisper for a minute or two before Randall propped his broom against a shelf and both of them disappeared into the late brightness of this afternoon which Roy felt he'd ruined with a smile.

7

Everyone at the laundry was terrified of Miss Ilgenfritz. Even Eureka's sisters were shocked into submission by the stern laundress who dressed in clothes unclaimed after six months on the rack. She reminded Eureka of the war: partly because she was German, partly because she dressed and ate and spoke with an economy that seemed a result of life on the front; a reaction to rationed staples, to hours spent in blacked-out basements waiting out air raids. Twice a day, mid-morning and late afternoon, Miss Fritz — or "the Fraulein," as she was called behind her starched back — rustled down the sidewalk to Lehmann's where she would stand at the end of the fountain and toss off an ammonia Coke ordered iceless.

"She smells bad, but she'll do you right," claimed Rose, the colored woman Eureka had been assigned to help. The Speight girls had integrated the laundry work force, even though Eureka's sisters had no interest in breaking the barrier. They complained to their father about what their school friends would think, referred to the place as the colored laundry though its clientele was exclusively River Road and white, and at work they clung together in a frail island, ignoring their coworkers with a disciplined insolence which made their days harder and longer.

After a day of guarded silence and instruction, Rose and Eureka fell into a rhythm of steady work broken by gossip and giddiness. And stories: Rose had spent half her life in Newburgh, New York, and three times a year took the train north, stopping off in Harlem to visit. She was saving money to take her family north again; when she talked of New York she talked fast and sassy, and Eureka felt as if Rose's words were pushing her along crowded streets, threading crowds, skittering over hot sidewalks.

Eureka had been there for three weeks before Miss Ilgenfritz said more than five words to her. Late one afternoon she was at her station in the very back of the store when Miss Fritz came spilling down the aisle.

"Act busy," said Rose.

They *were* busy, yet the Fraulein didn't seem to notice. She stood in front of Eureka, blocking her view of the plateglass and of daylight down the long steamy aisle. She put her hands on her hips and said to Rose, "Which Speight is she now?"

Speight she pronounced funny — Spite — as if it was German, thought Eureka.

"Her name's Eureka. She's one good worker, too, I tell you. Best help I had."

"She can come with me then," said Miss Fritz. "Wilson is sick again, and I need someone to help me make pickup."

Outside Miss Fritz climbed into the old panel truck, told Eureka to sit in the back. There were no windows, no seats. Eureka slid around on the ribbed floor, cushioned by bundles of linen.

At a stoplight Miss Fritz called back to her, "Please, you will pick up the weekly dirty. Go always round to the back door, please. Do not delay."

At the backs of houses on River Road she was met by uniformed maids who seemed drugged, who shared a manner of transcendental indifference, the same slow way of bouncing out the screen door with fingertips, focusing two inches above her head and saying "Yass?"

It grew dark. Miss Fritz took corners recklessly, never-minding a bit of curb. At the last stop, she called out to Eureka.

"This pickup is first week, new. They might not be expecting. The help may take awhile to gather the dirty. You be patient and don't bother."

"Yes, ma'am." Eureka pushed open the double doors and jumped into dusk at the dead end of a street she did not recognize. Dizzy from the long wild ride, she stumbled up the flagstones, knocked, then backed down the stairs.

Waiting, she felt weary, unsettled by an afternoon of not being able to see where she was going, thrown about the airless dark on her way somewhere that seemed a secret. She felt a deep fatigue that brought out in her a resigned awareness of the future. She'd felt it before, a fatigue when she could not only feel her bones but what her bones would feel like in forty years.

A bulb above the back door blinked on, spreading yellow across the highest steps. The door swung open and a man pushed out the screen to stand on the threshold. In the porch light the color of his trousers reminded her of soup served in grade school. He did not notice her at first.

"Who is it?" He spoke more to himself, a reassurance rather than a question. She stepped forward without speaking.

"My God," he said. "And so soon."

"I'm from the laundry."

"I thought I told him the courtyard."

"To pick up your laundry. From Miss Ilgenfritz's?"

158

"And not today. Saturday. I thought I said Saturday. It doesn't matter though. You're here. You came."

When he moved a few steps closer she noticed his limp, saw how pasty he was even in this pale light.

"I'm sure I said the courtyard, though. Did you bring the note?"

"What note?" she asked. The Fraulein had not mentioned any note.

"Preface to a thousand pages of foolscap," he said. "We won't get started on it today. But soon. A long story which I want to tell very quickly, get it out of the way first thing. The story of how I could think that I wrote one thing on a note of great importance and actually have written another."

"Nobody gave me any note."

"How should I do it is the question. Before the accident my inclination would have been to include everyone I'd ever met. Paragraphs on insignificant snapshots taken during family vacation. We used to take two weeks in Asheville every July. Grove Park Inn where Scott Fitzgerald used to hole up when Zelda was locked up in Highlands up the mountain. Once a bellhop named Carson showed me the room where Fitzgerald wrote those potboiling stories he made such a killing from, where he supposedly drank forty bottles of beer a day.

See, I'm doing the very thing I vowed not to. It's the medicine, I guess. Sometimes it makes me talk, even though talk is what I don't want between us, too much talk will kill us, we have to find a way to get there without all the wasted words. So many words wasted when you're trying to get to know another person. Surely you've noticed."

At the mention of this man who drank forty beers a day, she decided that he was drunk himself. Clearly he thought she was someone else.

"Still, I can't boil it all down to its essence. Some things you just can't summarize. And I'll have to allow myself a few extravagances. Maybe a side tour of Trent: you'd be surprised what I know about this place from a lifetime of not paying attention."

He talked like Randall would talk if Randall knew what he knows. An older, smarter, broken, drunken Randall.

"Though I feel compelled to mention that aside from my walk last week I have not been keeping up, with Trent that is. I've spent almost a full year inside, lying around listening to Beiderbecke and reading."

She thought of the Fraulein, who hated to wait and was waiting.

" 'Course I've started a lot more books than I've finished. Gide's *The Counterfeiters* I've started five times at least. My friend Thomasson sent it to me. He swears by it. Sleeps with it even."

He thinks I'm someone else, someone different but obviously not someone he knows well.

He leaned forward, thrust his head in the nearby darkness, lowered his voice. "I have to take medicine for my back. I was in an accident. You'll hear more about this later. It's a major thread of this story I have to get out of the way."

She began to wonder how long she'd been standing there, listening to him. He seemed to be talking to himself now.

"Maybe it's not such a major thread. Doubt I'll be able to tell what's important until we get down in the jungle and start hacking through. Listen, I realize my metaphors are a little rough right now but it's been a while since I've had anyone to talk to and of course once we get far enough in that turning back is a consideration equal to pushing forth — I've never known that, you see — then I'll hit my stride and my language I swear will show it. And when it gets going we can dispense with all this tiresome history by condensing it."

He beamed through the darkness. She understood only this: that he had wanted to tell her a story, that he wanted to tell it quick, that it might take him awhile to warm up. A car door slamming nearby brought her back to the moment, her purpose here.

"I'm to pick up your dirty clothes," she said.

"What? Oh, don't worry. Whoever that is, they're not coming here. I can't believe you came so soon. Your brother was right. I have to admit I didn't really believe he could get you here."

"Hal?"

"He told me his name was Randall."

Hearing footsteps and heavy breath behind them, Eureka turned to see Miss Fritz picking through the high grass. The Fraulein heaved to a stop behind Eureka's right shoulder, so close Eureka could smell ammonia when Miss Fritz half-whispered "What?"

Good question, thought Eureka. She would have answered had she known how, had his mention of Randall not distracted her. How did Randall figure into this? Had he given Randall a note for her? A note saying what and why her and how did he know Randall and what did he want? Question begged question, things he'd said came back to her, previously muddled torrents now made enough sense to keep her quietly pondering.

For a moment the three of them stood there awkwardly, as if they'd all interrupted each other and were waiting in overpolite limbo for someone else to start talking. Edwin moved in and out of the shadow line. Miss Fritz stared at him, then leaned in close to Eureka's ear and said, "Well?"

"Very pleased to meet you," said Edwin. And to Eureka: "This is your mother?"

"He doesn't have anything today," Eureka said quickly. "He was trying to decide what day for us to check back. Which day did you decide, sir? For us to come back and pick your dirty laundry up?"

"Yes, yes," said Miss Fritz, "Which, when?"

"Please come back on Wednesday."

"Wednesday then. Come along," said the Fraulein.

Eureka was halfway to the truck when she heard, or thought she heard, his voice echo through the high grass, two last words following her around the side of the house: "Come alone."

"Everything he said and did," said Eureka. "You tell me *now*."

They were sitting on the back porch steps shelling crowder peas. Randall tossed a pea at two hens nearby, studied the collision

163

of wing and dust.

"Everything."

Jumping up, Randall ignored her, kept the victor away with his foot while he fed the slower hen from his palm.

"In court, then," she said to entice him. Court was something they'd stumbled upon at the end of one of their afternoon explorations. They had gone into the courthouse to get a drink of water but once inside Randall had wanted to explore. She was against it — it didn't seem like a place they should be poking around in — yet no one paid them any attention. In fact, most of the people there looked at them as blankly as the blind woman who ran the concession by the front door and her sleepy Seeing Eye dog sprawled across the tile beneath her. Randall paused to stare at the woman and her dog, who wore a harness and lounged all day until it was time to lead her home. Eureka yanked him around the corner.

"Don't stare," she whispered. "She can feel your bug eyes crawling all up and down her."

"But how come people don't cheat her? How can she tell the difference between a one and a five?"

"Maybe they feel different. Besides, this is a courthouse. People in here are on their best behavior."

But the people they saw in the lobby seemed glued there like wallpaper, as dazed and broken a group as Eureka had ever seen assembled. There was no air of impatience or anxiety, no one seemed tired of waiting. In the lobby it was stifling and everyone smoked and swigged pop. When they finished with their cigarettes they spit in the empty bottles, tweezered the butts and pushed them through the narrow throats. Behind the long benches, alongside the green walls, bottles smoldered slowly as if part of a rite to ward off stiff sentences.

Despite the desperation, the courthouse fascinated Eureka. She listened for heel clicks on the waxed tile, floated down the hallway past the mural which changed hourly, a shifting parade of the long-suffering kin of felons wearing blond depressions in benches. Randall as usual was too curious to be distracted for long. She followed him through double-paneled doors and found herself in a half-full courtroom where a trial was in session. A man in a uniform grabbed Randall's shoulder, leaning over to whisper in his ear while she waited tensely behind, ready to bolt. But Randall scrambled down a side aisle, sat and craned forward in the pew as if about to kneel and pray.

"What'd he say to you?"

"Said sit down."

They sat through several cases that afternoon and they'd been back four times since and no one ever stopped them or asked them what they were doing there. Randall loved the form of the courtroom — the questions, the rebuttals and the demeanor of the stern judges who hid their intelligence behind country inflections and favored incomprehensible barnyard aphorisms.

"Okay," he said, casting more peas across the lawn for the hens to fight over. "Okay, but who's the lawyer?"

"Me. You take the witness stand," she replied, patting the steps beside her.

"What about the Bible?" he asked, and he started inside to retrieve their mother's tattered copy but she stopped him, told him to pretend. While she recited the memorized oath he held his hand palm down on his kneecap and stared solemnly toward a neighbor's garage.

"Please describe the events of last Tuesday," she said.

"Tuesday last?"

"You know what I mean."

"I went to his house to deliver a package from the drugstore where I am now employed as delivery boy. I have my own bike but just for business use only."

"Randall . . ."

"Okay: It was black as all hell inside his house and got dirtier the further back you headed in there. Got darker, too, like a cave. To get him to come that time I knocked on the window but know what, he came 'round to the door instead."

"The court is more interested in what this man said to you." She paced in front of the steps, erasing hen tracks with her bare feet as she interrogated.

"I'm not through describing that house."

"I've heard enough about that house. *There's this house has a face like Pa's.*" She mimicked her brother's high-pitched nasalese, then straightened her face and lowered her voice. "Tell about him, what all he said to you."

"He asked which sister was it with me in the courtyard that one day."

"He was there?"

"Guess so."

"Did you see him there?"

"I was in the tree, remember? I couldn't hardly even see you."

"Why was he there?"

"Maybe the suspect was hiding behind a bush."

"I said why, not where. And I never said he was the suspect."

"He's got to be if we're talking about him like this. Don't you pay attention? Maybe I should be the lawyer."

"Too late. You swore on the Bible. What did the suspect say next?"

"Suspect asked me could I get you there on Saturday."

"To his house you mean?"

"Courtyard." He was growing bored, she could tell by his terseness. He flicked another pea on the ground beside her, sending the hens to peck around her ankles.

"Martha catches you throwing food away she'll backslap you."

"Those chickens stay starved. Hal never ever feeds them enough when it's his turn. Sometimes I spy on him. Why do Martha'them hate those chickens? I noticed they'll eat them."

"Because they're prisspots. They think those chickens digging up this yard is the only thing keeping us from living out on River Road with the rich."

"How come they think that?"

She straightened and said, "Objection, your honor. All this about these chickens is irrelevant. Total waste of taxpayers' money."

"Sustained," said Randall in a jowly judge's bellow.

"Now, Mr. Speight, answer the question

please. What did this man tell you?"

"We have to think of a name for him," Randall said. "Besides 'the suspect' I mean. Can't just call him 'him.' "

"We know his name."

"Yeah, but it's not right for him."

"Why not?"

"Just wrong. Too big. He's too shrunk up for a name like that. His name swallows him whole."

"You're off the subject again. Am I going to have to threaten you with contempt?"

"He asked me could I get you there and I said no, sir. I said you worked on Saturdays all day long at the laundry. Then he asked me what about Saturday night and I told him our daddy likes us to be home by dark."

"I don't know why," said Eureka. At the end of the corridor that ran from back porch to front she made out the silhouette of her father reared back in his drinking chair. "It's not like we have family hour."

"When's family hour?" asked Randall.

"Never mind," she said. "Then what happened?"

"Then he gave me the money." Randall was shelling peas again; she reached down and grabbed the pot out of his lap and held both of his hands.

"Don't worry," he said. "I remember where I hid it."

"Why didn't you tell me he gave you money?"

"I wanted to wait and give it to you with the note."

"He gave you a note?"

"Yesterday at work. Said he'd give me more money to act like he wanted me to cut his grass. Said the druggist was going to ask what he wanted with me, which the druggist did ask soon's as I come back in the drugstore."

"Where is this note, Randall?"

"He plays records in his kitchen. There was a lumpy one spinning around but the needle wasn't hardly touching it."

"Go get the note. Bring the money, too."

When he was gone she noticed the hens gathered again at her ankles. "Get," she said, but when they didn't budge she scooped up a handful of peas and flung them across the lawn. She watched the hens peck each other and wished for the bone-weariness to take her away, to let her see ahead. She thought of *him* again, saw him beaming proud-childish over this story he claimed he had to tell her.

Randall handed her a crumpled note and two limp tens. She smoothed the bills, turned them President up the way she'd seen bored clerks do, then handed them back to him.

"Hide them somewhere Hal can't find them."

"You're not going to buy something new to go see him in?"

"Who said I'm going to see him?" She turned sideways and raised her shoulders when he hovered close. "As if you haven't already peeked."

"Wednesday dusk. Episcopal courtyard. Please come. Edwin Keane," he called across the yard.

"Sssssh." She gave him her big-sister-dangerously-irked look which he expected and returned with a loony smile. He was bluffing. She didn't believe that man could ever be so brief or direct, not the way he'd rambled on about people caught in the corners of snapshots. But as she unfolded the note she saw the sentence, scrunched in the middle of the page in careful blocks. His precision made her suspicious, as if it was an attempt to fool her. "Please come," printed so legibly, semed to neutralize the yearning, make it matter-of-fact.

Randall had crept close again. She felt him, a peripheral shifting of light, sun gone behind the clouds.

"Take after your daddy, sneaking up on somebody."

"Your daddy, too," he said. "And don't try

171

to change the subject."

"What?"

"This piece of evidence produced and you go hogging it."

"Who you want me to share it with, your chickens?" she said.

"Yours, too." An injured edge to these two words. It had become routine, his objection to the way she referred to things as his only — family, house, yard, chickens, Trent. It didn't matter to him that she planned already to leave because he didn't believe she'd do it, ever, and he hated the way she distanced herself with pronouns. She knew it hurt him but it was a question of purity, keeping separate what belonged to her so that when time to leave came there would be no sorting to be done.

"This evidence will not stand up in a court of law," she said.

"Why not?"

"How do we know he wrote it?"

"He *gave* it to me. I *brung* it here."

"You swear?"

"I already took a oath you don't need me to swear after every little piddly thing I say the oath'll stay good until you step down it's not like it only lasts for —"

"Okay," she said. She held the note overhead, the chickens roused to attention by her raised arm, bunching below her as she waved it about. "Exhibit A," she said. "Court adjourned."

During the next days his note began to irritate her. She was disappointed by the mundane chop of its syllables, by the absence of a formal closing, which Randall had pointed out to her more than once, since that week in English class he was studying proper letter writing form.

"He'd flunk Miss Harrell's," he said. "Where's his salutation? He just jumps right in there."

That fits, she thought as she remembered the way he'd rambled in the dark, the density of his monologue, words packed tightly into sentences like clothes stuffed into a suitcase you'd have to sit on to shut. She remembered images, too: a man who liked a book so much he slept with it nights. During the long dull hours at work she pictured this man in bed with a book on the pillow beside him, wind from a floor fan batting the pages back while he, asleep, inhaled its contents with the ragged draw of his snore.

Who does this remind you of, a voice asked each time the image recurred. Soon the sleeping man went from resembling Randall to becoming him, right down to the way he slept with one arm thrown out as if to save a troubled swimmer, down to the circle of saliva widening on his pillowcase, the metronomic cadence of his snore.

The man had mentioned a tour of Trent. She thought of this while folding linen, stretching the tour out over hours and miles, comparing it to those walks Randall had taken her on when they'd first moved to town. He might talk better, know bigger words, but the things he knew about this town would be dry, forgettable history lesson fare. He would not have Randall's knack for finding special places. She pictured herself walking with him through town, their pace set by his fountain of words. Something about him made her want to both burn through time and proceed with caution.

More and more that week she found herself thinking of him, imagining things. I have to *imagine,* she told herself, I've seen him only once, briefly in the half-dark. After ten minutes of crazed monologue and mistaken identity (even though she had proof to the contrary she still doubted that it was she he wanted, thought maybe she had a double around town, not identical but close enough to pass in shadowed dusk) what had she learned about him that she could call real?

Physical things: suit pants the color of split-pea soup, a patchy beard which reminded her of raked gravel beneath which wintry skin shone like sand. These were the real things; the things he'd told her were fragmented, blurred by the confusion of their crisscrossing purposes and the threat of the waiting fraulein.

After realizing the futility of basing anything real on that meeting she took pleasure in re-creating him. Her imagination became as charged as it had that day in the warehouse. As soon as she detached herself from the responsibility of reality she thought of him night and day.

She thought of him right up until the time she decided to go to him. Then she put him out of her mind.

At work on Wednesday she and Rose were folding work clothes for the City of Trent. "Where you been all week?" asked Rose.

Eureka was silent.

"Fritz get on you about something?"

"No."

"Didn't think so. She told me you were 'goot help.' "

"No she did not." Eureka slapped Rose's shoulder with a limp pantsleg.

"Sure did. Said you saved her the other day when y'all went out on pickup."

"She tell you about the last place we went?" said Eureka. Though she'd resisted, she was glad to be distracted from the stack of workshirts rising on the table beneath her. Usually she and Rose made a game of this chore, talking back to the names on the shirts, chiding Ed for his Extra Extra Large beer belly, shaking their heads at Calvin's dribbled tobacco juice stains, wrinkling their noses over Johnson's lingering body odor.

"What last place?"

"Some man's house."

"What man?"

"I don't know him. I mean I know his name but that's about all. Edwin Keane."

"I know all about them Keanes."

"What do you know?"

"I know they sitting pretty up to the end of River Road. I heard they living room about big as this whole building."

"He's strange."

"Strange how?"

"Didn't have his clothes ready. Kept talking to me like I was somebody else."

"Just because he didn't have his mess ready, that don't mean he's strange. Times I went out on pickup, half of 'em expecting me to go in they bedrooms and strip the sheets. And look: all of 'em talk to you like you somebody else."

"I tried ten times to tell him what I was doing there but he wouldn't listen."

"Who does he got you mixed up with?"

Eureka shrugged. "Somebody."

"Well, that boy . . . now that you talk about him I believe there is something wrong with that boy."

"What?"

"Don't quote me but I believe he got in that bad wreck back here about a year or two? Seem like somebody riding with him got killed."

"He did say something about an accident. And he limps. But he can talk," said Eureka. "You ought to have heard him talk."

"Must of talked sweet, way you been acting."

Eureka was ready to deny it when she saw the Fraulein headed their way, sending both back to work.

"I'm going," she told Randall after supper that night. They were on the back porch again, crouched on the bottom steps, hiding from Martha, who wanted them to do the supper dishes.

"Going where?"

She was shocked — how could he forget — until she remembered that the world had not spent the last few days in her mind, nor had she spent the last few days in the world. Things had gone on as usual for people next door, up in Raleigh, in Spain; people who had not shared her alternate spells of queasy indecision and fantasy.

No one knew but Randall, and he'd forgotten. She remembered how he'd winced at her pronoun strategy, understood better why it hurt him. She wanted to share it with him. His indifference bothered her even after she reminded herself of his age.

"To the courtyard. To meet him."

"Better think of a name for him first."

"Don't tell anyone where I'm going."

"You're going to tell a lie?"

"Of course," she said.

"Oh," he said. "What lie you going to tell?"

His disinterest concealed something troubling, but she did not have time for the battery of questions it always took to ferret out his hurt.

"Wait up for me," she said.

"Unless I go to bed first," he said, slinging an acorn at a nearby hen.

On the front porch she stood for a full minute above her father, reared back and napping in his drinking chair, twitching through a dream. His drunks are like sleeps, she thought, made of stages that repeat themselves like the stages of sleep: deep water dream, the shallow point just before waking.

"Pa," she said.

Waking, he blinked, let the chair legs bump to the floor, and after a few seconds during which he seemed embarrassed said, "How's it going over to the laundry?"

"It's all right."

He yawned. "German lady treating y'all all right?"

"She's been good to me."

"Your sisters don't do nothing but complain about her. Say she's a slave driver."

"It doesn't bother me, staying busy."

"Me neither. I'd soon them tell me what to do as not and the day drag on." He stared at her eyes for a moment, until she looked away. "For not complaining you deserve something." He took a thin roll from his pocket, extracted a dollar bill and handed it over.

"For not complaining."

She smiled her thanks but felt funny for accepting it: both slighted, as if she needed more than a dollar to distance herself from the rest of her sisters, and guilty, as if people were giving her money to do things unnamed and therefore suspect.

"Promise not to say a thing to the others and I'll give you some every month from what you earn over there."

"I want to go for a walk."

"Now? It's going dark directly."

"I won't be long."

"I don't like y'all out late here in town.

Not unless you take Hal."

"Hal's not even here. I'll take Randall."

"What can Randall do?"

"Talk them to death." It bothered her to make fun of what she considered a gift, yet she knew it would work. Her father shook his head and said, "He sure as hell can do that. All right, but hurry."

They did hurry through the grey downtown, gone quiet in the after-hours. The only activity came from the "county," as the local jail was called, and the Sir Trent Hotel, town's two tallest buildings. Inmates of each sat on stoops watching the last trickle of traffic, trusties of the county chaperoned by a single deputy.

Prisoners called from the dark barred windows as they passed by the county.

"Looking good, little girl."

"Nothing but the truth, so help me, Jesus."

In quick glance Eureka saw the glint of streetlight on the window screens, bones of bars underneath; still deeper the waist-up outline of felons all after-supper restless, their world going slowly dark. After she and Randall passed out of sight there would be only trails of headlights outside. The prisoners kept up their chatter until it turned lame and forced, like infielders trying to intimidate a batter long after they'd lost the game.

"That good stuff."

"Fifteen minutes you won't never forget."

"You're supposed to protect me," she told Randall, who'd stopped several times in midsidewalk, shielded his eyes in attempt to see inside the cellblocks.

"From them or from him?"

"I thought you didn't want to call him 'him' anymore," she said, grabbing Randall's arm and tugging him along.

"Haven't thought of a new name yet."

When they reached the church she paused outside the gate. "Stay here."

"Thought I was supposed to be protecting you."

"I don't need it from him. He's harmless. He just wants to talk is all."

She hadn't thought it until she'd said it, but saying it made the whole thing coherent and even obvious. *He wanted someone to talk to.* He said himself he'd been cooped up for a year, Rose said he'd been in a bad wreck, it would be harmless and charitable, like volunteering to visit the sick at the nursing home which her home ec teacher had forced them all to do one afternoon.

"How do you know he only wants to talk?"

She ignored him. "Just let me know if somebody's coming," she said.

"If you're only going to talk to him what

do you care?"

"What's wrong with you?"

"Absolutely nothing at all," he said, and he reached out to grasp the low limb of an oak and swung himself into the cloud of foliage above.

8

As she came into the courtyard she saw his cigarette rising and falling in a corner, the breeze sifting cinders and spitting them to the ground. He grew solid as her eyes adjusted to the darker patches of shadow. His shirt was unbuttoned to the breastbone, his tie dangled limply as if wilted by the humidity. When he met her stare she looked to the ground, studied his feet: canvas gym shoes with big toenail holes, white sock shining through like a sliver of moon.

"First of all I owe you an apology," he said. "I was confused last week."

"Me, too," she said.

"About the laundry. Your little brother told me you worked there but it slipped my mind, I was thinking ahead, it never occurred —"

"What else did my little brother tell you?"

"Let's sit," he said.

"What else did you *ask* him?"

"Nothing," he said. "Things: your name, where you lived, how many in your family."

The very things she tried to distance herself

from by using those carefully chosen pronouns; she wanted no part of them, he wanted to know them. This should be a warning, yet she was curious about why he would ask such boring questions.

"I'm sitting," he said. "I was in an accident and it hurts me to stand." He sat down on the bench and lit another cigarette, waved it between them in fiery loops which left trails.

"Shoos mosquitoes," he said. "Won't you sit?"

She did not speak or move.

"I can't see you." He squinted.

"I told a lie to get here."

"I hate it's so dark. Next time . . ."

"I told a lie to get here."

"And you don't want to waste a good lie to hear me talk about how to shoo mosquitoes. I don't blame you. Okay. I wanted to know all those things because I was interested. Actually what interests me is beyond all those things, but one has to get them out of the way. Sooner the better. You remember that day when you were here before?"

"I used to come here lots until some old lady tried to run me off."

"Lobster Woman no doubt. This being their sacred stomping ground."

"Lobster woman?"

"Long story," he said, waving his cigarette

wearily. "Later. I'm talking about the time you were here with your little brother gathering leaves."

"For school," she said.

"I know. Strickland's botany. Eleventh grade. I had to do it, too."

The thought of him bent to gather leaves, climbing a gum tree, his slick-soled gym shoes useless against smooth bark, was enough to soften her. She remembered how she'd resented the assignment, how she'd thought it had bound her to Trent and its traditions in a particularly anonymous way. But he'd done it, too, and he certainly was not tied to this place. He was only here temporarily, to recuperate; that much was clear from the first time she'd seen him. She could hear it in his talk, his sentences spinning their wheels in the thick Trent sand until he felt well enough to leave.

"I was standing in the corner over there," he said, pointing toward some boxwoods. "Eavesdropping and spying. I should tell you that I'm not in the habit of taking walks. As a matter of fact, before that day I hadn't left my house in months, a year almost I'd been inside if you count the time at home before I moved to the bungalow. But something drew me out that day. Something drew me here."

He was breathing heavier, his cigarette forgotten, a stubby sixth finger about to singe the hair below his knuckles. She watched the ember grow closer to his skin and readied herself for those stuffed suitcase sentences. Just sit and listen to the thick of it, she thought, like listening to rain without hearing drops.

"I don't think you understand how difficult it is to get to know another person. I say that not because I don't think you're bright but because you're young still. Once someone half-knew me and you would not believe how much effort it took to get there. It took years to reach the less than halfway point and when we arrived there I discovered I didn't want to go any further with her, but that's neither here nor there now."

She wondered about this "her": what she looked like, where she was now, who left whom.

"I'm not one who takes much pleasure in explaining myself to others. I get bored and embarrassed talking about myself." He stopped talking suddenly, flicked his cigarette into the gravel beneath them and stared at it as if he needed something besides the darkness of the courtyard to focus on.

"Sit down," he said, and she did, tucking her dress under the knees and touching down twice on the marble before settling at the far end.

"You know me," he said.

"No I do not."

When he turned to her his look was blank, as if she was his reflection in a mirror he'd been staring at so long he'd become dimensionless, background.

He said her name. "It's beautiful."

She'd never thought so. Teachers squinted at it when it appeared near the bottom of their class rolls, everyone misspelled it, most people repeated it when they first heard it, a tinge of disbelief in their tone as they ravaged it with shaved-off syllables and added R's — Eureeker, Rureker, Rurearker. When the word *urethra* came up in health class she'd laid low afterwards, finding solace in the fact that the term echoing tinny down the locker-lined corridors was too technical to be remembered much past midterms. The name of a town in California, a slogan for triumphant discovery: what did any of these things have to do with her?

"I never liked it," she said. "Even the sound of it. People cough it up from their stomach seems like."

"Oh, I love the sound. It *is* guttural, like you say, but it's exotic. Compared to most names. It's Greek, you know. You know what it means?"

She stared down at the smoldering butt until

he sensed her embarrassment.

"Anyway, it's wonderful, to me that is, I can understand if you don't like it though, I hate my own name. The sound of it *and* its meaning. Not its literal meaning, I have no idea what it really means, probably Son of a Lawyer or something, but the meaning I've given it."

"What's your meaning?"

"Son of Lawyer," he said. Her smile seemed to give him energy. "Actually, this is a good segue." He pulled an envelope from the breast pocket of his suitcoat and handed it to her.

Though she had no idea what "segue" meant she felt another torrent coming on, and she studied the envelope.

"What is this?" she asked. It was smudged with inky fingerprints and the flap had been torn open but carefully retaped.

"Sit tight. Your little brother told me your daddy doesn't like you out past dark and since we're violating curfew here I'll be brief. Before the accident I felt like I had my whole life laid out for me. Clean, linear, invariably boring. Between my mother and Sarah I felt like all the suits I would wear until the day I was buried in one had been already chosen, outfitted with coordinating shirts and ties. Somewhere was a bedroom the size of a stadium where all these outfits were draped over beds. It seemed I'd never have to face the day when I'd have to waste time with the question of what to wear. Do you understand?"

Since she had so few clothes, since all of them were cast off by the stair step of older, larger sisters; since she was near the bottom and the hand-me-downs came to her frayed, stained and shapeless; since she had no choice but to wear them with what little style she could muster, the question of what to wear was crucial, always worthy of the time it took.

She shook her head no, but he didn't seem to notice.

"Those days I dreaded the future. I became obsessed with the ideal of one day when I knew nothing of what would happen next. With her I craved above everything — above security and even bliss — a simple ambiguity. But with you, it's the very opposite. With you I want to know. I want to see ahead, to not be surprised."

First he'd made her think she had a double, now he was saying that somewhere close by was her complete opposite. She'd never once considered the possibility of either: not in the world, certainly not here in Trent. Though she wasn't too keen on the double, the opposite fascinated her and she became so caught up imagining her physically (blond and chunky and dough-boned, a girl who moved through her life like a snow woman melting with each step) that she quit listening, wandered back to him only when he stood to leave.

"Wait a minute," she said. She held up the letter. "What about this?"

"That's yours."

"It's not money, is it?"

"Must run in the family."

"What?"

"Your little brother didn't seem to care too much for money either."

"He's hardly ever seen any."

"What kind of currency do they take out at Speed's store?"

"Credit," she said.

"But what do you pay your tab with?"

"Cukes, peppers. Chickens and hogs and even tractors if it gets way out of hand."

"So money means nothing out there?"

She handed him the envelope back. "Means nothing to me either place."

He laughed, but it wasn't a relaxed laugh. He stuck his cigarette in his mouth and sucked so long and hard that the ember flared bright red.

"It's not money," he said, handing it back. "It's a letter I want you to read. Now we'd both better go. I'll let your little brother know when we can meet next when he brings me my medicine."

She'd forgotten about Randall, hadn't thought of him since he'd disappeared into the tree. She looked to the branches above where he was no doubt hiding, watching and listening like someone in one of those Tarzan books he loved so much. Spying and eavesdropping just like Keane had confessed to doing to them that day last week. He'd heard everything: her whining about her name, Keane's talk of her opposite, that crazy tirade about a place where suits with matching ties were laid out across beds.

And he'd seen him give her the letter. It would do no good to hide it, there was no way to hide anything from him anyway, even though she wanted to: for the first time she'd discovered something she didn't want to share with him, something which she hoped would not sag beneath the weight of his childish questions. Earlier his lack of interest had hurt her, but now she welcomed it.

Such a quick turnaround made her not trust herself. She didn't trust Keane either, or the notes and ten-dollar bills and letters. She'd just give the letter back, say no thanks, no more meetings please, so what you love my name and hate your own, it's not worth risking Randall over for me to sneak out and hear how once there was someone it took you years to not get to know. A rustling of leaves above confirmed it: if not Randall shifting on a hidden branch it was the wind of him laying claim to the days they'd shared. She honored its whisper, reaching out with the letter in hand to the empty dark where Edwin had stood, where the last of his cigarette sent up thin, ribboned smoke.

Late the next afternoon, Eureka waited until Miss Fritz went for her ammonia Coke, shut herself up in the laundry bathroom, tore open the letter and began to read.

Dear Eureka,

I have only the best intentions in telling you these things about myself and would not dare set myself to such a task if I did not think that there was the slightest possibility of obstructions being washed away by the flood of my confessions, obstructions that could quite possibly otherwise cause you to turn away. So I feel that in volunteering this information oh already this is hopelessly stodgy and muddled and filled with the kind of maudlin language favored by failed politicians with something to hide I'll start over, let me start over.

Dear Eureka,

This is the first of several installments of that thousand pages of foolscap I mentioned. Don't worry: it won't *really* be a thousand pages but it may seem that way, and the weight it will lift from both of us will seem like thousands of pounds. I've told you of my reluctance — inability, actually — to talk about my life. What I've decided to do is give you several letters which record incidents revealing sides of myself which I feel you need to know about. These aren't good sides.

There were quite a few things I thought important enough to include here, but after a day's worth of mulling-over I managed to whittle it down to several. The first is bad but by no means the worst. Right now you are probably asking yourself why any lover would want to lead his hand with a list of atrocities committed in cold and mostly sober blood. Remember: this is offered to save us valuable time, to avoid that so-called "grace period" which so many lovers naively trust. I've made that mistake before, and I'm telling you, it's kiss-of-death.

This happened while I was still in college. A weekend near the end of the semester, Thomasson (the only one of my fraternity brothers I could ever really talk to) and I had been in the library all night. We went back to the house where at eleven a party was just beginning. Everyone was on their first drink, the music and talk were not yet loud enough to drown everything out. You could still eavesdrop. I sat down midway up the steps with Thomasson, waiting for that moment in parties which I've always liked, when time lags into drunken slow motion. I was watching for it, sort of making a game out of it. I like the way this split second makes people feel as if they are a part of something spontaneous and monumental, even when they're only bobbing heads whose fixed smiles substitute for ideas. I'm just as guilty sometimes, only that night I was too tired and distracted to elbow my way into it. I sat there on the stairs with the sole purpose of making fun. Thomasson got disgusted and said so.

"This is deer hunting with headlights," he said. "No sport. Targets should be moving, Edwin." He stood up. "Good night, sitting ducks," he said, but no one heard him of course and he went upstairs to bed. I should have listened — should have followed him — but it felt too good to stop.

So I sat alone on the landing and watched and passed judgment. I thought bad things until, finally — and it took awhile — I started to feel bad myself.

I was about to join Thomasson upstairs when I happened to notice a boy approach a girl. He said something to her. She answered, smiling. I sat back down and from that point on I kept my eyes on the two of them.

At first I thought I knew them both, but decided after closer scrutiny that I only knew their type. She was pretty but nowhere near striking. I had no doubt passed over her several times during my room sweeps, skipped right over her because she seemed, standing alone, so easily pegged. Marginally affluent, city schools until puberty at which point something all-girl. Summers spent at the family compound out-side of Linville. Tri Delt legacy, early childhood ed. major. This is what I might have surmised during my first sweep, but now, in the shadow of this boy she seemed to bloom. I know that sounds horrible but this is what I thought at the time. I couldn't stop staring at her. That borderline wholesomeness I had passed over the first time evolved into an intolerable sexiness: she stood by him looking incredibly clean as if she'd never ever been dirty. I wanted to smell her hair, which was black with a purplish glint where the light hit. I slumped down further on the landing to check her legs through a clearing in the thicket of couples surrounding her. I didn't care who caught me staring.

Women are quick and uninhibited when it comes to commenting on each other's looks but for a man to say one word about another man's looks is to all but emerge from that three-dollar bill closet. I'll admit that I stared as hard. I noticed everything, even the way his pants hung off his hips. I checked him out as thoroughly as I'd looked her over. He, too, seemed so goddamn clean: a clean like hers that went beneath the skin, a clean you're born with, that makes showering and bathing only a formality. There's something unreal about someone that clean-looking, especially to someone like me, who feels filmy with dirt from years ago. It's *unnatural* to be born so clean I realize but that night it was so intriguing, these two clean people standing together laughing and talking. At one point he went to get her a drink and alone she looked vaguely into the crowd, let her eyes drift until she stared right at me but didn't seem to see me, *I really was a fly on the wall.* He came back and handed her a cup, she reached for it and swayed a little, he grabbed her forearm and held onto it, I saw for the first time ever into the future, two clean people on taut white sheets. The thought of watching these two moving against each other in bed drove me crazy. I wanted to be there.

In just five minutes while sitting on the stairs in the midst of an otherwise boring party I'd gone from self-disgust to longing. The two of them seemed at the height of a youth I'd never had (maybe that night was the pinnacle and I didn't realize it), a youth to which they remained oblivious. The whole room was oblivious; they danced and draped their arms around each other and shouted and ignored the only thing they had going for them, youth ticking away. But this couple seemed to represent my youth, which I could only experience *through* them.

At first I was confused. I didn't know if I wanted them to defile my youth with sex or ratify it with sex. I knew only one thing: that I wanted to watch.

I left when they did, threading the crowd without being noticed. He opened the door of his car for her, I crouched behind a streetlight and watched them make out, she half-turned in the passenger's seat toward him, he standing outside with his head thrust forward into the car. A small square of overhead light blinked off and on as he pushed on the car door, just enough light for me to see their expressions, which had passed from the affected aloofness of people trying to survive big parties into intimacy. Looks which made me think that they knew each other completely. Two people whom I had previously thought incapable of knowing anything at all had accomplished it in a matter of minutes.

People were leaving the party now, I had to be careful, several times my obsession almost got me caught but I tell you I don't think I was ever actually aware of what I was doing or what I was about to do. I didn't think of what they were doing as private either. Back then, you see, I was ignorant of propriety where my curiosity was concerned (I've always been what they call *impulsive*), meaning that if something interested me I didn't give a good goddamn whether it was any of my business. That's what business is, something which interests you.

So there I was hiding behind a streetlight while girls streamed away reluctantly, damning their too-early dormitory curfews. Just at the point when it was the most crowded he bolted around to streetside, climbed in and cranked up. I ran for my car, which was parked a block back, didn't give a damn if I was seen. I got in the car and broke about ten laws tailing them.

Finally he signaled, pulled up in front of a fraternity house and went around to open the door for her. Please, I'm saying, or praying — that might have been my first prayer since Vacation Bible School — please, I'm praying, Please Please let it be a ground-floor room. The house was wide-open, all lit-up. I followed them right inside, chanting my pitiful plea under-breath the whole way, please let it be ground-floor. There were no fire escapes, three stories of slick sandstone, no chinks, no trellis, not even a nearby tree to climb. But I was lucky. They fooled around in the hallway for a while, I hid in the foyer, peeking around a pillar, a bad movie version of a burglar. Finally he went for his keys and unlocked a room to the side. I went out and found the window. Pulled up a few sticks of stove-wood from a neighbor's pile to stand on. For five minutes I stared into a dark room, then a lamp flicked on. They stood in the narrow space between two single beds. He was wrenching his shirt from his shoulders. His tie was still buttoned into his shirt collar as he pulled it off, kicked both loafers under

199

the bed, unbuckled his belt and slid it smoothly from the loops. Every movement fluid. Unbuttoned his pants, unzipped. His pants dropped straight to the floor, bunched up around his ankles, yes, I thought, finally, this is it, this is where he'll bungle his agile act, but he just stepped out of it one foot at a time, kicked away the lump of clothes with a graceful flick of heel.

I was jealous. I've always been bad at undressing during the heat of the moment. He turned it into ballet. With me it's like shedding inhibitions — each article of clothing grows heavier, harder to part with, each successive article an inhibition more deeply ingrained.

I pressed my face against the window screen and could feel the grid pattern across my cheeks. The screen smelled of rust, the windowsill of rotting wood, the night air of blown-up dust. He put thumb and forefinger above each hipblade, slid them under the elastic band of his shorts, eased them off until he stood naked with his back to me. Then he stepped toward her.

Be patient, Eureka. All I ask is that you give me the benefit here and try to understand how in the long run this will help us.

Her hair was mussed and one strap of

her dress had strayed from her shoulder and clung loosely to her upper arm. She stood there fully clothed for a minute, looking him up and down, before she started to undress.

She wasn't quite as graceful as he was, but she was much sexier. As I watched her pull her dress off, my face started to itch where the screen pushed against it. Further proof of obsession, what pain and physical discomfort you're willing to put up with in order to be fulfilled. Mosquitoes stung my ankles, my neck pulsed with a painful crick, my feet tremored from the tiptoe I had to sustain in order to see inside. He tossed her bra across the room, she stripped her panties off and pulled him close again. She pressed herself against his chest, only the edge of her nipple visible. She stood back then and the sight of her breasts resuming their shape, freed from his press, the sight of those breasts falling slightly and holding was one of the most beautiful things I've ever seen. Can't do it justice here. It was something I never would have noticed had I been involved, had I been in the room with her instead of him. The perspective would have been all wrong. I had what I thought of then as a great realization: that the perspective of onlooker affords much more aesthetic appreciation than the very narrow and selfish view of participant. Not that I still believe that.

She pressed against him again, backed them both up to the bed. She lay on her back sideways, her head resting on the wall. He stood in front and surveyed her, holding both her hands. When I rushed the fraternity they had a dirty film night we were required to attend, a sequence of short jumpy sex acts between sad older women and Cubans who wore black socks during the entire reel. That was the only sex I'd witnessed aside from what I'd been personally involved in. Undoubtedly the actors in these films were down-and-outers pulled from the streets and paid in drinks and reefers. And face it, economic instigation does not make for impassioned love. You can go out to my neighborhood, old money River Road, and find proof of that. The shorts I'd seen in the dark parlor of the frathouse were like dry educational films that tell you what to do should there be a sudden attack from the air or sea. I had always thought that there could be nothing more boring in the world than watching two people in bed. But these two proved me wrong as I stood in the bushes and held my breath, watching them grow more and more frenzied until finally it was over.

And because I did not want to see them go through those awkward moments when the lust wanes and there you are naked with another person in a state no longer very animal, and most of all because I did not want to see them with clothes on again, I left. More carefully than I came. Climbed into my car with the unmistakable signs of peeping tom-ism — the distinct weave of window screen — printed across my face for all the world to see.

It wasn't until much later — actually until I sat down to write this letter — that I realized fully what I had done.

I devote so much space to this incident for two reasons.

One: it would be pretty difficult for me to sum up what I have just described to you. Despite the obviousness of my infraction against those two unsuspecting lovers, the experience was so rich that I could very well have gone on for another ten pages, had my medicine not run out. During the middle of this letter I had to call the druggist for more and am awaiting your little brother as I write.

Two: this incident seems in retrospect to have been the beginning of something. The start of my giving in to every impulse that was strong enough and singular enough to induce action.

Enough for now. There's more — two more major entries which will make this seem in comparison like a little white lie. But I don't have the strength to go into them now. Later. Sometime when my medicine holds out, when I don't have to interrupt my thoughts to harangue that self-righteous druggist down at Lehmann's.

Know that these confessions are not meant to shock or disturb but to save sacred time and to prepare you — prepare us — for our future.

Love,
Edwin

She folded the letter, pushed it back into the envelope, slammed the lid down on the toilet and slumped there. She'd been in the bathroom for twenty minutes reading and rereading while her sisters and coworkers had rattled the door. She'd kept quiet, hadn't answered the "who's in there?"s, had barely noticed the knocking until Rose came, shook the door on its saggy hinges and asked if she was sick.

"Yes," she'd replied in a frail voice she'd not had to fake. She was at the place in his letter when he'd described the girl's breasts falling after the boy moved away from her, going on and on about it as if he was describing an eighth Wonder of the World. She wasn't sick, though it was easy to sound so. She wasn't shocked, either. So many worse things were imaginable that this seemed mild: she was sure he'd embellished, she could feel it in the push of his sentences, in the extravagance of some of those words which she admittedly did not understand.

Yet she was less confused by vocabulary than intent. What was she supposed to make of it all? What did he want her to do now that these confessions had begun? Stay away? Pull her shades close nights from now on, spread the news that he's inclined to peep-tom?

She began to talk to herself, filling the closet-sized bathroom with whispers and worry as the knocks came and went. "He says he's doing it to save time and why shouldn't I want that, time saved now means I leave here sooner. I should trust him after all he's older he's been through a lot he's smarter. If him sending me these letters and confessing his big sins saves time then it's fine by me. I don't have to say one thing about them, he'll never even ask me what I think, it's not something he'll want to talk about doubt he'll even bring it up."

"Sounds like she's got somebody in there with her," she heard a coworker say just outside the door.

"I do," she said, clutching the letter and standing on the toilet lid to look out of the high window above her head. No way for her to squeeze between the rusty bars, no way out; the letter had cornered her here in this bathroom with its tic-tac-toe games pencil-scratched above the toilet paper holder, and the thickly chemical smell of the Lava soap ends the Fraulein scrubbed with at the end of each day.

But if he really wanted to save time, why not skip over all this? She thought this instead of saying it, now that she could hear them gathered outside, whispering. He was the one who complained about his past, how hard it was to explain. If this peeping-tom bit only happened once, why take the time to drag it up, especially since he was so big on saving time in the first place.

She needed someone to talk to, but could think of no one she could trust. Only Randall, and given the content of the letter this was impossible. Even if she tried talking about it vaguely, his curiosity was so persistent that it would break her down. Her sisters? Without a doubt they'd see Edwin as someone like Jay Jay Drawhorn or Edna Rivenbark, a town

206

crazy to make fun of.

Outside she heard the Fraulein's voice.

"We're lined up to go to the bathroom," said Martha. "Our sister's in there, won't come out after about a hour."

"You know it hadn't been no hour," Eureka heard Rose say. "She sick, Miss Fritz. I was just headed in there to take her some aspirin."

"You girls get back to work," said the Fraulein. "Rose, see to her now."

"Girl, what is *wrong* with you?" Rose whispered as she squeezed through the door.

"I'm sick."

"You better act like it after I went and told Fritz a lie. I don't like lying to her. Y'all think just because she don't speak English good she stupid but she know when you lying. Wilson got himself fired for all the time calling in sick, like she couldn't smell whiskey on him next day 'cause she German. I might as well sit down while I have the chance."

Rose lowered herself to the floor, watching Eureka fold the letter, stuff the envelope down her knee sock. "You in here all this time reading mail?"

"It was a real long letter."

"I'm out there telling lies for you and you in here reading a letter?"

"Sorry, Rose. I messed up, didn't I?"

"This is my job, 'Reka. You just come in

207

here after school for a few hours but I'm here all day, going be here 'til I get out of this town. Fritz and me have got to the place where we understand each other. She know all I want's to work hard and get paid good and not put up with any of her ammonia mouth."

"I *am* sick," said Eureka. "It's not really a lie."

Rose cut her eyes to the bulging sock. "That Keane?"

Eureka nodded.

"What's he writing you letters for when he just live 'cross town?"

Eureka hunched forward. "Tell the truth, Rose. What would you do if a man sent you a letter describing all these bad things he'd done in his life?"

"I'd be glad he writing them down instead of doing them."

"But see, what if . . . I mean, has any man ever done that to you before, set you down and told you all about his past sins before he even asked you out?"

"I never went with a preacher. Besides, that sound like something only a white man would think up." She leaned in close to Eureka, and said, "We been in here long enough. I'm going tell her you sick. That I sent you on home. And look: like I told you, this is my job."

"I know, Rose."

"When I open this door, you act like you about to fall out."

"I won't even have to fake it," Eureka said, and as she stood her legs seemed feather-weight and wobbly, like rope ladders unfurled from a rescue vessel to save someone from seas high and wild.

For once, Randall seemed to be listening and not talking. At least that's how it looked to Speight, who was washing the plateglass windows when he saw, reflected in a just-scrubbed swath, his son standing next to a strange man on the far sidewalk. The glass was so clean, the reflection so clear, that Speight could make out the man's mouth moving, could almost read his lips.

They talked for two or three minutes after Speight spotted them. The whole time the man talked and Randall nodded, which was what kept Speight interested. Had Randall been the one holding forth, Speight might have thought less about it, might have figured the boy had cornered someone to ask some crazy questions about the clock inside the parking meter, might have returned to work and missed that moment when the man handed something to Randall. After the man limped away — he appeared slightly crippled — Speight watched his son bolt across the street, intercepted him in front of the store.

"Whoa," he said, curling a hand around his collarbone and clamping down hard. "Who was that you was just talking to?"

"That's a Mr. Edwin Keane," said Randall. Delivered in a proud singsong pitch, as if he was Trent's official tour guide and had been asked about a prominent citizen.

"How come you know *him?*"

"I go see him sometimes."

"What for?"

"Take his medicine."

"What was he talking to you about?"

"About me taking him some medicine."

"I seen him giving you something."

When Randall squirmed but didn't speak, Speight tightened his grip. "Did I not see him give you something?"

Randall dug into his pocket, placed the carefully folded ten into Speight's extended hand.

"This for his medicine?"

"No sir. Customers don't pay me, drugstore bills him."

"I know that. What's this money for?"

Randall swiveled his head about, looked across the street, then up and down the sidewalk.

"He didn't touch you did he?"

"No sir."

"Then what?" Usually Speight couldn't

get the boy to shut up; his holding back seemed a bad sign.

"He pays it to me so I'll hurry," Randall said. "To bring his medicine as quick as I can."

"Why wouldn't you hurry? You haven't been goofing off again? Going down to the river when you're supposed to be working?"

"No sir. It's just he wants his medicine right then, he can't wait like normal people."

"Does the druggist know he's paying you?"

"No sir."

"Anybody else know?"

"Nope."

"He's give you money before?"

"No sir." It was easier to lie this time; that's the secret to it, Randall thought, it gets easier and every time you feel a little less bad.

"If he pays you again you bring the money straight to me. And from now on, do whatever he tells you to."

"Yes sir."

"Keep him happy," said Speight, and Randall promised to try.

9

That ring again, slicing the drugstore quiet. Roy wondered how Keane managed to make each call come through like fingernail raking blackboard.

Twice Roy had been wrong. Twice he had winced at a ring he thought unmistakably Edwin's only to pick up on Dr. Sawyer's nurse phoning in a prescription, a mother trying to track down her truant son. Both times he had let the ringing continue for as long as possible before picking up. This time it didn't work.

"Lehmann's, druggist."

"I need it now," said Edwin.

"Beg pardon?"

"I said I need it now, Green. My medicine. I'm sick."

"Won't argue with you there."

"Within the hour."

"I don't know how much more familiar we can get here," said Roy. "You don't even bother to identify yourself anymore. What if it wasn't me who'd answered? You'd have felt pretty foolish telling Ruby you need it now."

"Maybe she'd listen."

"According to my records, tomorrow afternoon is when your refill comes up. Shall I send it over then or do you want to give a call around noon to remind me?"

"Don't do this. Don't make me do this again."

Roy forced a thin laugh. "I can't make you do anything. Can't make you help yourself, can't make you listen, certainly can't make you understand my position."

"Why waste time trying, then? If you understood anything at all you'd just let me have it and go on back to work. Let me have it when I want and you can eliminate all the dirty dealing, all that going over your head you hate so much. Yet you hold onto your tenderfoot ethics. Play your tired trump and keep me waiting all day."

"It's my only trump I guess."

"Well, you're wearing it out. I'm hanging up now. Send me my medicine."

Roy started to scheme before he even laid the phone down, calling Randall up from the stockroom and filling a bag with empty vials. Lehmann took a two-hour lunch on Saturdays, and Roy often took an extra half hour himself. If Keane managed to reach Lehmann before Roy returned, Lehmann couldn't send the boy

213

if the boy wasn't around to send. He'd have to come up with something else for the rest of the day, but he felt sure he could manufacture enough deliveries so that Edwin would have to wait until Monday. I'll have to do it by the goddamn hour, he thought, which seemed fitting, since after seven years and countless requests for a yearly salary, Lehmann still paid him by the hour.

But if he could keep the medicine away for even one hour he would be doing the boy some good. Hours add up, he told himself, ashamed of the thought but swayed by its simple truth in Keane's case. I am the only one who can save that boy, the rest of the town would as soon keep him doped up and hidden away until one day — not long off at the rate he's headed — he takes too much. At which point they will blame it on a car wreck he could have recovered from had he not been surrounded by cowards and snobs, people so shallow that the sight of one of their own limping down the street in unpressed pants makes them want to treat him like a broken-legged nag.

For seven years Roy had been trying to leave this town; for seven years he'd talked himself into staying because of his job. However humiliating and unfulfilling, it was daily rhythm, a physical act ingrained by movement and senses. He'd grown used to the idea of it as shelter, a dark cavern where he hid from the blinding afternoon. He'd been sequestered too long now; away from Lehmann's he would wither.

Now he had a reason to stay, and this reason supplied an energy he'd not felt in years.

"Remember your first day here when I sent you down to the river?" he asked Randall.

The boy looked away from him, gave his slight Speight nod.

"Go down there again, but this time stay longer."

"How come?" Randall wasn't his usual eager self; he fell sullen at the mention of the river.

"How come? Because it's Saturday, that's how come. And you've been down in the basement helping your daddy all morning and you need a break. I don't want to see you back here before three-thirty at the earliest."

"Last time I did that I got blessed out," Randall was saying. "By that man."

"Which man?"

"The one's after my sister."

Kid talk, thought Roy. He handed Randall a bag to use for cover and told him to get lost, take your time, have fun.

People will tell you the most embarrassing

things, Eureka thought while trailing her sisters home from the laundry for lunch. People will confess their biggest sins to you, convinced you'll see it all in a sympathetic light. If they didn't think you'd react the way they anticipated, they wouldn't tell you these things in the first place.

Since she was still unsure of what to think about Edwin's letter, she'd decided to ask him what he *wanted* her to think. Obviously he'd intended her to see all this his way. She only had to ask which way that was.

She lagged until her sisters passed up the sidewalk sloping into town. When she came to the Episcopal church she ducked into the courtyard in case they noticed her missing and sent someone back for her. Rose had told her how to get to Edgecombe Street. Talking to Rose had helped, but she still had the letter to deal with, and even though Rose's advice made sense at the time, during the hours she'd spent wandering around town after leaving the laundry she'd picked Rose's words apart in the same way she'd done his letter. Rose had said she'd rather him write those things than do them, but what was to prevent him from doing both? Rose had said it seemed like something a white man would think up, but that didn't help either; white or colored she didn't care, she only wanted to know how to take it.

After she'd decided to see him, once again she'd spent the hours leading up to the visit thinking of him, hearing as she walked and ate and slept the wordless burning cadence of his speeches. Listening to him made her feel as if she'd been led somewhere blind-folded, then allowed abruptly to see. The moments when she understood him were often too sharp, blinking at a sudden brightness. Yet however foreign or vague the things he talked about, she could always figure out his thrust, from inflection or rhythm or context, from the weather which cloaked him as he spoke: storm cloud or sun burst, heat lightning or downpour.

She'd given up trying to figure out who he was to focus instead on who he was not. He was not the composite husband she'd resigned herself to that day in the warehouse, wasn't the slick, silent boy who'd woo her half-heartedly, ferry her to his Trent in a brand new Buick.

She needed only to peel off that thin layer of neglect when studying his image, skin him lightly with squinted eyes to see what he'd looked like once and what — with work and rest — he'd look like again. Summers spent swimming in the river and down at the beach had flared his shoulders. Had he not been hurt he'd surely become one of those middle-aged men who showed age only in the slightest sag of stomach and under the eyes in a certain slant of late afternoon light. Beneath his disheveled surface lurked features which would emerge vibrantly and dominant in offspring.

But what of the other beneath-the-surface which she would not want to crop up in children, that hidden side of him described in the letter which could have even begun to show itself without her realizing it during the brief time she'd known him?

Know's not exactly the word to use here, she thought, and the realization that she'd been wasting her lunch hour wondering how his looks might translate to offspring sent her on down the street.

He was sitting at the kitchen table shirtless, pale skin greasy with sweat. Saturday noon noises rose from both sides of the bungalow, raucous snatches from Johnsontown, yard-work sounds from Edgecombe. He sat motionless in the cross fire, smoking a cigarette and staring at a book propped on a crimped percolator.

When she knocked he focused on her slowly, recognition evolving into a childlike smile. The purity of his reaction unnerved her, and she almost turned and ran.

"I brought this back to you," she said, holding the ragged envelope out to him. One dog-ear of the read and reread letter bulged in a corner, the breeze from a fan atop the refrigerator fluttering it.

"Keep it," he said. "I meant for you to."

"But I don't understand it."

"Good. That's a reasonable response. You couldn't possibly understand, so why should you drive yourself crazy trying?"

"I don't need it," she said. "This isn't something I need to know."

"Of course you don't need it if you want to know me. To the extent that you can know me through what I confess in one gushy letter. I'm not sorry I sent it, and I plan to send others — at least one — but you're right not to put too much emphasis on it. I was just trying to take a shortcut, avoid that seeping stage, those months and months when things crawl. Talk about need. We don't need that. Slow death of love. It should all come completely, instantaneously, the way it has for me, or not at all. Not in bits and pieces."

"But you just said there's more, right? Other pieces coming?"

"Yes, but they'll be short, I promise, and besides, it's necessary. At this stage big truths are rare, whether they come in bits or at once. People hedge for at least a year. A year's a long time. You'll be out of school in a year.

219

This is just to speed things up. By the time we've known each other six months we'll have accomplished what it takes most couples three times as long to wade through."

"I don't know," she said.

"Sit down."

"You're always telling me to sit down."

"You're always standing up."

"I've always got to go."

"Where have you got to go?"

"Back to work."

"No you don't," he said.

"I do, I swear."

"Don't swear." He sat down on the cot, plucked the letter from her hand, tossed it toward a drift of papers on the floor, grabbed both her hands and pulled her down beside him. She was awed and weakened by their last exchange, the speed of it and its simple cadence: *I've got to do this, what, this, why, because, okay.* It crackled along smoothly like the talk of people who've been together for years. She knew it was dangerous to trust such a thing — she'd heard of girls who'd ruined their lives over five minutes of thin domesticity, married into misery over a tomato sandwich slapped together for a hungry boy on a school field trip — yet it flowed like blood and was as undeniable. It was a type of communion which rose from the rhythms of child-

220

hood, satisfying in the same intuitive way as countless conversations with Randall.

Maybe it was working, this shortcut of his. He was right, in a year she'd be through with school and ready to leave here forever, but how, who with, where to?

"Before you came I was getting sick," he said.

From being so close she felt faint herself: the air of the kitchen soaked her, heat flashes dried her out. He pulled her closer. She felt the heat, the alternate drape of cool, heat again, and thought of her dwindling lunch hour.

"But now I feel much better," he said.

On the fourth ring Roy pulled his head out from under the pillow and picked up.

"Where's the goddamn delivery boy?" said Lehmann, slicing the long drowsy *o* from Roy's hello.

Roy rose up on the bed and looked across the room at the clock, saw that he was only forty minutes late.

"Where's the boy? And where the hell are you?"

"I'm in bed. About the boy, long story. One that can surely wait ten minutes."

"Keane's been bugging me, he's got his mother on my ass, she's called here three times, where the hell are you and what'd you do with that boy?"

"Asked his father?"

"Speight said you sent him out, but I've been back an hour and a half and the boy's nowhere around."

Roy lowered and softened his voice. "He's at the river. I sent him there. He's a hard worker. Needed a break."

"I don't pay people to take goddamn breaks. And it's not your job to send people to the river because you think they're hard-working."

"Okay. You're right, Walter. I sent the boy to the river because Keane called me, too. He was begging for an early delivery and I wanted to make him sweat a little. To make him realize how bad off he is. Figured if I made him wait, he might lay off some."

"You think they're going to nominate you for the Nobel Prize for making some smart-ass rich kid dope fiend wait three hours for a delivery? Do you really think you can help that boy? Are you that goddamn dumb?"

"Must be."

"That boy's a lost cause even to his mama, hear her talk. She's been talking my goddamn ear off all afternoon, complaining about you mostly. Said you were rude to her and her boy, said you were quote belligerent and insolent unquote and said you'd been trying to work some kinda cure on the boy which she was wanting to call practicing medicine without a license."

"That's ridiculous. All I did was delay his deliveries for a few hours a few times, deliveries which legally should have been delayed anyway. It wasn't a cure, it was just an attempt to get him to realize how bad off he'd gotten. It was just a start."

"Now it's a finish," said Lehmann. "I'll pay you two weeks severance since you've been with me so long. Seven years is it? Seven years and you haven't learned a thing."

"Slow learner, I guess," and he hung up and rolled over into the side of the bed where he never slept, where the sheets stretched taut and unwrinkled.

The first time she pulled away but he didn't give up. He came back quietly and kissed her and she let him. She was willing but restrained.

Not that she hadn't had to rebuff boys at school. She'd seen other girls go into the woods beyond the playing fields and come out red-skinned, chafed, changed. It did not seem to matter if they enjoyed it or not, whether they picked their way out of the blackberry and privet hedge smiling or frowning. It didn't matter if some tie had been made with the boy they'd followed through the brush. It didn't much matter; either way they emerged red-skinned from the prickly floor of pine forest and the stucco-rough hands of their suitors. Chafed and changed.

She could as well emerge red-skinned, chafed, changed from this kitchen; the only difference was in the one who'd enticed her here. Even though he was not the one she'd imagined, beneath that scraped-away surface he was no longer someone with attractive genes and good looks but a man snaking his arms tighter around her waist, lifting her close, lips on her neck now.

She wanted to lose herself so deeply that each movement was involuntary, a simple and isolated reaction. But that would be unfair to him. It would dilute his passion, reduce his caresses to light taps on the knee to test reflex, a banging shutter causing her to tremor and wince.

She'd thought of it often and decided that if the time came and she was someplace secluded (far from the schoolhouse during recess where an audience for the pickup games hung on the playing field witnessing quickly formed couples slink off and claw back through the scrub) it would not matter that much *who with,* first time being to her mind something to be gotten through like the first fifteen seconds in frigid pond water, a submerged numbness necessary to limber up enough to swim. She would not waste time waiting for the precise moment because it occurred to her that the precise moment is the one most often missed, that it was more important not to miss the moments following.

As he licked and caressed he pushed out streams of words which never quite congealed into sentences and she marveled at how quickly they'd come to this intimacy. She believed, suddenly and wholeheartedly, in his shortcuts. She saw his words forming a quicker route, a dotted line severing a map of the next year of her life, her time left in Trent, which she knew would stretch out endlessly. During it she would be prone to crucial mistakes, as in the restless last half hour of a car trip when the lights of passing cars disorient and the electric eyes of roadside animals hypnotize. In that moment she believed in his power to get them there quicker. He knew time. Let the letters come, she'd read them and save days, months, they were only a leg of this route he'd discovered which took off across fields with the glorious forging of the escapee.

She stood to shed her dress, shuddering involuntarily when his belt buckle hit the floor with a thud. Slow mist filled her marrow. Naked, she felt light enough to float.

As he kissed her stomach she saw the two of them climb into a car, *his mouth a slow wet minute on each nipple and he was moaning,* not a new car but a rusted tub that smoked and squeaked, *he hugged her waist* and the car headed out of town *pressed his face against her stomach* through the outskirts, miles and miles of outskirt *the features of his face distinguishable to her flesh* used-tire stores and mill outlet sheet and towel shops *his nose against her lowest rib then lower* for hours they drove while the town straggled limply alongside, a tireless competitor keeping up in tin billboard, cinderblock storefront *his eyelashes fluttering* occasional open space *she reached down to weave her fingers through his hair* but around a bend another barbecue stand another couple crammed into a green metal glider peddling wholesale shoes, odd sizes *her fingers bleached bone-white by her laundry work threading his warm, wet hair* another roadside tavern another auto parts store another

As she kneaded live bait and cigarette shop *he pulled himself up by the sides of the cot to fit his feet beneath hers like rungs, frantic gasps now* neon-lit *craving the full breath the countryside would bring and when he entered her she did not shudder, thinking nothing now is invol-*

untary as they began to move beneath a traffic light blinking caution above more stores, more outskirt, more remnant of Trent.

Breath is a dirty thing, Speight decided while cleaning the plateglass, and each person's is different, dirty in its own way. He'd just dipped his rag to rinse when Lehmann came through the propped doors.

"Hold off on them windows."

Speight dropped his rag in the bucket. Clean windows had always come first to Lehmann, sometimes he'd have Speight out twice a day not counting the touching up he did now and again when the kids came after school to window gawk.

"Run this package out to this address quick, then drive out to the river and find that goddamn boy."

Speight took the bag and the car keys but made no motion to leave.

"You got your license, don't you?"

"I've had 'em," said Speight.

"Well, what?"

"Which boy is it I'm looking?"

"Forget his name but you ought to know, since you more than likely had a hand in naming him."

Driving across town, Speight thought of Randall, wondered more than worried about him. There were things he didn't know about the boy, things he just couldn't figure out: how the boy would react and what would interest him, for instance. But he'd felt he knew him well enough to get him this job and trust him to do okay by it. If the boy rebelled it would be against the curfew of sundown, against darkness preventing him from finishing a half-built fort in the woods. Against the limited intelligence of a teacher or a big sister claiming to be bored. But rebelling against his father, the job his father had gone out on a limb to get for him? Not for a few years yet, if then.

He found the address and knocked a few times on the front door, but there was no answer. Probably spying from behind their pulled curtains but won't take deliveries unless they're brung around back. He was rarely asked to make deliveries, which was just as well because he hated it. People were always rude and it struck him as undignified work for a grown man. To compensate for the embarrassment he always knocked on front doors first.

He started around back, pushing through knee-high weeds, thinking of the way Lehmann had talked to him on the sidewalk: "That goddamn boy." "You ought to know, you more than likely had a hand in naming him." In fact he had named the boy himself, no say-so from Barbara. Named him after a uncle from down around Elizabeth City, captain of a freighter, a swaybacked, red-bearded man of native intelligence and nasty habit, buried at sea one winter near Martinique. Naming Randall seemed sentimental to him now, unlike him really to get messed up in that. Barbara had named the others and he'd learned the names she'd given them slowly as if memorizing state capitals. Barbara called them all after her own people except for Eureka, God knows where that came from. He'd since heard it was the name of a place out west. Sometimes he wondered if the girl hadn't suffered under such a strange name, it hadn't shamed her or made her skittish. If it wasn't part reason why she seemed so uncomfortable here in Trent.

The back door was an inch ajar. Speight stopped in the grass to check the name on the package, then started up the stairs.

Halfway up he heard the noises. In broad daylight with the damned door half open, no wonder they didn't answer up front. He'd misjudged, they weren't lurking in the curtains ignoring him so he'd shuffle around back like an old uncle fieldhand. These folks weren't concerned with putting delivery boys in their place, least not today they weren't.

He looked up at the house, noticed the paint peel on the shutters, the overgrown yard: this wasn't the type place where people put on airs. He stood there frozen, thinking of sex, something he usually remembered on the porch nights. He hesitated over moving, over making a noise that might distract these folks (he looked down at the bag again — Mr. and Mrs. Keane) from their pleasure. But it felt foolish and wrong to wait there for who knows how long, so he started up to prop the bag against the railing and leave.

Bending over, he heard her. Recognized her voice even though she wasn't speaking words. A cross between a coo and a deep-chested cough repeating itself in uneven, heightened takes. He saw her fleeing away down the long hall of the house, turning to take stairs, dress hazy, hair streaming above her shoulders.

He thought of Randall hiding out down at the river when he was supposed to be delivering this man his medicine. Remembered the man on the street he'd seen slipping his son money and it was as if during one of his nightly porch drunks dusk's breeze had finally blown in answers. On the landing he tugged open the screen door, unleashing hot shadows from the dark room where her gasps harmonized with a deeper, raspier moan. He heard her scream, heard the same man he'd seen with Randall say wait a minute. He met and held her stare before focusing on the pale frame stretched above her, a white blanket of change he would remember all his life. He did not move or speak when Eureka rolled the man off the cot, stood and covered herself, screaming at him to go away which he did, finally, taking the bag with him.

10

The way the men were spaced in the mouth of the garage reminded Eureka of bad teeth. As she watched from a thicket in the woods below, stray words tumbling past like trash dumped down the bank of the steep ravine kept her wide awake and shivering, made her want to climb the hill to Rose's house. But Rose had five kids and her husband Henry's mother all in a two-bedroom house, and Eureka didn't think Henry would welcome a bedraggled-looking white girl storming hysterical up on his porch on a Saturday night when the neighbors were out, the streets were full, everyone could see. Rose wouldn't mind — Rose would take her in — but why risk getting her into trouble?

Besides, these woods seemed the only place for her, the appropriate place: where else should she be forced to lay low because of a man who confessed his secret sins but a place where secret sins were routinely committed? Winos came here to strain rubbing alcohol through molded heels of bread salvaged from the trashcan behind Pasteluccia's Bakery. This was the most open practice performed here, the least surreptitious act. Down by the creek bottom, idle boys lured girls into the Johnsontown woods. It was the office of many who kept their office hours in the half-dark of after supper, when the streets swelled with potential, when the vacant lots of J-town were rivers silver with fish.

After her father had left the bungalow she'd pulled on her dress, grabbed her shoes and fled out the back door. Edwin, standing naked in the doorway, had called to her as she hurdled the brush at the edge of the yard and disappeared into the woods.

First light flushed her from her bed of soggy pinestraw. Except for the occasional rooster crow, Johnsontown was quiet. The mouth of the garage was dark now and toothless, frozen in a wide, silent yawn. She took a side path which wound through the wood to a clearing where she could see down Edgecombe. The kitchen window of his bungalow was the only light on in the neighborhood; yellow slanted from the curtainless square, still bright enough to shine through the dim adjustment of daybreak. She sat beneath the tree until the light fell impotent, then picked her way through the brush and across the yard, up the stairs and into the bungalow.

When he awoke he found her asleep in the chair beside him, her feet propped on the cot, her face buried in the fold. He thought of his mother, how she used to visit just after he'd had his medicine, slump in the wingback and talk about her life.

This was his first thought. Next he realized that he was looking at Eureka and seeing his mother.

His third thought was that he was out of medicine. Fourth, it was Sunday and the pharmacy was closed.

He stared at her again, noticed the scratches on her arms and legs, some as long as incisions with smaller cuts crisscrossing like sutures. After she'd left him he'd taken the last bit of medicine he had stashed away and sat nodding on the stoop all night, staring into the woods until dawn when he'd collapsed into the cot.

He thought of yesterday and craved her again but the morphine lingered inside him like a shadowed patch of snow that the sun couldn't reach and he thought of that old saying he'd heard as a boy: snow slow to melt's sure sign a new storm's coming.

When she stirred he did not even wait for her to shake away the sleep.

"Where've you been? I waited up forever."

She drew her knees onto the chair, hugged them to her chest. "It's about a thousand degrees in here," she said, and she got up and switched on the fan, then sat again. "Are you all right?"

"Sorry," he said. "I'm afraid there's trouble ahead."

She nodded. "I didn't go home. I was going to pick up some clothes but I was afraid he'd be at home waiting."

Then he *was* her father. He'd guessed so from the way she screamed at him to go away, her voice at once defiant and tentative. She wouldn't have screamed that way at any old substitute delivery boy, wouldn't have pulled her dress on and bolted out the back door like a surprised fawn.

Though this was not the trouble ahead he'd been referring to, he had to act as if it was, and once he began to consider it he realized how complicated her situation was. He'd not thought of where she would go, had assumed she'd gone home, even though he'd suspected that the gaunt, black-eyed man standing on the threshold was kin. He didn't know if she had friends to stay with. She didn't seem the type to ride out a storm with a favorite aunt or a married cousin.

Come to think of it, he couldn't really imagine her being kin to anyone. He'd only met a few people like her in his life, people whom he could not imagine kin to one other person in the world, much less the requisite two. Her little brother said he had five sisters and a brother. It shocked him that she came from such a large family, but then the fact that she was connected by blood to anyone surprised him. Two or twenty seemed superfluous. He thought of her as having shown up in the world at just the exact moment she showed up in his life. She appeared in the moment without history or a past, and everything she did was performed with an ethereal fleetness: calling to someone invisible above, making leaves disappear between manila pages. Only much later could he connect her presence there with an assignment given to hundreds in this town, including himself. To admit that she was there because of Strickland's fifth-period botany instead of by miracle was difficult, but even afterwards, when she *admitted* it, he still doubted it. In his memory of that afternoon, the way she went about plucking up leaves and pasting them into her photo album had nothing to do with botany, Strickland's fifth period, high school, Trent.

"I've run out of medicine. When I'm without it for long I get sick."

As he spoke he began to shiver, and as the day heated up he grew sicker. She brought him water that he would not drink. First he sweated, then he grew so cold that she covered him with a quilt and two blankets. Underneath the covers he continued to sweat, even though he claimed to be freezing. His eye sockets darkened to the purplish-black of a two-day bruise. She heated up some bouillon. He sat up in bed, but that was all. He could not have eaten anyway, she realized. When his jaws were not trembling they sagged uselessly.

Finally he drifted into a sleep punctuated by palsy, like a dog quivering in nightmare. When he awoke he seemed worse, and asked for a soup pot. She brought one and for the next half hour listened to his convulsions which were relentless and loud and largely dry, producing spit first, then bile.

Very late in the day when the temperature peaked and began its imperceptibly slow wane, after he'd retched the hours away while she sat helplessly beside him, he rose up on one arm and said, "A doctor got me like this."

"Like what?" He looked calm, more tired now than ill, although he was still pale and seemed to have sweated away pounds.

"My own uncle."

"Got you like what?"

"Long story. No time now. Want you to run an errand for me."

She didn't want to leave the bungalow and

said so. "What if I run into him? Or the Fraulein? What about my job? I'm sure I'm fired."

"Forget it. You don't need that job anymore."

"Tell my father I don't need it."

"You can tell him if you want, if you want to see him before we go."

"Go where?"

"Away. Anywhere. I've got a driver and I've got a car."

She sat up and studied his face for lies. "You feel better then?"

"Eye of the hurricane," he said. "Won't last. Look, you won't run into anyone on a Sunday morning."

"I just might."

"Sooner you run this errand, sooner we can leave here."

"What errand?"

"I need to see the druggist. He lives in that apartment building across from the high school. Go get him and bring him back here. He can help us."

"How do you know he'll come?"

"He will. He has nothing else to do."

She said nothing, wondering if she might be able to think more clearly away from him. She needed to get out, but she had nowhere to go now. Before there had been places reserved and secret, places Randall had shown her or the churchyard, all of which were closed to her.

"Please, Eureka," he said. It was the first time he'd called her by name, and something about the careful way he said it — as if it was a foreign word to him and he was pronouncing it in earnest, trying to make himself understood — moved her so much that she rose and left the room.

The stairway creaked and swayed as they descended, Randall first, his father following a few steps behind. Below the fifth rickety step the slats became invisible, as if they stopped suddenly in midair. Randall held tight to both railings and lowered his foot, feeling around for the step below, but Speight kept coming, sent them both tumbling.

Randall opened his eyes to slivers of weak daylight winking through the recessed windows. For a long time his father was quiet and still. Then very slowly he sat up, spat once and began to pat the dirt around him.

When he'd returned to the drugstore from the river, his father was gone and so was the druggist. Mr. Lehmann had acted mean as hell without saying why, snarling at him to go on home, wasn't nothing else for him to do today, put the bike in the basement and get. At home he'd found no one there, had sat in the backyard talking to the chickens until his father appeared around the side of the house and without a word yanked him up by his shirt loop, pushed him through the pantry to the basement door. Randall was left standing there trying to decide exactly what he'd done wrong while Speight went for his belt.

Listening for his father's footfalls, he'd opened the door and peered into the blackness. It smelled of clay, wet cardboard, cave crickets. Hal had told him once that beatings hurt more down there in the dark. "Can't see the damn belt, don't know where the thing'll hit next," he'd said. Once when Hal had been suspended from school for stealing a pair of cleats from the field house, Randall climbed down in the leaf-clogged pit where the windows were sunken to witness his beating. He heard the belt whoosh through the basement air, saw Hal limp out finally. He wasn't wearing a shirt and his skin was splotched red except in places where it had already begun to bruise purple. Once outside he started to run, dragging his hurt foot through the thick leaves in the backyard, rustling away into the woods like some pitiful monster, Randall would tell Eureka later, from Transylvania. Randall caught up with him halfway over to Johnsontown. "Goddamn him to hail," Hal said. "Sonbitch even whacked my nuts. Goddamn him: he could see me but I couldn't see him."

"How's that possible?" Randall had asked. "Dark's dark. Same for him as you down there." It could have been pitch out then for all Randall saw of Hal's wild swings. "Goddamn you, too, with your questions," his brother said as he beat him up on the sidewalk near Johnsontown, in broad daylight, in what passed over there for public.

"Can't see," his father was saying. He patted the dirt in another direction, feeling for his belt. Randall could see him a little better than before; his torso in silhouette reminded Randall of the cheap, badly cracked bust of Beethoven at the public library.

"You hurt?" his father asked.

"No," he lied.

"You know why I brung you down here."

"Eureka and him?"

"Taking money to set up your favorite sister." His father's voice crackled like radio talk awash with static. "You know what they call that?"

"He paid me because he wanted to see her again. I tried to give her the money but she said for me to save it."

"What do you mean again?"

"First time was in the courtyard of the church."

It was quiet so long that Randall grew sleepy.

"You mean to tell me . . ." His father wheezed. "You mean to tell me that you set your sister up in a churchyard? And you not yet twelve?"

Flattered that his father remembered his age, he said yes — yes without thinking. It was not until the thick belt snapped against his cheekbone that he thought of anything, and then he thought of the belt, of which way it would come from next.

Just past dawn, Roy remembered having heard once of a bootlegger who would sell it to anyone, sight unseen, cheap, open all hours, even this time of a Sunday morning. He dialed the number of his next-door neighbor, the milkman, who consented sleepily to the loan of his car.

In the borrowed Plymouth Roy drove west out of town through streets the eerie dead of Sunday morning. At a stoplight he slapped open the glove compartment and rifled through the milkman's personal belongings. Not very personal: a dandruff-flecked comb, green at the roots; an old lady's plastic rain bonnet; a map of the mountains of western North Carolina and east Tennessee. He unfolded the map carefully, propped it against the steering wheel to study it. The Smokies were stained a smudgy charcoal color, the Blue Ridge was not all that blue. The stoplight switched to green. He checked the rearview. The only movement behind was a sign swayed loose from its post, sand shifting in the gutters. He went back to the milkman's map, which was the type you buy at a tourist trap, points of interest colorfully and disproportionally represented right alongside highways. A black bear reared hind-legged from a spot in Avery County between Pineola and Linville, flanked by two fat cubs. Just to the left of Asheville a mammoth French château rose beside a network of intersections: the Vanderbilt estate. Near Franklin, smoke curled from a tepee leaning toward north Georgia. Roy imagined the milkman and his mother striking out during the milkman's annual two weeks off, following this map westward and uphill, expecting roadside bears where the map said there were bears, tepees near the mammoth tepee. Idling at the stoplight he let himself be seduced by the map. He liked the way the attractions had been misrepresented, liked how ridiculously embellished and grand they appeared.

He folded up the map and stuffed it into his breast pocket.

The light changed again above him. He sat

there, consumed by the feeling that he should leave then, today. The only reason he'd found to stay — helping Edwin Keane — was no longer possible since he'd lost his job. But leaving today would be acting in haste. He never acted in haste.

Hours later when the knock came, he was sitting in his chair by the window fan sipping whiskey. On the coffee table in front of him the stolen map was spread. He was not drunk, though he'd been sipping for eight hours almost. He wanted to be drunk for several reasons — to forget about Lehmann and Keane and the pharmacy, to reach that obliviousness to passing time he'd discovered once in drunkenness; because getting drunk after getting fired seemed the manly thing. Yet the more he drank, the more he thought of yesterday, the slower the second hand's tick.

"Who?" he said without rising from his chair, but he wasn't surprised when the knock came again without explanation. Standing, he felt the whiskey, as if now, with someone at the door who would spot the nearly empty fifth, his sobriety was calling itself into question.

A girl stood at the top of the stairwell, an "Am-I-in-the-right-place?" skittishness in the way she looked at him and then away. Obviously wants next door, he thought, and he stared past her at the steps falling away toward the overscaled bears of the milkman's map.

"You want the milkman? Next door, but if you're wondering where your quart is, Sunday's his day off."

"You work at the drugstore?" she asked.

"Used to," he said, thinking how strange this sounded.

"You don't work there no more?"

"Nope." He looked at her closely for the first time. She was pretty in a way which grew on you, *interesting-looking* he remembered having dubbed this style on others. But before he'd used this term approximately, when conventional adjectives failed. Her looks did interest him: the blend of dark skin and black, tangled hair, the bones in her face which had a way of altering the contour of her profile every time she moved or spoke. Roy noticed the shape she was in: her skin was scratched, her hair matted, skirt mud-stained.

"I'm not a pharmacist anymore and I never was a doctor, if you're looking for someone to treat those cuts."

She looked down at her dress and shook her head. "That's not it."

"Well, what?"

A door down the hall opened; Taft Crumpler's widow stuck her head out then pulled it back inside, leaving in the corridor a yellow odor of boiled chicken.

When she said nothing he asked her in.

"Sorry," she said when they were seated.

"About what?"

She shook her head again, clutched her knees. "Just, I don't know." She stared down at the map spread across the coffee table. Her slow gaze and the sparseness of this place where he'd spent the last seven years embarrassed him.

"You could tell me your name, maybe."

"Eureka. Speight. Randall's my little brother. The stock clerk at your pharmacy? He's my father."

"Randall's mentioned you."

"We're close." She looked down at the map again. Whatever it was she wanted, he would have to pry it out of her.

"Is something wrong with Randall?"

"No," she said, then: "I don't know. I haven't seen him since yesterday early. Anyways he's not who I came about."

"Well?"

"Edwin Keane?"

Roy leaned back in his chair. "What about him?"

"He's sick."

"Besides that."

"You knew he was sick?"

246

"He's been sick since I've known him."
She seemed surprised.
"You must not know him very well."
"No," she conceded.
"Just how *do* you know him?"
She sat loose and glum-looking, as if she'd never talk again.
"I mean he's not so far as I know a very sociable creature."
"I met him at church," she said.
Roy's abrupt laughter brought out all he'd had to drink; it sounded maniacal even to him, and he worried if he'd scared her.
"Okay. He's sick, so he sent you to me. Well, I can't help him."
"He thinks you can. Something about his medicine."
"No doubt."
"He's been throwing up all day. Shaking and sweating. Goes from hot to cold, can't eat, he looks awful. If you won't come I'll have to call his doctor."
"That won't do him any good. His doctor's the one that got him like he is."
"That's what he says, too."
"Although there are others to blame, including himself. How long has it been since he's had a shot?"
"A shot?"
"His medicine."

"He's not had some today while I've been there. Won't you please just come look at him? Even if you can't do anything, you know more about what to do than me."

"I don't see what good it would bring, considering first of all that I'm a bit under the weather myself as you might have noticed and second that I no longer have any professional credibility."

"I don't think that matters. I mean he wouldn't've asked you if he didn't think you could help."

"What he wants me for doesn't have a damn thing to do with my professional credibility, you're right. That's the problem in the first place. It's because of him that I have no professional credibility."

She focused her gaze so that it bore through him, as if now that he was refusing to come along with her he did not exist.

"Look, I'm sorry. It's confusing to you, I'm sure. Lots of ancient history here. Lehmann, Keane and me, we form sort of a sordid triangle. I still don't understand exactly where you fit in."

Standing, she turned toward the door.

"Maybe it's evolved into a sordid rectangle now. You're the new angle, I suppose."

She wheeled around so quickly that she created a draft; he felt it hit his face, her annoyance lacing a hot breeze. "What do you want to know? Just ask me so we can quit wasting time and I can get back to him."

Her reaction intrigued him. Obviously she was more than just a courier like her little brother; she wasn't just delivering the message, her concern was obvious from her reaction. But Keane? How had they ever even crossed paths? Keane's path, so far as Roy knew, stretched only from bed to telephone.

Considering Keane's fifteen grains a day, the mention of *loss of sexual desire* as a side effect would be as absurd as saying *this medication may cause drowsiness.*

She didn't know much about him, that was clear. Regardless of how they'd met, they hadn't known each other long. The moment I'm no longer any good to him he finds someone else to manipulate. It's useless, he thought; if anything it should make me want to pack up and leave. And surely the fact that her father works at the drugstore is no coincidence.

Again he noticed her muddy shoes, her swollen knees. What had he done to her?

"Okay," he said. "You're right, it's none of my business how you know him. Wait here."

He went into the kitchen and fetched two bottles of paregoric from a top shelf, put them in a bag, grabbed the suitcoat he always wore to work.

"I'll come with you," he told her, "even though I'm telling you there's nothing either of us can do for him."

"Good lord," Roy said as he followed her into the kitchen. "Open some windows to start. Get some air in here."

It was past dusk, but the room seethed with the gathered heat of the day. Eureka wrenched open the windows above the sink, leaned against the counter with her arms crossed to watch. She was already tired of this druggist who seemed nosy to her, half drunk, sad in a way that was somehow offensive. As if he chose sadness, preferred his life lived in the back of drugstores and stuffy upstairs apartments. She had walked five feet ahead of him on the way over so she wouldn't have to talk to him. The druggist had not tried to keep up. He seemed to slide into a dark, mute mood as soon as they left his apartment.

He scooted the wingback close to the cot.

"Bad news," he said to Edwin. "Your buddy Lehmann gave me the boot."

Edwin, shivering, asked Eureka if he was serious.

"I'm here as a friend," said the druggist.

"Not exactly the capacity I had in mind,"

said Edwin. The shivers chopped his breath and Eureka remembered how Randall used to speak through the floor fan, how his words would emerge wavy, diced into syllables.

Roy pulled two bottles from the pocket of his suitcoat. "Heat some water," he called over his shoulder, as if he was the midwife, she the stunned father-to-be.

"That won't last," said Edwin. "I need something that will last."

"Call your uncle if you need more than a friend. Or less than one."

"What can he do on a Sunday night when the pharmacy's closed? He'd just have to call you to help."

"I told you I don't work there anymore."

"You turned in your keys already?"

Without a word Roy stood and started for the door.

"Wait," said Edwin. "You've got to help me out of this. I'll die otherwise."

"Not die," said Roy. "You'll just be sick for a few days. Then, who knows, maybe if you're strong enough you can go without."

"That's what I want."

The druggist snickered, a phony snort which embarrassed Eureka.

"Since when is that what you want?"

"Since yesterday."

"Pretty sudden. What, I mean if you don't

mind me asking, what caused such a turn-around?"

Edwin sat up to drink the paregoric she brought him, mixed with warm water in a coffee cup. He made a face at the taste but almost immediately stopped shaking.

"Combination of things," he said.

"Including the red-letter arrival date of Miss Missionary here?"

Edwin winced — whether at the aftertaste of paregoric or the question, Eureka wasn't sure.

"What's that supposed to mean?"

"She told me all about how you two met in church."

"Oh, don't bother lying to him," Edwin said to Eureka.

It's not a lie, we met in the churchyard, she almost said, but instead she blushed and wished she was elsewhere.

"He's not worth wasting a lie on. Besides he's on our side."

"Was, until it got me fired."

Whatever was in the coffee cup worked; she could feel him warming up to talk like he had not done all day, since yesterday when she'd first arrived to give him back the letter. "He sees through lies. Hears through them on the telephone. It's amazing, his ability to sniff out the chaff. While I waited for him to come to the phone I used to speculate about which moral compunction would motivate him next."

"You got me fired."

"That's ridiculous. I kept you from being fired for months. The way you talked to me, the way you treated me — one phone call to the boss from the right person, we both know who that would be, and you'd have been fired months ago. No, you got yourself fired somehow. How'd that happen anyway?"

"I'll tell you. Before I went to lunch yesterday I sent the boy down to the river. While I was gone, your mother kept bugging Lehmann until he called me at home and, when I told him what I'd done, fired me. Over the telephone, which figures, since this whole thing has played itself out over the phone wires."

"You blame all that on me?"

"Sure. If someone else had the guts to say no to you, none of this would have happened."

"See what I mean?" Edwin said to her. "Mr. right from wrong." He turned to the druggist again. "Surely you knew they'd can you for that."

"At the time I thought it was worth the risk. For several reasons. First I wanted you to be inconvenienced. Also I had some stupid notion that I could help you. I figured if I

253

kept the morphine out of your veins for an hour in the long run I'd be helping you adjust, learning to live again without it. I'll be the first to admit it wasn't very well thought out."

"I'll be the second," Edwin said to her.

"And then I had another ridiculous idea — your situation seems to breed bad notions. I thought of you as a victim. Of Lehmann and the way he sucks up to your family, of your soft-hearted uncle, of plain bad luck. That accident, the Teague girl. All that which I figured you couldn't help."

"Sounds like you no longer see it that way."

"I changed my mind the day I saw you paying off the kid."

"Which had nothing to do with anything you're talking about."

"Right. You were hiring him to do yardwork. Trim your hedges, mulch your flower beds. He did an excellent job. I was just thinking while walking up the drive how you ought to be on the Home and Garden tour this year."

The druggist gave her a grave hope-you're-listening look, then turned back to Edwin. "It has everything to do with what I'm talking about."

"He sounds tired, doesn't he?" Edwin spoke to her but stared at the druggist. Both of them were using her as a backboard, banking their words off her, bringing her into whatever troubled history they shared. It made her uncomfortable. She stared at the druggist, too, at his wide forehead and thinning blond hair, the part of him always visible behind the high counter from anywhere in the drugstore.

"Sounds like he's going through the motions," said Edwin. "Do-gooding without conviction, as if he's just trying to earn a merit badge. I could be the little old lady he's helping cross the street."

"Could have been. I'm through with you."

"You mean that just because you don't count fucking pills anymore you have no reason to want to save me?"

"Long as I don't have to put up with you."

"I can't believe that. Not coming from the moral center of the universe."

"You have a strange way of asking for help. All you've done since I've been here is insult me."

"Sorry. You're right. Maybe I ought to try bribery."

"You've tried that already. I have some savings."

"Enough to live on?"

"That's none of your business."

"So you're looking for work elsewhere?"

"Nothing for me here."

"We'll sure miss you. But one last thing before you take off. This paregoric won't last but an hour at most."

"I brought a couple bottles. That should get you through the worst of it."

"Then what?"

"I thought you said you wanted to go without. No time like the present."

Noticing both of them staring at her, Eureka looked to the floor again, thinking that her presence here was both unbearable — to them and to her — and necessary. As if she was keeping peace, but the peace was not something which should necessarily be kept.

"Yes," said Edwin. "But it's not that easy. Even with reasons to try it's not like I just sit down to sweat it out."

"There's the hospital I told you about."

"The one in Kentucky? The place for addicts?"

"I told you I did some checking up. They have a high success rate treating medical addicts up there."

"What about people like me?"

"I suppose you've been throwing up all day because of food poisoning."

"Call it what you want. Doesn't matter to me, because the truth is I'll be sick again when this paregoric's gone, too sick for a trip to Kentucky. Too sick for a car trip around the block."

She felt the druggist's gaze again.

"We might could work something out," he said. "Of course I'd have to be sure you were going to Kentucky."

"You're saying you'd find enough medicine to last the trip?"

"Of course I'd have to be sure you were going to Kentucky."

"I'm confused. I thought you were through with me."

"Should be. Soon I will be. But I like to finish things, Mr. Keane. I hate loose ends. Since I've got to leave this town, I might as well leave feeling like I tried."

"And that's why you'd do it? To make yourself feel better?"

"There are other interests at stake here."

"He means you," Edwin said without looking at her. "I don't believe he approves of us."

"Never said that. I'd just rather no other innocent people get sucked into your melodrama like I was."

"I can't believe you're still blaming me for your problems at work. You were hired to count pills, which you refused to do, so they fired you."

"If that's what you want to believe, fine. Now, since you're not interested in Kentucky, I've got packing to do."

"Packing?"

"Headed back to Michigan. That's where my family is."

"How about if I gave you a lift as far as Kentucky?"

"I'd have to make sure you checked in, too."

"You don't trust me, do you, Green?"

"You said yourself once how desperate pain can make a person. There's a minimum stay of a month. You're prepared for that?"

"If that's what it takes." Edwin nodded her way. "Of course she'd have to come along."

"I don't believe they have double rooms. More than likely a dormitory situation. No room service. No conjugal rights."

"I'm not leaving her here. In fact, after Kentucky we'll probably head north ourselves. I'll rent a place for her in town."

"Sounds exciting, doesn't it?" the druggist asked her. "A month by yourself in a strange town in Kentucky."

"Maybe you could stay and keep her company."

Can't be me they're talking about so brazenly, she thought, though she knew it was. Pulling a chair from the table, she carried it over to the door and facing the dark backyard.

"Thanks but no thanks," the druggist said. "I'm a pharmacist, not a baby-sitter."

"Think of this as a paid vacation. I've even got a driver. At your beck and call. Good-natured guy named Deems. Native intelligent. Energetic. Might rub off on us melancholy types."

The druggist was silent. His quiet unnerved her, made her think he was deliberating. She imagined him sitting on the front porch of their rented house in Kentucky, a younger and slightly more sober version of her father. She fought the urge to turn to him, focused hard on the woods.

"We know you like to see a thing through, Mr. Green," said Edwin. "We know how you hate leaving those loose ends."

11

Walking through town, Roy mumbled the phrase over and over as if it was a name or phone number or some vital information he would lose without repeating. At times the phrase was muted by the buzz behind his eyelids, the almost-audible throb of impending hangover. But he never lost it. He kept time by it, set his pace to it.

I know what I'm do-ing, I know what I'm do-ing. Clarity was what he was after — this was a crucial move he was making — and he worried that the phrase was too simple, the say-it-and-it's-true philosophy of the hopelessly naive and shallow.

Yet Roy was driven more by cadence than by meaning; syncopated against his heartbeat, the chant reassured him, for synchronization seemed suddenly a very bad ideal to him. What could be more limiting than having everything aligned so that a life was driven by a single beat? So much better to time things so that they missed slightly, so that they produced a rhythm which caught his body off guard.

He knew what he was doing. Yesterday after Lehmann had fired him, his choices had seemed infinite: free to leave Trent, free to leave North Carolina, free to leave the country if he wanted. The next day he was more light-headed from the possibilities than from the whiskey he sipped, until the girl showed and he agreed to follow her back to see Keane. After an hour of listening to Keane, the infinite field of his future had narrowed enough to fit in the low-ceilinged, cluttered kitchen where they sat. Other towns the world over would be as hard to penetrate as this one. He would be a stranger if he went back to Ypsilanti now after twelve years away and wherever he went, this business with Keane would follow him unless he finished it.

He was working on the last vial when he heard the back door of the drugstore creak open. He thought he'd forgotten to lock it, that the policeman checking doors had come in to lecture him. "It's me, Roy Green," he called. He was working under a small desk lamp at the drug counter and could not see far beyond its fuzzy radius; he felt movement in the nearby darkness but did not look up.

"Left the door open again, did I? I'll be damned."

After a lengthy silence Lehmann said:

"That's a hell of a goddamn casual response from a man's just broke and entered."

Roy put down his work and reached back to flip the light switch. "I thought you were the police."

"You'll get to see them soon enough."

There were tense moments while Roy explained the situation, but he was surprised at how well the truth went over. Leaving Speight's daughter out of it, he told how Edwin had sent for him, how he'd begged and offered bribes, how he'd finally promised to give the place in Kentucky a try. Lehmann relaxed and gave Roy his familiar world-weary look which meant he was about to take him into confidence.

"It's the pain in the boy's back causes him to act so pushy. He doesn't mean anything by it."

This was a favored expression of Lehmann's — a favorite expression of half the people in this town — and it had always annoyed him. *If he doesn't mean anything by it, why does he do it,* he felt like saying, and he realized that in the space of three minutes he was back to squelching comebacks, withholding things he felt he ought not to say.

In the alley they leaned against Lehmann's idling Cadillac, Roy tremoring from the hip as he tried to think of something to say. Finally

Lehmann cleared his throat and offered Roy his job back, which Roy declined.

"Well, then, I want to thank you, son. I appreciate you doing this thing for me. The boy I hired doesn't come in 'til the morning and I guarandamntee you Keane's mama would have got me out of bed if you wouldn't of come down here. You know I could get in hot water filling the thing myself."

I'll be damned, thought Roy, he thinks I did this to save his ass.

"Hired a boy over the phone. But I swear if you'll decide you want to come back, now or on down the road, I'll just put him right back on the bus. To hell with it."

Smiling, Roy picked up his chant again.

"I'll have the uncle write us out a script tomorrow to keep the records up. Don't, the government'll be on us for sure. You know, I don't even mind you coming down here tight. I can't blame you for going off and getting tight. Seems like the right thing to do, I mean after I fired you and all."

Roy reached in his pocket and pulled out his store keys. "I know what I'm doing," he said, handing them over.

Lehmann looked him over and said he'd never doubted that one minute, there were no hard feelings, he hoped Roy got what he wanted from life and one last thing — considering all he'd done to help that Keane boy, there was bound to be a reward for him in heaven.

Early the next morning they were halfway up the long driveway when Edwin asked Deems to stop. Eureka leaned forward to see the edge of the house, a high line of red brick surrounded by boxwoods.

"I'll walk from here," said Edwin. "Need the exercise."

True, she thought, he does need it, there are worse excuses. But then he'd botched it by telling Deems to back out, the driveway was probably blocked, no place to turn around.

Not that I really want to meet his parents now anyway, she thought as he handed her two twenties and told Deems to take her to Trelawney's to buy some clothes. She wasn't exactly presentable, still wearing the dress she'd left for work in on Saturday morning. Edwin had given her a raincoat to wear over it but she looked just as odd in a man's slicker on a clear, hot day. She'd had a bath since at least, but cleaning the dried mud away had only made the cuts and scrapes more noticeable.

At Trelawney's the woman who waited on her was curt and nosy. Terrified that her father or the Fraulein would burst in and drag her away, Eureka piled clothes on the counter, chosen by size, without consideration of style. The woman rang it all up slowly, each ring buffered by interminable foldings and fidgeting with tags. Eureka stared sullenly at the pneumatic tube which sucked Edwin's money up to a bald man on the mezzanine.

"I'm in a hurry," she said finally. The clerk moved even slower then, announced that she had to go to the back for a bigger bag.

"I don't need a bigger bag," said Eureka.

"All this here won't fit in a little one," said the clerk.

"Try two little ones," said Eureka, and Deems, who had been amusing himself in the shoe section, checking workboot tread by running his huge fingers over the grids, heard her and snorted.

She ignored him. Already the clerk thought she was *with* him. Though she hadn't yet had the time or energy to look twice at Deems, being mistaken for his companion made her miss Edwin.

But they'd had two more hours to kill while Edwin met with his parents. In the Dodge, she pinned Edwin's raincoat to the upholstery and made a dressing room out of the back seat. Dictating directions, they'd circled Edwin's part of town while she tried on dresses

265

and Deems watched the raincoat sagging in the rearview.

After a half hour the raincoat came down. Deems slanted the rearview and whistled.

"Look where you're going." She sunk into the upholstery. After thirty more minutes of repetitive directions he realized that they were killing time and assumed a cursory pattern of his own design.

They rode around. She thought about things. As much as she wanted to see Randall before she left she convinced herself it was a bad idea. It would slow things down too much, she was on her way out now. To explain to him all that had happened since she'd seen him last would have taken days, and she had only an hour. He'd be hurt — he might even hate her for a while — but he'd survive. Her flight would make it easier for him to leave when the time came.

Still, she fantasized coming upon him on a side street, spotting him a half block away. As they passed him, he would glance sidelong into the back seat where she sat among shopping bags. She smiled, imagined how his eyes would bulge, how the front tire of his bike would hit the shoulder and he would wrestle the bike out of a swerve and slam on brakes and she would order Deems to stow the bike in the trunk and open the door for their passenger . . . and then what? Take him home? Take him along? So much was new and foreign that she was better off leaving without seeing him or saying good-bye.

So much ahead to think about: this hospital business, which she didn't understand. Edwin had promised to explain it all when the time was right but the night before, after the druggist returned with the medicine, he'd taken some and gone straight to sleep. And the druggist: was he really coming along to keep her company? She couldn't imagine how she'd get through a month of him, what she'd ever talk to him about.

An hour later they were on their way out of town, and she abandoned her worries to consider how odd a mix the four of them made, like people thrown together in dreams. Edwin slumped beside her, nodding in time to the potholed highway. From the front seat floated a laugh so swampy it seemed to grime the window glass, neat whiskey laugh of larynx and lung.

"Deems, Deems, Deems," said the druggist, who for once was in a good mood.

"Say what, doc?" said Deems.

"Do you go 'round deeming things?"

"I deems things this, I deems things that," sang Deems in a pretty fair tenor.

The druggist switched the radio on to drown out the Deems song, picked up the tail end of Houston Carter's gospel hour.

"Houston!" shouted Deems.

"You know him, I take it," said the druggist.

"Runs a bug-killing business outside his preaching. Drives a motorsickle. I asked him to let me borry it one time. We was all down to the river and he was busy dunking 'em but he wouldn't lend me it. Said I's reckless, claimed I'd wreck it. Stingy son of a bitch for a preacher."

"Why is it that if you ask someone from Trent if they know someone they give you a biographical sketch instead of saying yes or no? Probably comes from reading those who's who books all you people buy to shelve next to your family Bibles."

"They say Houston knows every gospel tune ever wrote," said Deems.

"I gather you know him then," said the druggist.

"Yeah," said Deems. He smiled when he spoke, as if a smile made everything he said funny.

They followed the river out of town and into the swamp that surrounded Trent on three sides. Serenitowinity it was called. Eureka knew because she had grown up on its easternmost edge, and Randall, who loved the names of things, loved its name. A few miles out of town the swamp dipped even lower than normal and the road ran high and shoulderless above the black water. This section was so dark and dangerous that road signs advised the burning of headlights during daylight hours and the speed limit dropped to a cautious forty-five. Deems ignored both signs, barreling headlightless along at a steady sixty until Edwin rose suddenly and told him to pull over.

"Say what?" said Deems.

"Stop, goddammit."

"Where's he think I'm supposed to pull off at, doc?" Deems asked the druggist, but the druggist stared ahead at the pavement, black and slick from a recent rain, steamy tar.

They fishtailed to a stop in the middle of the road. Edwin swung the door open and stuck one foot onto the pavement, testing the blacktop with a wingtip toe. Then he got out and walked away, straight down the dotted line for a few hundred feet; he stopped and hugged his arms across his chest. While the three of them watched, Edwin picked his way down a path emptying into a logging trail. When Deems switched the car off, a crescendo of tree frog song rose immediately from both sides of the road, converging in a place between Eureka's ears.

Sometimes this swamp can spook even someone who grew up in the thick of it, she thought, especially this time of year. The sight of Edwin about to disappear into it terrified her. She watched birds fly in and out of black shadows and thought of all the people lost there over the years. It entered your bones, entered your head, too. She remembered the people who lived in its recesses, bootleggers and trappers she'd see sometimes walking along the roadside. In full light they seemed skittish, out of place, possessed. They walked slow and looked swollen, waterlogged in body and spirit.

Just before he passed out of sight, Edwin looked over his shoulder at them and they swiveled about-face in vaudeville unison.

"Now what in hell's he doing?" Deems asked.

"Maybe he needs more medicine," said Eureka.

The druggist laughed. "No, he doesn't need more medicine. Right around here was where his accident occurred, I believe."

"Oh, yeah," said Deems. "I remember hearing about that. They towed his car up to my granddaddy's body shop. 'Forty-nine Packard. Won't much left of it. Somebody with him got killed, right?"

"Who got killed?" said Eureka.

"The Teague girl," said the druggist.

"But who was she?"

The druggist turned to her. "Sarah Teague."

"But who was she to him?"

"He went with her for a long time, didn't he? Seem like they got together back in high school," said Deems.

"You knew them in high school?" the druggist asked Deems.

"Everybody around here knows a person dies tragic in a car wreck, doc. Even if you never laid eyes on them you swear you was close so you can go down to the graveyard and fall out when they crank them down in the ground. They was engaged, won't they?"

"You might be right, Deems," said the druggist. "I don't know that much about it." He turned around again, his gaze ranging above and beyond her before he lowered his sun-blind squint to her face. "You're the one who ought to know."

"He told me most of it already," she lied.

"Sounds like you got the abridged," said the druggist.

"Maybe she don't want to know," said Deems.

"Here he comes," said the druggist, and they fell into a thick, self-conscious silence as he climbed back into the car and said, "Okay." For the next half hour no one spoke. She watched the piney swamp and ditchbank slide by until the new world blurred by the roadside and she grew drowsy. She leaned her head on Edwin's shoulder and soon they slept, collapsed against and supporting one another.

When she awoke they were entering Raleigh. The fringes of the city blinked, signs shining through white noon, an outskirts aura even to the features of the people they passed in traffic. An hour later they made their first official medicine stop. Eureka went in with him, sat at the counter of a diner drinking a cup of coffee he'd told her to buy. She watched a man grow impatient with the locked men's-room door and jiggle the handle before storming out to his car. Edwin was inside for ten minutes, fifteen, twenty. The diner smelled of an aftertaste, a belch of fried breakfast. It was deserted enough for the waitresses and the few other customers to know her business, know she was waiting for that skinny man who'd gone in to the men's but hadn't come out. The waitresses bunched up at the end of the counter to wonder what he was doing in there. Smoke streamed from the corners of their mouths like gossip, wispy but tenacious, clinging to the late afternoon light. For the first time Eureka sensed the strength of his medicine, felt its power. She was ready to go; it was keeping him back, holding them up. She wondered if she might be wrong about the druggist, if he really was trying to help.

When her waitress approached with a coffee pot, Eureka said, "No more, thanks," and bumped her cup across the counter. She got up and walked without looking back to the men's room where she knocked on the door and called his name until he cracked it.

"Almost," he said through a lopsided smile.

She pushed in easily, bolted the door behind her. "Guys have been trying to get in here. You okay?" she asked. She breathed through her nose, stared at the urinal, warped and yellow tiles beneath it, rotting plywood black beneath the tiles. She thought of her family wondering where she was in the world, what they'd think if they could see. Told you so, her sisters would say, though she wasn't long gone enough to feel remorse over witnessing the inside of a men's room in Siler City.

"The good kind of sick," said Edwin.

"What'd you go down in the swamp for?"

"Ancient history. Couldn't begin to explain now."

"You're right, this isn't the place. Let's go." She led the way across the dining room, past the waitresses crammed into a front smoky booth.

Back in the car Edwin was loose-limbed, amiable, car-trip giddy. The druggist took one look and refused to be sucked in by this sudden exuberance. He folded his suitcoat into a sad pillow and slept while Edwin questioned Deems about the hit parade and both of them sang poorly along with the radio.

At dusk they coasted down into Black Mountain, then began the steady westward climb up the Swannanoa Valley. Eureka stared at the mountains loping along the roadside, spindly timber on the ridges backlit by the last of the sun. Darkness came slower to these valleys, dusk lingered in shades of grey instead of the bright orange bathing she knew from flatlands. An hour past Asheville they stopped for the night at a small cluster of roadside cabins.

"He's a moody sapsucker," said Deems when Edwin went inside to pay.

"Don't you talk about him," she said.

"Whoa," said Deems. The druggist laughed. She disliked them both, wondered why she'd allowed herself to be lured into their vaguely mutinous allegiance when Edwin had disappeared into the swamp. She knew why — because they were saying things she needed to know — but she still felt she'd betrayed him, and she vowed not to talk about him behind his back again.

"You boys are up the hill in number nine," said Edwin, tossing a room key into the druggist's lap.

She followed him to a cabin farthest away from the rest. Inside he pulled her onto the biggest bed she'd ever seen. It took up all of the front room but a sliver of hallway, grazed both pine-paneled walls. He hugged her head to his chest and held it there. They sank deeper into the too-soft bed.

"This bed could spoil me rotten," she said, but her voice boomed through the quiet cabin, and she fell into shamed silence. Ten minutes of tongue and touch: she was halfway to some point fluid and irretrievable when he let her go, rolled over and off the bed, disappeared into the bathroom. Water drummed the metal of a stall shower. She rose, fished a sack of coffee from a box of food they'd brought along. The vibrant orange of the oven eye, tightly coiled and ablaze against the drab paneling, reflected off the bottom of the pan and made her feel warm, comfortable, almost in control.

When the coffee was ready she stepped onto the back porch, brushed leaves from a metal glider and sat. Mountain air was ten degrees cooler, the texture different: instead of the yellow she associated with air down east, this seemed blue-green, rich and wild but thinner and more dry than what she was accustomed to. It made her dizzy, and when her ears popped she swallowed like Edwin had told her to in the car crossing the eastern continental divide. The longer she sat, the richer the air grew, the muskier its odors: rotting tree trunks, damp moss, a trace of skunk. Everything's wet here, she thought; mountains towering in the dark above must be filled with water. She thought of Randall, how he used to wake her early mornings claiming to have heard the sea.

Inside she lay on the edge of the bed and stretched her legs out tight, her feet blocking Edwin's way when he emerged wet and groggy from the bathroom.

"Where are we really going?" she asked.

"You sound like our Doubting Thomas druggist." He fingered a fleck of tobacco on the tip of his tongue, grimaced and said, "Lexington, Kentucky."

"To that hospital?"

"Yes."

"I don't understand all this."

"I know. I'll explain."

He pulled the curtains to, locked the door, flopped beside her. "It's all about blood, see."

A car passed close by outside, headlights

streaming in a slow arc across the walls, lighting parts of them: his forehead, her elbow. Gravel crunched beneath tires. After a second's silence she heard the car squeal off down the mountain and imagined it was the druggist and Deems fleeing, marooning them in this kitchenette.

"There came a point in my life when blood assumed a different purpose in the scheme of things." He shook his head, began to mumble. "That's pitiful. I told you how hard it was for me to talk about things like this. It sounds so stuffy always, so goddamn serious. It's embarrassing. So much easier to write it down."

She'd forgotten about the letters. Compared to the changes of the last few days, his peeping tom letter did seem silly. Still, she wondered about the letters to come, which sins they'd include.

"Before the accident . . . ," he was saying.

"What accident?" she said. "Tell me about this accident."

He raised up on one arm and looked at her, seemed perturbed by the interruption. "There was an accident."

"I know *that*," she said, kicking him lightly, trying to tease him into elaborating, but it didn't work. "I can't talk about it now. Have to write it down."

Dangling her feet in the dark space between

bed and wall, she had the eerie feeling she got when wading in murky pond water, a fear of what she could not see.

"Before the accident my blood did the same thing yours did. Same as everyone elses. Even Deems. Some people, you look at them and you just can't believe that they have blood in their veins, that their bodies work the same way. Well, I might look that way to you now, but a year ago I was normal and healthy and fit."

He stopped, winded. "Maybe I exaggerate. Anyway, the accident. Where the blood kept me like you — alive, I mean — the medicine kept me numb. I needed to be numb for two reasons: so I wouldn't feel any pain, and so I wouldn't remember certain people, places or things. One place and one person in particular. More later in part two of our ongoing one-sided correspondence."

"When?" she asked, but again he ignored her.

"Medicine comes with side effects. This medicine I take has some major ones that I didn't think I'd have to deal with until recently. Last week, in fact."

"What side effects?"

"It has a way of killing a part of me that we both want alive."

"So quit taking it."

"It's not that easy."

"Why not?"

"My body's too used to it. You saw what happened when I went without it for one day. You saw how sick I was."

He had slipped into a contemplative daze, as if weighing what he was about to say.

"When the druggist first mentioned Lexington, I agreed to go just so I could get more medicine. I knew it was the only way he'd get it for me and I was sick, I needed it, I would have agreed to go to Antarctica. I figured we could ditch him anywhere along the road. Frankly, the druggist can be a self-righteous son of a bitch when he wants."

"You lied to get that medicine?"

"But then things changed. The druggist is right: I can learn to live with the pain in my back. It's mostly imagined anyway. And as for the other pain I mentioned, those people and places, as soon as I met you I could forget. I don't know the hows or whys, but when I'm with you those things fade. The only thing left is the minute we're sitting in. And you're a lot better for me than morphine."

"Morphine?"

"That's what the medicine's called."

She'd never heard of it, but she didn't think she liked being compared to it. Since she'd known him, she'd been forced to think of herself in strange terms: her double, her opposite, now this medicine.

"You favor comparisons," she said.

He smiled, reached for her, crooked an arm around her neck. Laughing, he pulled her close. "Thanks. You're right. Sometimes I'm too busy looking for metaphors to recognize the thing itself. But sometimes the thing breaks through, like it did the other day in the kitchen, to show me how pretentious I am. That was something of a miracle, you realize that, don't you?"

"What? What are you talking about?"

"Remember the side effects I was talking about earlier? That part of me it kills that we want alive?"

She nodded.

"Easier shown than told." He stood to wrench off his shirt and pants. He was right, he *was* clumsy when it came to taking off his clothes. She could see why he was impressed with that couple he'd spied on. It took him forever to unbutton his shirt and when he tried to kick off his wingtips without untying them he lost his balance and fell beside her on the bed.

She stared at the space between them. The ridges of the tan bedspread were worn and frayed; up close the tufts of twisted cotton ran in raised rows like furrows. She thought of that field behind the schoolhouse in the country where couples met during recess and lunch. She squinted until the bedspread was blurry and she saw the field again, blond sand blending with his pale skin. He reached for her hand and held it as they crossed the playground behind the schoolhouse toward the line of trees where boys led girls, girls led boys, boys boys girls girls into that dense thicket of indelible secrets from which one emerged chafed, changed. He squeezed her hand so hard nerves tingled then went numb, placed it palm-flat against his stomach and began to guide. They pushed forward through the woods, southwards along the line of thin hair flat against his skin; he forced her hand past the elastic band of his shorts and soon after sighed, pulled his hand away. She opened her eyes to see him smiling triumphantly, as if he had made some amazing point. As if these last five minutes had been some heated debate he'd won after endless struggle.

But she did not know the subject of debate until now and it seemed hardly debatable to her, as cool and lifeless as it felt. Instead of releasing her grip, she closed her hand tightly around him and kept it there. Then, slowly, she pressed her palm to his skin and traveled back up the same route he'd forced her to take until she reached his waist, where she detoured until her hands rested against his hip blades. She rose on her knees, shed her dress and lowered herself to him again, holding tight to those sharp bones as if they were handles of a huge pail and spending the next half hour trying to prove him wrong before falling onto the bed in silent and exhausted concession.

"The other day was a miracle," he said. "If it happened again, there'd be no reason for me to go to Lexington."

It was hard to think of the state she was in as proof of anything but a frustration tingling everywhere: eyelids, toenails, tonsils. As she lay beside him waiting for it to pass, she imagined herself in those terms she'd already begun to question: a double, an opposite, a pain reliever capable of erasing his past, and a miracle which — fortunately, he claimed — occurred only once.

"What if," said Randall, "and I know it's a big if but what if you found out all of a sudden that your brain was like that ant farm Dwight Sutton brought to school one day, your whole head a ant farm and everybody could see your thoughts shooting off down tubes, passing other thoughts or running smack upside them and the tunnels your ideas make right out there for people passing you on the sidewalk to see. Might get lucky, sun might be out bad, there might be a glare on the glass or say your hands could be dirty and the glass could get smudged from where you run your hand through your hair and then they might not be able to see all the way through to the truth but what if —"

"Enough," said Speight. They were walking to work, Monday morning early, no one up but yard boys at work in the wide lawns up West Main. Randall kept in step with his father's stride while Speight, oblivious to the game, sucked smoke from cigarettes he'd rolled at the breakfast table, flicking them into the gutter when the ember neared the yellow calluses of his forefinger and thumb. By the time they reached downtown the sun had risen high enough to singe the dew from the grass and burn away the fog, leaving the smoke from Speight's butts drifting up from curbs between work and home.

"In the dirt between tunnels, dumb-ass ideas would be buried," Randall said as they walked up the alley toward the back of the drugstore.

"I said enough," said Speight, though there was no need: they were at work now, such talk was impossible. Speight disappeared down the basement stairs, his low "Be good" lingering in the corridor. He'd grown so gaunt in the last few weeks that Randall had imagined he heard the bones in his feet clinking against the concrete when they walked to the store. Since she'd been gone he'd taken to staying out on the porch all hours of the night.

Since she'd been gone, Randall talked to his father nonstop, even when Speight told him to shut up. He seemed to have forgiven his father for the basement, though the bruise was the slowest to heal of any Speight had seen, yellowish-purple long after it should have darkened to black and blue. Speight tried not to look at the boy. The bruise reminded him of how he'd stretched alongside him in the dark and felt a misery as deep and paralyzing as any he'd felt before, misery that seemed to come up from the cool earth between them. I've lost them both, he'd thought then, the two who were mine.

When the bruise did not heal he made Martha take Randall to the doctor but the doctor sent him back in the same swollen way, said nothing could be done, time would take care of it.

The bruise did not fade, nor did the helplessness Speight felt. The past few days had been filled with drink, Randall's constant chatter and the nagging regret that he had not done things differently. He knew he wasn't the type to run home for his gun — the reaction didn't even occur to him until the next day. Even then his thoughts of violence were forced.

That night after supper he called his children into the kitchen and sat them all down at the table. They whispered and fidgeted and did not look him in the eye.

"It's about Eureka."

" 'Reka's run off," said Randall.

"Shut up and let him tell it." Martha reared back from the table and smirked.

"Y'all must know something. She's not been home these three nights, nor at work."

"We figured she retired," Martha said. She'll make it hard for me because she senses I had something to do with it, thought Speight, even though Eureka had never gotten on good with any of her sisters. She was closer even to Hal who had just stamped in, his clothes stiff with red graveyard clay, his breath sweetening the room with fumes of afterwork beers. Yet despite their differences (he doubted they'd have ever exchanged more than a greeting if they hadn't been born sisters), Martha was possessive about Eureka. Thickness of blood: her mother had been that way, too, forever protective of people she'd once shared a name with though she hadn't spoken to half of them in ten years.

"She's run off," he said.

"Where to?" Martha shot back.

"Don't know."

"Who with?" Ellen and Marianne said simultaneously, their timing touching off giggles.

"How come?" asked Alicia. The innocence of her question — she was thirteen — drew irked looks from her sisters, looks that let Speight know Eureka didn't need a reason to run off, only some place to run to, someone to run with.

"Oh, boy," said Randall, rolling his eyes. "Y'all are all gone nuts. She'll be back in a few days."

Everyone ignored this, turning to Speight again.

"Who with?" asked Martha. She did hold him responsible, he could feel it.

"Don't know the man's name."

"Man?" said Ellen. Giggles again among the younger girls, Martha swiveling around to silence them.

"He doesn't really have a name," said Randall. "What I mean is he doesn't really have a name that fits him."

No one even looked his way. It's like without Eureka here to listen he don't exist, thought Speight. Like the riddle the boy kept bugging him about on the porch last night, a tree in an empty forest falling on deaf ears,

286

does anybody hear?

"Poor thing," said Martha. "She don't live in this world. She don't have a clue."

"What goddamn good's a clue?" said Hal. He'd been leaning against the stove stirring a pot of beans left simmering on a back eye for him. He mumbled through a mouthful, touching off his sisters' giggles.

"Go dig a grave," Martha said to him over her shoulder.

"What good you think a clue'll do her? Think she'd of stayed here if she had a clue? Ask me, I think people're better off without a clue."

"It ain't hard to see why you'd think that way," said Martha.

"I guess you're supposed to be an example of somebody with a clue?"

It went on like this but louder, Martha and Hal spraying each other with insult while the younger girls egged them on and Randall sat silently in the corner, looking for all the world like his father who, trapped at the head of the table, searched for an easy way out of this room where history had always worked against him.

12

Edwin had been promised a hospital but when they arrived in Lexington what little they saw from the road — a gatehouse, a formidable fence, the tips of two fat smokestacks visible through the highest diamonds of the chain link — looked more like a prison.

"Goddamn," said Deems. "That's a hospital I'd hate like hell . . ."

"Probably need to check in over there with the guard," said the druggist. He saw the shock curtain Edwin's face, cringed when Deems had said what they'd all been trying not to think. It was a miracle that they'd managed to get this far; Roy hadn't counted on seeing the Kentucky line. He'd figured Keane would leave him at a rest stop somewhere in West Virginia. Late at night in one of the motel rooms they shared he'd made Deems promise not to abandon him.

"What you worried about, doc, he likes you I can tell, besides you got something he wants, right?" Deems said before rolling over.

"Not much left." If the morphine ran out

before Lexington, Keane would order Deems to U-turn the moment the dregs seeped into his veins, would head straight back to Trent where the new boy waited at Lehmann's, ignorant and eager to please. Even if the new boy had principles there was always a grace period in which disgust built, resistance germinated; if eventually he stood up to Lehmann and was given the boot, Lehmann would find someone else overnight, the eastbound Trailways might as well install a revolving door to accommodate the turnover.

Drunken late-night word of a lubbock whose only loyalty was to his new high life, to Keane's daddy's money. Thick-slabbed syllables uttered five seconds before ragged snores of drunk-sleep, *Don't worry, Doc I ain't about to leave your ass' side the road with the groundhawgs.* This slurred promise his only insurance. Eureka couldn't stand him. She would not slant the rearview to watch him shrink in dust-plumed distance if, while he did his business behind a roadside pine, Edwin gave the order and Deems gear-grinded away.

So he'd made this trip with the knowledge that every leg could be his last. He held his bladder until someone else called for a pitstop. When they stopped he made sure Edwin saw him slap open the glove compartment and stuff the vials in his pocket. This may or may not have saved him from abandonment; by the last few days he didn't care. He'd lost the thread of his chant and at times found it difficult to remember why he'd agreed to come along. Something about seeing this thing through.

Yet he had to admit that a trip out of town — his first in years, except for weekends in Norfolk or Raleigh and a week back in Ypsilanti for his sister's wedding four years ago — brought things into perspective. In Trent his vision was myopic, obscured by his early afternoon reveries. Outside, he found clarity, even if it was misguided — a sharp sense of the four of them entering into a renegade excitement he'd never known. Sometimes as they sped along, skirmishes of small talk erupted. Repetitive smart-ass fare, but he found it seductive. He enjoyed those moments even though he was always conscious of what lay ahead — like in gangster movies which made prison seem worth three weeks on the high-life lam.

They sat in the car staring at the miles of fence twisting off into the distance, their silence interrupted by a transistor blaring a Nat King Cole tune from the barred window of the gatehouse. Finally Edwin got out, pulling the girl along with him, and as Roy tilted the rearview mirror to watch them lean into each other by the bumper, he had a new idea of how to see this thing through: while Keane was away he'd work on the girl. If I can't save Keane from himself, I can save Eureka from Keane.

Edwin thrust something through the window, a card full of scribbled names and numbers.

"Find rooms in town. Don't scrimp. If you need more cash, call one of those numbers and they'll wire it to you. Keep yourself in the manner in which you are unaccustomed and keep Deems in Kentucky bourbon but don't let him crack up the car."

A paneled truck appeared at the top of the hill, waves of heat radiating from its hood. Roy watched it wind down to the gatehouse, then glanced outside: Keane and the girl so close by he could ruffle their clothes with his breath. The window framed them from neck to waist; Keane's suitcoat draped most of her as they embraced and she shrank almost out of sight until Keane released her, stuck his head in the window and told Roy to keep her happy.

"Oh, I will," said Roy. "I'll treat it like a job."

"You're in good hands, then," Keane called up to Eureka. "He won't stop until you're ecstatic."

★ ★ ★

Inside the hospital Edwin was fingerprinted, strip-searched, led into a shower room where two guards watched him shiver beneath the feeble stream. Next a huge man who called himself Nurse Jane gave him a shot, then led him down a repetitive forever of yellow corridor. In a spare office a Dr. Covington offered him a seat and asked him dozens of questions about his history. Edwin was as expansive with Dr. Covington as he used to be with his mother, perversely amused that his history here was measured in grains, was not connected to family or lineage or River Road Trent.

"Now we come to the most important question of all," said Dr. Covington. He leaned forward, casting a shadow over the ink blotter. He had the khaki coloring of someone employed too long by the government, someone filed away to yellow and mold slowly. "Why do you want to quit taking morphine?"

"I've found something better."

"Let me guess. Heroin?"

"With an *e* on the end."

The doctor smiled. "Unfortunately, the libido is one of the first things to be affected by morphine addiction. Still, I'm afraid the desire to return to normal sexual relations might not be sufficient impetus to remain clean once outside."

"You make it sound like I checked in here to get my libido fixed."

The doctor said, "We rarely see patients here with habits like yours. What kind of doctor would keep this up for so long?"

"One that hates to see people in pain. One that is my uncle."

"He should have his license revoked. I'm surprised the druggist didn't report him."

Edwin shrugged. "Small town."

"Then the druggist should have his license revoked."

"Actually, the druggist is a conscientious fellow. Very much by the book. He's the one who got me in this place."

"Time I explained this place to you, Mr. Keane. How it works."

Edwin watched clay-colored chimneys belch black smoke outside as the doctor talked about the difference between voluntary patients like himself and those who had been convicted of crimes and were placed here in isolation from the general prison population. Most were small-time thieves, said the doctor, but there were murderers and armed robbers among them, and *this place* (the doctor repeated Edwin's phrase with a self-conscious emphasis which quickly became annoying) was started to keep smuggling and the black market out of other federal pens by collecting them all and, if not curing them, at least maintaining their habits.

"Seems safe enough in here to me," said Edwin. But the doctor ignored him to drone on about how a few years ago they had begun accepting voluntary patients. These were mostly nonmedical addicts off the street but also a few "meds" whose addictions stemmed from illness, injury or treatment from inept or crooked doctors, and who for some reason wanted to taper off.

"The reason is crucial," said the doctor.

"I understand," said Edwin.

"And your reason is this woman you've met?"

"Not good enough?"

"My concern is that you stop to please yourself."

Edwin said, "First of all, it's been awhile since I did something to please someone else. Second, she doesn't even know what morphine is. Since she doesn't know, what she wants isn't that important to me right now. See, I could have both if I wanted, but why waste the energy to juggle two things which serve the same purpose?"

Edwin looked out the window at the withered hills and smiled. "I never once thought I'd find something that worked better. Inconceivable to me. I figured I'd waste away inside that bungalow, carried off finally by pneumonia. That must have been what I wanted. I think that's what other people wanted also, and I can't say I blame them. After Sarah, I never once thought I'd want to get involved with another woman."

"I'm listening," said the doctor.

"She came out of nowhere, that's the thing. No one's ever done that to me before, I've always been able to see people coming for miles."

"How did you two meet?" said the doctor.

Edwin squinted. The doctor had disappeared for a few seconds, but now he was back, as cardboard paternal as before. "I can explain this whole thing to you in a single sentence, doctor. My addiction is and has always been metaphorical. That it's a metaphor is all you really need to know," said Edwin.

Late-afternoon light from a high window laminated the doctor's face, making his smile seem all the more patronizing. "We have a hard-enough time treating opiate addiction in this place, Mr. Keane. We'll have much less success, I can guarantee, in treating metaphors."

"We'll save money this way instead of paying hotel rates," Roy claimed. "He'll be in longer than a month, you can bet on that."

He had rented an apartment above a corner grocery in a neighborhood of small businesses, factories, black-bricked apartment houses. No one stayed around after dark, no one seemed to know anyone else. At first the grocer downstairs watched them closely, suspicious of their presence so suddenly in Lexington, Kentucky, but they paid a month's rent in advance and were good customers. Deems went down every two hours for cold beer until, on the third day, the druggist rationed him to twelve Miller High Lifes and two packs of Lucky Strikes daily.

In the late afternoon children returning from school played in the alley which ran beneath their rooms. Outside the kitchen window there was a fire escape which had rusted in place five feet above the pavement, rendering useless the complicated system of weights and pulleys. The children scoured the alley for refuge and heaved bottles and shards of flower pots at the landing. They came every day to do this. The druggist, driven wild by the noise and wilder by the fact that this was happening to them in a town where they knew no one and should by all rights be anonymous and invisible, finally called down to the kids near the end of the week, but he was too scared to enter the line of fire. He pressed himself against the window sash and threw his voice out like a ventriloquist. It floated to the street like ash from a crosstown fire, wispy and innocuous. Deems, watching from the kitchen table, laughed and said, "They ain't going to do nothing if they don't see you."

"You stick your big head out there, then," said the druggist.

The assaults continued into the second week. One afternoon the druggist said to Eureka, "Here we are, strange people in a strange town, and these kids have to come taunt us." She thought him pathetic for saying this though she was as bothered by it as he was. There didn't seem to be anything they could do. If they were at home they would know the words — the names of the children, their parents, a neighbor at least — to get them to stop. Here they had no knowledge, no authority. Every time the noise would start up she and the druggist would sink into a shared mood of misery and helplessness. Deems ignored it until the first Saturday, when the barrage began a little past seven and woke him. He appeared in the kitchen with a chair in hand, opened the window wide to toss it. There were bratty squeals, and Deems leaned out the window to hock obscenities, then went back to bed. When the children came again they spied from the cover of a Chevy abandoned down the block.

Most days the druggist started hitting the Scotch in the late afternoon. He read the Lexington papers with a thoroughness that stretched the morning edition right up until the evening boy arrived at the stand downstairs. He read the obituaries of dead Lexingtonians, he read the ads for used vacuum cleaner motors; he read the court docket, the tax listings, the price of potatoes.

Eureka drank sodas and waited for him to finish, hoping he'd want to talk. She didn't especially like his conversation but Deems took to going out a lot after the first week and she grew bored. But the druggist was busy with his newspapers. She rifled through his castoffs — evening paper first thing in the morning, morning at night — but only pretended to read anything except for the human interest stories. The Lexington paper was more sophisticated than the *Trentonian* and did not feature pictures of elephantine gourds and muddy bream caught in irrigation ponds, but there were a few weekly social columns she enjoyed making fun of at first, though their rhythms — so-and-so motored across town to see so-and-so, a group of ladies from Rosemont Garden ate dinner at the Ballantine's downtown — soon depressed her. It seemed no one in Lexington went out any more than she did.

In the early afternoons the druggist took a long walk. One day while he was gone, Deems asked her to play spades. With each beer his moony smile widened. He licked his fingers to shuffle. He licked his lips and with each beer seemed to take up more space at the small kitchen table.

When she could no longer avoid his stare, she met it.

"You know what they say," he said.

"What do they say?"

He grinned and held up his hands, palms outward as if to deflect criticism or blame. "Big hands, big . . ."

"Head?" She stared at him. Threads from the pullover sweater he wore clung to his five-day stubble and were lit by the sunlight streaming in over the kitchen sink. The druggist called Deems reckless, but he seemed for all his clunky energy invincible to her. He wasn't as stupid as either the druggist or Edwin thought; he had just been raised not to feel things that got in his way, trained to get there by crashing through fences even when the gates were open. Like her brother Hal. Like her father, too.

"You're smarter than that," he said. "Don't need to play dumb with me."

"Big mouth?"

He laughed his smoky white-liquor gargle laugh. She was both affronted and drawn in by it: like everything else Deems said or did, it showed nerve ending. "You ain't so quick around *him*, I've noticed."

This caught her off guard. All Edwin ever talked about was moving things forward, yet he did not seem to want her to move any faster. She listened, she didn't ask questions, she accepted whatever ideas he presented. After all, she'd wanted things to move faster if that meant leaving Trent sooner, yet she still felt that since she'd met him her life moved slower.

Deems sucked smoke from his cigarette, laid it on the table edge, scattering ashes. Grinding them into the linoleum with his boot heel he said, " 'Course he's a dope fiend. That hospital ya'll put him in's for dope fiends. Found that out first afternoon I was here. That's why they got that prison wire wrapped around the place, old boy I met in a bar told me those dope fiends break out and head straight for town get 'em some dope. They water it down out there I guess. You take dope, too?"

She slapped a card down on the table. "Your turn," she said.

"Naw, you don't take any. I can tell by your ass. Your ass wouldn't be so round if you was to take dope ever day."

"Play," she said.

"I watch y'all. He don't hardly even touch you. Don't even talk to you that much. Just goes to sleep on your shoulder like a little bitty brother."

She picked up his beer. "Want another?" She'd seen him grow sullen and quiet when drunk, figured it was worth a try. He grabbed the bottle and turned it up, kept the backwash bubbling until the last drop sucked down the neck. Belched, grinned, said, "Ready."

She got another from the icebox, rummaged in the drawer for the churchkey, turned to find his eyes level with her waist.

"What?" she asked.

"Missed a belt loop."

She was wearing a sweater and a pleated skirt, beltless. When she handed him the bottle he said, "What do you want to go with a dope fiend for?"

"What are you doing here if you hate him so much?"

"Ain't sleeping with him, that's for sure. Making good money, better than I ever could beating dents out of wrecks back home."

"How'd you get picked to be his driver anyway? Take some kind of road test?"

"See, me and his daddy has kind of a business deal going. He did some work for us and instead of paying him in cash, which we're a little short, I'm agreeing to offer my services as a driver to his invalid son."

"You hired his father as your lawyer?"

"Well, it was my granddaddy hired him, but we're — you might call us partners."

"I used to go to court some, maybe I sat in on this case. What did it involve?"

"I don't know why I'd care to tell you but I'm getting tight and tight's when I start telling the truth and nothing but it so help me, you hear?"

"I hear you, Deems," she said, taking up her cards again, rearranging them into suits, busying herself to hide the fact that she was having fun. It was the kind of fun she couldn't count on, excitement based on stirred-up dust. "What was the case against your granddaddy?"

"Who said it was against him? Accused of turning back odometers."

"He got off?"

"Keane's daddy's a good lawyer."

"So you're not making any money on this trip?"

"Hell, yes, I'm making money."

"But your wages go against the debt, right?"

"That's right."

"Not even your debt, right?"

"Grandaddy's the one raised me, I *been* owing him."

"Do Edwin and the druggist know about this arrangement?"

"What do they care? Keane just wants a driver and the druggist, beats hell out of me what he wants."

"Beats me, too," she said. This place the druggist had chosen for them reminded her of his upstairs apartment in Trent: steep flight up from the world he preferred living above, though it felt like a cavern, had the light of a basement. Maybe he wanted some place that reminded him of Trent. She'd heard him bad-mouth Trent to Edwin, but he complained too loud, like her sisters would when it didn't pan out for them, their whining laced with the resentment of being snubbed and desire for the power to snub back. She'd heard him say that Edwin reminded him of the job he hated, and if this was so, why was he hanging around? Keep her happy, Edwin had told him, keep her company, but the druggist had done nothing but drink Scotch, read the paper, take walks and ignore her.

Deems had shown her double the attention just today; though she didn't much trust it, she was beginning to warm to it.

" 'Course it's obvious why Keane lets him ride shotgun, you know that, don't you?"

She stared at her cards until Deems reached over and folded up her hand like it was a lady's parlor fan, brought it to his chest. "Soon's he gets out he's going to get the druggist to get him some dope."

She told Deems he was crazy. His beer breath was hot and sweet on her cheeks. "Give me back my cards."

"You don't know what dope is, do you?"

"Medicine for his back."

"You really think he's gonna come out of there a athlete college boy again?"

"I don't care for athletes or college boys."

"You don't care for him?"

"Didn't say that."

"Okay, so he gets out and he's all cured. Then what? Y'all going to get married?"

"Play cards," she said.

Deems turned his beer up, drug his knuckles across his lips and said: "The two of us is of one type. And the two of them is of another. They got the sleeping arrangements all wrong on the way up here, see what I'm saying?"

"Yeah," she said.

"You think I'm talking out of my head because I'm getting tight but when I'm tight's when I do not tell a lie. I'm getting ready to tell you something directly that's nothing but the truth."

"You keep threatening. You're so good at lying, I don't know why you'd want to bother with the truth." She stood and went over to the window. People in the world were leaving work; the street was clogged with traffic, sidewalks thick with pedestrians. She watched the colored tops of cars and buses pass and said, "Let's go out."

"Say what?"

"I haven't been out of here all week except downstairs to buy soup and crackers."

"Asking me for a date?"

"I'm asking you for a ride."

"Nothing's for free."

"Is that the big fat truth you keep promising? Well, it's a lie: you already been paid to drive me around. So drive me, Deems."

"You sound like him now."

"Maybe he's rubbing off on me."

"That'd be about all he could handle."

In the car Deems said, "You going to try on clothes in the back seat again?"

"Forgot my raincoat."

"Good."

"Just get us out of this neighborhood." They were burrowing deeper into an endless Johnsontown, a Johnsontown twice the size of Trent. Roosters halting traffic in the rutted streets and patchy vegetable gardens spangled with tin pie plates to ward off crows. Thin-limbed ghosts in ladderbacks and metal gliders along the loping parade of porches, all of them following the Dodge with eyes she could see anywhere, especially back home.

"I haven't lost nothing in the great state of Kentucky," said Deems.

"Just passing through myself."

"On your way to where now?"

"Don't know yet. Haven't decided. Edwin says maybe Canada."

" 'Edwin says maybe Canada,' " mimicked Deems. "You'll be back in Trent by the end of the month."

"What are you talking about?"

"Druggist said so."

"The druggist is going back?"

"Nah. Says he's going to Michigan. Told me I was going to have to take you back to your daddy."

"He might check with me first."

"I believe he's fixing to."

"He hasn't said a word to me since we got here."

"You seen the way those kids aggravated him. If you ask me, the druggist has got screws loose. That's what I keep trying to tell you: two of them is of one type, two of us is another."

"What type are we, Deems?"

"You know what they say."

"We played this game already today."

"You can take the girl out of Serenitowinity

but you can't take Serenitowinity out of the girl."

"If I believed that I'd have drownded myself before I could even crawl." She turned to him. "I thought you grew up in town."

Deems shook his head. "Ivanhoe side. Went to school over to Harrell's store, got called Swamp Thang 'til the day I quit."

"Nobody ever called me Swamp Thang. But I'm different from you, Deems. I kept clean. I never went inside that swamp and I never let any of it get inside me."

They'd reached an avenue which skirted Lexington, farmland and open pasture on one side, city stirring in neon fits on the other. As Deems drove he dropped an arm to the seat and dug his hand under her thigh. She shifted her weight to escape but his long arm followed, snaking deeper, his fingers spread out like the latticed bottom of a chair. She scooted against the door, yanked his sweaty palm off the upholstery with a sound like ripped fabric, pinched a finger by its nail, handed the whole appendage back to him.

"I know why I scare you," he said.

"Who said you scare me?"

"It's because you know me so good."

"Your big truth just keeps on coming," she said. "I'll never listen to you sober again, if I ever get the chance." They fell silent as they circled the city, Deems negotiating traffic, Eureka staring at the hamburger and ice cream stands and considering Deems seriously for the first time since she'd met him.

Certainly he was closer to the man she'd imagined for herself than Edwin Keane. He was right about one thing: she did know him, knew exactly what he was going to say, unlike Edwin who from the moment she'd met him had surprised her with those sentences which seemed to spring from some wild and private dark, which struck her as both out of sequence and in some oblique order soon to be revealed.

"You're right," she said. "I know what you're going to say before you even say it."

"Let's hurry then. Motel rates go up after dark."

"I want to go where some people are."

"You're lucky I'm thirsty."

He drove them to a gravel road paralleling the highway. "Call this a access road because down here you got access to about anything you want," he said. They parked the Dodge and walked across the wide gravel lots from one bar to another, emerging each time to a brighter stripe of red sunken lower in the western sky until it was dark and the parking lots were lit by streetlights dimmed by halos of bugs. Deems pretended they were ballpark lights and ran imaginary bases between pick-ups, a cigarette stuck between his fingers and an Ike jacket stolen from an abandoned coatcheck tied around his waist. Sometimes his drunken exuberance was infectious but mostly she worried she'd have to call the drug-gist to come for them in a taxi.

She sat at a series of rickety formica-topped tables, sopping up puddled beer with napkins and shredding the sheaths straws came in. Ate home fries and a cheeseburger steak and drank Coke after Coke until Deems weaved back from one bar with a bottle of Miller's which she sipped instead of wasting because after all it was Edwin's money they were blowing. Deems brought people to their table: women who worked all day in factories and distilleries and fell after work into this block of bars as if it was bed (she could tell by the way they smoked and watched the front door that even if bone-tired and dead-bored they couldn't leave before closing); men named Wharfrat and Choo-choo, one man with a thumb miss-ing and a white cross of bandage where once was his nose. Old buddies of mine, Deems claimed, and though he'd met them by the pool table five minutes before it did seem as if they'd grown up together, they spoke the same language and shared the same caveman laughter.

Deems talked her into one dance. "Keane wouldn't ever take you to a place like this," he said.

She *had* been curious about this life but she'd seen through it instantly, had been a step ahead of it all night long. As soon as Deems ushered another friend over to the table she absorbed and moved on, *yes okay I got it what next?* Her curiosity was only as deep as its subject, which seemed repetitive; nothing moving forward but blood alcohol levels and the sluggish trash-talking which might or might not lead to a gust of parking lot love.

She wasn't *above* it — it wasn't worth her putting on airs — she just wasn't interested. Deems and those like him (including her own Deems, the Deems she'd always conjured for herself) would seek it out because it was there always to slip in and out of, only an access road down which the tethers of work and home were loosened and hours passed as if floating on innertubes in a body of water hopelessly landlocked. What struck her as most tragic was that it was only good for a night; even a library book you could keep for a week. But people didn't come here expecting something eternal, they came here to sleep standing up, like horses.

"You're right, he wouldn't," she told

Deems. "Thanks for showing me around but I want to go back now."

"Miss the druggist?"

"Not hardly."

She walked out ahead of him and was almost to the car when she heard his brogans churning gravel and turned to see him flying toward her with arms wide and Ike jacket flared behind like a cape. He wrapped his arms around her, lifted her to the hood of the car and kissed her, his tongue thrusting around her mouth and his hands sliding to her hips. She felt *something*, enough to let him arrive at the natural end of what he considered a kiss, to not break him off. She wanted to experience his rhythms which, though rough, weren't faked. When he finished she pushed him away, satisfied with her choice.

"What?"

"This isn't right." He could take it however he wanted, she meant it several ways: we shouldn't be doing this to Edwin and this is wrong for me. She knew because when he kissed her, nothing moved but his lips and his hands and his groping tongue, but when Edwin touched her body he touched off her thoughts. In her mind she moved places, Johnsontown or schoolhouse woods or dense outskirts of Trent.

He hid behind a sheepish beery Deems grin.

311

"That's okay. I'm patient."

"Well, I'm not," she said. "Never have been and doubt I'll ever take time to learn how to be."

13

Edwin turned in his bed toward the high bank of windows at the end of the dormitory. It was first light out, five-thirty he figured. Rows of single cots with sagging metal springs stretched to the far wall. Even this early, half of the men were hunched over cigarettes, staring at the space between bunks. Edwin had awakened in the middle of the night to a chorus of exasperated insomniac sighs; even the breath of the sleeping had sounded desperate, the breath of people being chased.

During the day he kept to himself, sitting in the middle of the day room over back issues of magazines donated by the Lexington Junior League, half-listening to talk of how to pick locks, which doctors in Philly could be blackmailed. Most of his time he tried to think about Eureka, making plans for when he got out, but often — even after his shot — his plans were interrupted by memories he'd managed to stave away for months.

One day in the middle of the third week he found himself helpless and bleeding in the tannic slush of Serenitowinity. The image drifted up without warning, overtaking him in the middle of a *National Geographic* article about Nepalese sherpas. He was paralyzed: the early afternoon stillness of the swamp muted the day room noises — sharp-edged chatter of the Chinese addicts, monotonal street talk of the others. Staring at the tiny print, he saw himself muddy and contorted a few feet from the wreckage, saw Sarah's dress snagged on the broken windshield. Tree frog song drowned out a discussion in Chinese of the price of Mexican heroin in San Diego. When the noise faded and he found himself back among the sherpas, he rose and hurried down the long corridor to the infirmary.

"How's your metaphor feeling?" Nurse Jane asked him. Dr. Covington must have told the whole staff, one of the orderlies in Population had sneaked up behind him the other night to sing this song, accompanied by the swish of pushbroom: "Check your metaphor at the door/Don't, I'll have to sweep it up off my floor."

"I need a shot."

"Six o'clock, buddy-ro," said Nurse Jane. He hauled up his flabby forearm, thumped a boneless wrist. "Let's me and you synchronize our watches."

"Can you call Covington in?"

Nurse Jane rubbed the belly which preceded him through the world, his T-shirt lifting to expose pale skin rippled with stretch marks.

"Dr. Covington is at home with his fine family. He has a home life complete with basement workroom and swing set for the kids and beefsteak tomatoes grown in his backyard which sometimes he brings me."

"Can you call him at home?"

"Feeling puny, bub?"

"I'm in pain. My back — I broke it, in case Covington didn't tell you — it's hurting."

"Sorry to hear it, but can't do squat about it. You go on back down to Population where you belong and when Covington gets here I'll tell you wasn't feeling good."

Edwin returned to his magazine and read without interruption for an hour. But midway through an article about a famous Civil War photographer his attention flagged again as he dropped into a place he'd not thought about since the accident: the scrub surrounding Lake Mattamuskeet.

It was the detail — sulfuric odor of the savannah, talk of Tremont and Skipper recalled down to contractions and dropped *g*'s — that made him most uncomfortable, that forced him to ask to see Covington again. He could have tolerated brief shards, like the fragments that had sometimes pierced his morphine fog, a flash of swamp as it had appeared out the window that day, Sarah's face gauzy in the distance. But it was the clarity of the memories — the sight of Camp Tremont's beer-bloated face, so seemingly real that Edwin began talking back to him, causing the man nodding out in the next chair to move across the day room — that made them unbearable.

With the return of these memories came his hatred of Tremont; stronger than before, and even harder to articulate or rationalize. He began to miss Eureka and her way of containing him within the moment, holding past and future at bay. *This would be so much easier if she were here with me.* For a while he even considered asking Covington if there were not some way to work it out — he even thought of asking to finish his cure in town, under the druggist's supervision — but when he finally got in to see him he was too put off by the institutional air of the office, and the man himself, to ask for anything.

"We've got you down to three grains a day," said Covington. "In a few days you should be ready for the next phase. We'll switch you to another ward and substitute the dolophine with barbiturates. They should help you taper off."

"It all seems a bit rushed."

"You're in pain?"

"Not so much physical. It's hard to explain, but I'll try: morphine had a way of blocking certain things from memory, things I wanted to forget about? Now that I no longer have the morphine, I can't get these things out of my mind."

"We all have to learn to deal with the unpleasant realities of this world."

He's the druggist all over again, thought Edwin, treating me like a child who's trying to get out of going to Sunday school. He disliked the doctor more than the druggist, because the druggist was too confused himself to maintain such paternalistic smugness. The druggist was falling apart — Edwin saw that before they even left town — but still he felt he could trust him. The druggist was too self-absorbed not to trust.

Undeterred by Edwin's sneer, Dr. Covington continued his lecture.

"There's a widely held theory that people become dependent upon morphine because they are hypersensitive and have a chronic need to feel less. Some doctors feel we have a responsibility to maintain their habits, to shield them from the world as it is. I am of the opinion that a thin skin is kept thin by this type attitude. Do you follow me?"

Edwin looked out the window and said nothing.

"Do you really want to go through life feeling *less*?"

It's not that simple, he wanted to say, this is a complicated matter that you could not begin to understand after leafing through a file or two, and besides I feel more doing my fifteen grains a day than you feel cold sober. He thought of Tremont again, of how he'd never feel *less* about this man whom he hardly knew but who had become a magnet for all his rage. Even now, after all that had happened with Sarah and after all the time that had passed, he hated Tremont as much as he ever had.

He thought of explaining it all to Covington, but felt the same frustration when faced with trying to explain his past to Eureka. He'd rather stare out the window than oversimplify things for Covington, although it occurred to him that he already *had* oversimplified things. He remembered with shame all his talk of blood and metaphor, remembered the night with Eureka in the cabin, how he'd forced her to take him in her hand as proof of some hazy theory, how dramatic and wrong that seemed now that he was coming clean and could think again.

"When can I leave?" There seemed nothing else to say. The sooner he returned to Eureka, the sooner those memories would disappear.

"You're here by choice. You can leave any-time, but I recommend you rest for a few days, then work awhile with us on our farm. Physical work does wonders at this stage. Given your history, I can assure you that you won't be assigned anything too strenuous."

"Given my history and my chronic need to feel less," said Edwin.

"I recommend you stay for another month at least," said the doctor. "I don't think either of us want to see you back here again."

On the way back to his ward, trying not to think of Tremont, Edwin remembered the letters. She'd all but begged him for another installment, and besides, hadn't Thomasson once suggested he try to put it into words, the way he felt about Tremont? Stopping by the infirmary, he asked an orderly to find him a typewriter.

"Give him whatever he wants," Edwin heard Nurse Jane say when the orderly ducked into the next room to repeat the request. "He'll be back soon, and a little less a pain in the ass next time."

Wasting the rainy afternoon away in bed with a movie magazine, Eureka heard a rustling and rose to see an envelope flitting back and forth beneath her door. Eureka held on to the doorknob and stared at Deems crouched in the hallway, his hair slicked back with rain-water.

"Love letter from your number-one in-valid."

"Next time knock." She tugged the letter from the vise of his thumb and forefinger.

"I reckon he satisfies himself on paper now like the rest of your convicts. Is it any good for you, girl?"

His laugh lingered as she slammed the door, climbed back in bed, ripped the envelope open, swept movie magazines onto the floor.

Part Two: he'd promised, but she'd forgotten all about it except that it was supposed to make the confessions of the first seem like little white lies. Plucking the letter from the envelope she noticed how anxious she was and she laid the pages on the pillow beside her, breathed deep to slow herself, considered her anxiety. Was it because she was bored? Or because what had confused her at first she now craved, won over by the power of these letters to bring them closer together quicker?

She was bored. She made a point of leaving the apartment every morning while Deems lay crumpled along the sofa and the druggist sat at the kitchen table with his coffee and news-paper. She crisscrossed downtown Lexington, staying out of the shops and stores: browsing and even window shopping reminded her of her sisters and those shopping trips they'd hauled her on during their first days in Trent. Not only had they exhibited a remarkable flair for the obvious but because they never bought more than a spool of thread they had drawn disdain from every clerk in town.

Not that she was broke. Edwin had given her fifty dollars' spending money and there were certainly things she'd like to have, even things she needed, but Lexington did not seem the place to acquire them since Lexington itself was only temporary, a layover on their way farther north or west. Anything she bought here would seem temporary, too, would more than likely have to be replaced once they settled.

That was why she was bored: they had no real business here but waiting for Edwin, and to connect, learn the names of streets or the hours of the public library, seemed pointless. The wait had made them restless, especially during the last few days when the rains had come and the grey-white pallor of the sky draped the city. Landlocked sky, sky of saltless Canadian breezes frenzy-whipped by lakes they called great. When the rain set in she finally admitted to missing a few things: Randall, Rose, the way down-south rain swelled up from the ocean as if siphoned by the sky, clouds ushering deep seas fifty miles inland to release in drops salty-white as sweat.

She was bored enough to put her trust in anything which promised to move things forward. What had confused her about his first letter was why he even thought it necessary to explain his life to her; not once had she considered explaining hers to him. She understood that some people felt the need to pick over their past more than others (she suspected that what kept her father so late on the porch nights was an endless and tortured accounting of what he could have done differently to hold onto the farm) yet Edwin seemed — she fumbled for the word — obsessed. And his obsession seemed suddenly frightening, as if beneath it was hidden something she'd rather not know about.

Which could very well be lurking in the pages sitting on the pillow beside her.

He was right, she realized; the first letter *had* moved things forward. If she hadn't gone to his house to return it, she'd still be in Trent now, sweating out the afternoon in the back of the laundry. It seemed these letters possessed the power to challenge time by any means available. And the way days had dragged in Trent, the way they dragged away from Trent, primed her to accept these means.

Once, near the middle of the third page, the druggist knocked and asked if she wanted the paper. He was through, he was going out for his walk now even though it was raining, could she believe how it was coming down? She detected boredom in the way he forced his words through the closed door, his chipper tone, but she told him she was napping and returned to the banks of this Mattamuskeet she'd studied in her North Carolina history class, the lake the Whigs had lost all that money trying to drain.

Though the Mattamuskeet Edwin described had nothing to do with history: a flat place, hot and still and silent except for gunshots, black flies buzzing, the tired stories of this guy Edwin kept saying, over and over, how much he hated. She read along, annoyed by his asides, especially the longest one — a page and a half — about how trapped he felt with this Sarah, how he had chosen this Tremont as a symbol for all he hated about his life.

She read on, heard the gun go off, saw the men rise from the ground with faces scared sober. She wasn't shocked. So he shot at them, so what? She'd grown up on the edges of Serenitowinity where people were shot at daily for less reason, not only shot at but shot dead. It had turned out all right, no one was hurt. She could see why it bothered him enough to include in his letter, though she was unfazed until she reached the part when he described running into his friend Thomasson (wasn't he in the last letter, the one who slept with his favorite book? She felt she knew him, liked the blunt way he spoke, liked the fact that she'd come to know him well through Edwin's letters — it seemed further proof of their power) and claimed to have been "stretching the truth" when he told Thomasson it was a complete accident.

So he had meant to shoot instead of shoot at. Or so he said: she didn't know whether to believe him or not. Wasn't it possible that he didn't remember it quite the way it happened? He had been sick for a long time, people tended to see the worst while laid up, and what did it matter now anyway? She had only to believe that these letters would save time, move things forward, bring them closer together. What was in them was less important than the fact that he was writing them. She decided to trust them regardless of content, to sit back and wait for them to work their magic.

"Why don't you go out and get us some food, Deems?" said the druggist. He sat across the table from Eureka, scowling and sipping his Scotch. It was raining still, dark in the room; the overhead light was powerless against the shadows, bunched and hovering

in the corners like low clouds in the sky outside.

"It's cats and dogs out there, doc."

"People eat when it's raining," said Eureka.

"Did I ever tell y'all how come I'm so good
with cars?"

"He's been like this all morning," the druggist said to Eureka. "I think it's time for his
nap."

"Y'all haven't never heard it?"

"Is this a long story, Deems?"

"It's a story from long time ago. Goes like
this. When my granddaddy was young he was
out in the yard one day working on his tractor.
Got it going finally and was adjusting something with a screwdriver. Went to hammer
on the screwdriver and the thing slipped and
punched a hole in the oil line. He won't one
to waste, so he put his finger over the hole
and pressed down hard but the pressure was
so high that the oil went right on in his veins.
In the hospital six months. They didn't know
whether to work on him in the operating room
or the garage. Had maintenance men and sur-
geons in there examining. To this day we got
to take him back down to the barn ever six
months and do a oil change."

"That explains it," said the druggist.

"Explains how come I'm so good with cars.
We understand each other. It's in the blood."

"Then why don't you climb in that car you understand so well and drive down the street until you meet up with some lunch?" asked the druggist.

Standing in the doorway, Deems leaned against the jamb and hooked his thumbs behind his belt, wide leather creaking as it stretched.

"She's hungry?" he asked finally.

"I could eat," said Eureka without looking up.

"Oh, I got it," said Deems. "Y'all two want to be alone."

"He pays you to drive, so drive."

"What the hell, doc, he's the one paying. You just sitting around boozing until he gets out. I don't see where that gives you the right to —"

"Go, Deems."

"I already tried my damndest, doc. She don't even put out for him. They do it through the U.S. Mail."

"Stay gone long as you like."

"You're like me, I reckon," Deems said as he grabbed his coat. "Not in your nature to take somebody's word for it."

"Are you going to talk to me or are you going to hide behind that paper?" the druggist asked when Deems was gone.

She put down her newspaper, asked if he

326

wanted some coffee. She needed something to do, the newsprint was not thick enough, the druggist so close in the half-dark.

"You must have inherited your father's fear of words," he said while she filled the pot with water.

I'd talk to you if you weren't so damned druggist, she thought, if you didn't always respond as if I'd asked how to get rid of a rash. But he was right, she did fear words. She had no idea how to weave them so that they held together; she thought of Edwin's sentences which appeared like strings of streetlights in the middle of some dark plain. When she tried and failed to translate a thought into words she felt awkward and wasteful, as if she'd tossed money out a car window. It could well have been inherited, like the druggist suggested. Her mother talked only a little more than her father; if she opened up it was when he wasn't around, and it seemed to Eureka as if what her parents shared had been established and maintained by nerve endings. She'd seen marriage and family controlled by sharp eyesight and careful gesture. Her mother tongue was look and touch.

"More I think about it, the more I realize how amazing your little brother is. I'm taking for granted that everyone in your family is as tight-lipped as you and your father. Slim chance he'd learn to talk at all among people who hoard their words so." He was quiet for a moment, then said, "Speaking of your father, I wondered if he's called the authorities on Keane."

"You needn't worry about Pa calling anybody," she said. "He'll just think I run off, which I did. Wouldn't make a difference to him if I run off with Edwin or with Deems."

"Why didn't you run off with Deems, then?"

"You know why." Then, quietly, she said, "Deems is who I always figured I'd run off with."

The druggist's laugh was low and phony. "Deems?"

"Not Deems, but one like him."

"So you're with Keane because he's not who you thought you'd end up with?"

"It's a lot more than that," she said. She blushed, exasperated — all these words, their accumulating failure.

"That's good, because that kind of reasoning doesn't take into account how absolutely lost Keane is. Which is something you ought to be aware of, even if you're only tagging along in hopes of a side trip to Mammoth Cave."

"I thought you were trying to save him.

Seems like you'd have a little more faith."

"There was a time when I did. When I knew exactly what I was doing. Seeing a thing through, I called it. But here I am sitting around drinking Scotch all day and lording over the two of you. Only thing I'm seeing through is my own slide. I come up here to see that he gets straight and I end up just like him."

"I still don't understand what you thought you could do up here," she said.

The druggist sighed and looked wearily her way. In the month that they'd been here he'd lost weight except in his face, which was swollen and pink.

"With him gone there's nothing left there, nowhere else to go. Until something breaks between us, he and I are inextricable, understand?"

"No," she said. "What's inextricable mean?"

"It mean's he's not who I thought I'd run off with either. Similar situation to yours: you imagine one way for yourself and when it fails to turn up you get a little dizzy and make crazy choices."

Her awkwardness with words seemed preferable to his skill with them, since he could not manage a straight answer. She decided to try again.

"You still haven't said what you're doing here."

"Because there's nothing left. The only thing left over from my life is sitting in that hospital room a few miles up the road."

He paused to slurp Scotch. "I can't allow myself to drift. I tried to be as aimless as Deems, going with the best deal that comes around. Or you, running off with what seemed the least bit exotic. But it's not working. Can't do it. I wish I could — the way I live gets in the way of living."

She had the feeling that he was talking to himself now, yet she'd made it this far and felt compelled to keep talking.

"What are you going to do when he gets out of the hospital tomorrow?"

"A part of me says 'take off tonight.' But another part won't allow me to imagine my work over so easily. That would be like a missionary deserting his prospects after First Communion."

The druggist stared at the cup of coffee in front of him, then pushed it across the table, reached for his bottle.

"I don't think it matters anymore why I came along. Since I've been here I've turned into the person I risked it all trying to help. Sitting around this hell-hole all day like Keane cooped up in his bungalow, going out like him to walk down the street like a goddamn ghost."

He poured more Scotch and sat still. He seemed to want to blend into the premature darkness of the afternoon.

"Maybe you need to get out of here. It's just a drizzle out now, you could take your walk."

"Am I frightening you?" he asked.

"No." Once again she felt an impulse to fill the room with words, yet he seemed so near the edge of a darker mood, and she sensed he was on the verge of saying something she needed to hear.

"How can you help if it's not with the medicine? You're a druggist."

"What I was trained to do is no longer an option, thanks to him."

"So what are you now if you're not a druggist?"

"Someone who knows what's best for him. And what's best for you, too."

"What's best for me?"

"Leave here."

"I am leaving. Tomorrow, remember?"

"Tonight. Without him."

She felt duped. She felt as if the twists and asides of this entire conversation — everything worth remembering — had been erased and what remained was a calculated line ending in his last sentence. Everything was reduced to this advice, and it made her see the druggist in a harsh light she'd never allowed herself, a way that made her crave quiet and isolation.

"If you're not going for a walk, I am."

"I've hurt your feelings," he said, but she was already out of the door.

An hour later Deems came back, drunk and obviously upset — he threw his weight around the kitchen, sideswiping furniture and filling the room with heat, body odor and petulance. He seemed to want to provoke a fight, but when Roy failed to react he gave up and sat down at the table with a beer.

"Spent all the money you give me," he said.

"Fine," said Roy. He went back to his paper.

"She's asleep?"

"Went for a walk."

"How was it then, doc?"

"We missed you terribly."

They were quiet. After a minute Deems pulled a crumpled letter from a back pocket and tossed it onto the table.

"Groceryman give it to me. Another love letter."

The druggist lowered his paper to look. The envelope was fat and wet, the inked address had bled. He picked it up, weighed it in his palm.

"Maybe you ought to go out and try to find her," he told Deems. "She's been gone a long time. I told him I'd take care of her. Don't want her out walking the streets at midnight."

"I'll need some more cash," said Deems.

"She hasn't eaten. Take her somewhere to eat. Must be a diner still open out on the highway."

He papered one of Deems's palms with bills, dug deep in his pocket to fill the other with silver.

"In a generous mood, ain't you, doc?"

"Feeling selfless as always, Deems."

As soon as he heard Deems revving the Dodge on the street below, the druggist had the letter out of the envelope. Later he would wonder what he'd *expected* to find, but he was never able to focus for long on what had motivated him, so distracted was he by what he'd discovered: a way to see this thing through, a way to regain his dignity. When it came down to it, a reason to live.

14

Dear Eureka:

No introduction this time. You know what these letters are for, understand by now how much time they will save us. I'll start right where I left off: after Mattamuskeet.

Back at school I kept to myself, avoided everyone — even Thomasson, especially Sarah. I wouldn't take her calls, and I made excuses about how much schoolwork I had to do when she managed to get through. I was trying to break up with her, knew the more I saw of her the harder this would be.

Finally I finished exams, took off for Christmas break. At home I started going for long drives in the country. I must have driven every back road in Simpson County but mostly I'd take the same route every day, the road we took leaving town, through Serenitowinity. I'd never been out that way much before, if I had

334

I'd never really noticed it.

But during those weeks of aimless driving I happened on that road and was enchanted. The road ran high above the swamp; in places I could look down on the tops of small trees. There was no shoulder, just steep bank beyond the white line, so when I wanted to stop I just parked in the middle of the road. But it wasn't as magical a place when you weren't moving through it. Driving, I saw black water sparkling in the moonlight. And the road was so smooth, so straight, I hardly had to drive at all. I was left alone to think, but this place affected my thinking in the way that early afternoon used to — stimulating but sort of eerie.

I took Sarah there one day. She called me up the night before and told me we'd been invited to a party at Betsy Rivenbark's daddy's house out on the river. She chastised me for ignoring her, told me everyone in town was talking about me, saying I'd been locked up in South Wing, the hospital for loonies in Chapel Hill, all semester. I didn't give a damn what they were saying, but I agreed to come by for her after lunch the next day. What was the point in putting it off any longer? The sooner I broke it off with her the sooner I could get back to living my life. But I dreaded it: I didn't sleep at all the night before and on the way over I stopped at Frank's Place across from the cotton mill and had a couple of beers. I suppose I needed to drink to break up with her. It seemed then to be the biggest decision I'd ever faced. In a confused, egomaniacal twenty-two-year-old way I figured breaking up with her would affect everything: interest rates, NATO, the food chain. I was certain it would separate me from my family forever. I didn't think they would ever look at me in the same way again, and to this day I don't think I overreacted. It would have devastated my mother. It might have been more traumatic to her than what happened instead.

What happened instead: we stopped at the state store for gin. Sarah got quickly tight, but the more she drank the more sober I felt. She told stories: who was seeing whom, what had happened at all the parties I'd missed. I passed the turnoff for the river and reached my network of secret roads. She talked, I drove, the roads worked their magic: I felt relaxed and a little numb. Sarah's voice sounded distant and what she said didn't touch me. It was like listening to a radio report of a storm in Kansas.

"Where are we?" she asked finally.

"Weren't we supposed to turn?"

I said I thought we'd ride around for a while. I told her I had these roads I liked to take, that I drove through there a lot those days, that it had a way of calming me, taking my mind off things.

Skipper says you've been acting strange lately, she said. Of course I don't believe all that about you trying to shoot him. But Skipper says ever since then you've been real moody.

"Have you been to Camp Tremont?" I asked her.

She looked at me for a second, then laughed. This laugh she was obviously sharing with someone else, only that someone else was not me. She bent over to light a cigarette, slowly drew in smoke, giggled. Put her hand on my shoulder as if to steady herself and blew a mouthful of smoke against the windshield.

"Camp Tremont is not a place, you silly. It's not a summer camp. It's a he. This friend of Skip's."

"I know," I told her. "I met him."

"At the hunt, right? Why ask something so crazy, then?"

I couldn't answer her, could not tell her that in my mind the idea of Camp Tremont had broadened to include all categories of

337

nouns — person, place, thing; that Tremont was a person and a thing and he might as well be a place, since he'd come to cover the world; that it was true what he said that day at Mattamuskeet: wherever he happened to be was Camp Tremont, and he happened to be everywhere I went.

"You hate him, don't you?"

I didn't say anything.

"Why do you hate him so much, Edwin? You hardly know him. What could you possibly find to hate?"

"Well," I said. "He seemed . . ."

But after these two tentative words I shut up. *Seemed, hell,* I thought even as I said this, he didn't *seem* any goddamn thing, either he was or wasn't. I decided to take it slow. I wasn't in any hurry, and I realized that if ever there was a time to treat words with respect, this was it.

There were hundreds of things I could say about Tremont in answer to her question. I tried hard to narrow it down, to find the one thing I objected to the most. I sensed that I had to strike a valid, unquestionable nerve. Sarah, like my mother, was prone to dismissing people due to the slightest distinctions: because the chairs in their living room didn't go with the rug, because they drove their maids home themselves instead of calling a cab, because they arrived at church too early or too late or only came Christmas and Easter. To criticize Tremont on moral grounds was not only dangerous but unheard of. I wanted to point out to her all the things that mattered to me the most. I wanted to point out the things about Camp — about all of us, myself included — that bothered me the most.

But if I told Sarah all this she'd have sighed and started in on what she called the "chip on my shoulder." Like my mother, she was convinced that I had an inferiority complex — that if and when I pointed out all the arrogance, greed, ignorance and cowardice of the people around me, what I was really saying was that I felt they were better than me. You've got to learn that you're just as good as they are, she used to always say.

I still hadn't finished my sentence. Both of us had been silent since I'd started it, yet the sentence still hung about in the air. I felt the need to finish it, even though I had the feeling that not only whatever I said would be rejected but that I would be rejected, too.

I realized then — and you must have realized this yourself by now — how little this had to do with Camp Tremont. The sentence might have started out about him, but if I finished it it would be summing up everything I hated about my life and was too chicken to change. And Sarah's asking me about Tremont, about why I hated him, had nothing to do with him either. What she was really asking was, what's so wrong with the way we live? And what have you got to offer me that's any more honest and noble?

The car had filled with smoke and I cracked a window. Once outside, her smoke joined the mist that rose from the swamp, a thick fog moving in low, hugging the road. She sat there, silent, sipping gin, waiting for my answer.

Soon the calm of Serenitowinity began to fade and unlike the morphine there was no druggist to call for a refill. I tried to find the words but couldn't. The swamp struggled up, the words came, the tug of war weakened and confused me.

I thought then of Mattamuskeet, where I had been spared at the last moment. It was easy to believe that it will happen again, but what could have possibly been the equivalent, on a shoulderless road running through a swamp, of the vine across the path? I didn't waste time worrying. Couldn't intervention take any of a thou-

340

sand forms? And wouldn't most of those forms seem improbable — even impossible — if considered beforehand?

No, I didn't worry about how it would come. I just convinced myself that somehow it would come, that somehow I would be saved, as I jerked the wheel sharply to the right.

Trust me.

We'll talk soon.

Love,
Edwin

On the threshold of the bungalow Eureka froze, paralyzed by the stale air rolling out of the kitchen door like flames.

"What is it?" asked Edwin. He bumped against her, stooped under the load of suitcases.

Heat and moldy dark and ancient air, she thought, the same old air trapped here for weeks. She thought of things breeding in isolation while they were gone, like moths shut up in a closet.

Another sign that they never should have come back. They'd been sitting around the apartment when Edwin had shown up, pounding on the door and pushing past Deems to lift her off the linoleum with a hug that came close to rupturing things. The druggist was the only one in the room who had not been caught up in the swirl of the moment, had not once smiled; he had a game of solitaire going and after a brief look Edwin's way had returned to his cards. When they sat down to supper — steaks pan-fried by Deems and new potatoes boiled in his special bubbly mix of salt, onion, beer and tapwater — the druggist finally spoke to Edwin.

"Why did you waste money on a cab when you have a driver sitting around waiting for your call?"

"Thought I'd surprise you, Roy."

"We were packed and ready to go. She told us that we were to pick you up at the hospital and head out of town from there."

"I take it you're tired of Lexington?"

"Been tired," said Deems.

"What about you?" Edwin asked her. "Are you ready to leave, too?"

"Yes," she said.

"Plain and simple's what I mean," said Deems. He leaned across to Edwin. "Cat's got her tongue since you been back, boss."

"Okay. We'll take off in the morning. Hell, we can leave tonight for all I care."

"One question," said the druggist. "Where are we going?"

"You wanted a lift to Michigan, right? I

think we can manage. What about it, Deems? Think you can get us through downtown Detroit?"

"Motor City ain't got nothing I can't handle."

"Actually, I was thinking of heading in the other direction," said Roy.

"Florida?" asked Edwin. "Texas? You do look like you could use some sunshine."

"Trent," said the druggist.

"There's a Trent in Texas," said Deems. "Learned about it in school. Also they's a Trent in O-hiya and one in Wessconsun."

"*Our* Trent," said the druggist. He spoke to her, not to Edwin, as if Edwin came from one of those Trents Deems had named.

"We left town in a hurry to say the least. I need to get my affairs in order before I leave for good."

"You have affairs, doc?" asked Deems.

"Why can't we just put him on a bus?" Eureka said. She returned the thin smile the druggist leveled at her, frozen as if both were finalists in the penultimate moment of a beauty pageant.

"That would be horribly rude, wouldn't it, Deems?"

"Horribly." Deems swept his beer off the table and lifted it as he spoke, his pinky raised in a mockery which Edwin ignored.

"We'll give you a lift, Roy."

Later Edwin yanked the covers over their heads and whispered, "What's going on between you and the druggist?"

"He likes to tell people what's good for them."

"Don't I know it," said Edwin, laughing. "According to the expert, what's good for you?"

"Not you."

"He tell you to leave me?"

"More than once."

"But you didn't. You stayed, and I'm glad." In the low white tent he pulled her to him with strength noticeably renewed, spoke so close to her ear that his words rustled inside. "I'm glad you're here and I'm glad I came here. Just to be able to write those letters — God, at home, in the shape I was in? It would have taken months to get all that down."

"About that last letter . . ."

"Sssssshhh. Later. Let's finish with the druggist first. We'll take him back to Trent. We owe him that. If it weren't for him I'd never have come here, and there's no way we could have gotten out of Trent with me in the shape I was in."

"What does all that matter if we're going back now?" She turned away from him, drew the pillow to her chest. "I don't want to go back. No telling what my daddy will do when he finds out."

"We won't be there long enough for him to do anything. It makes sense, actually. We don't need Deems anymore. He's in the way. Also we might not be back for a long time. Don't you want to see your little brother before we go?"

"Of course I do, but I won't. It'll just make things worse for him and me."

"You want to take him with us?"

"It wouldn't work, having him tag along. Be like I was at home still. No, he'll get out on his own soon enough if I just let him alone."

So she'd resigned herself to coming back, though he'd promised it would not be for long.

In the kitchen he opened the window facing the wood, noises from Johnsontown whirlpooling in the shadowed corners. He crossed the room and wedged her against the counter, then led her into a front dusty bedroom she'd never seen, a room across from the parlor with two high windows facing Edgecombe, a double bed pushed against the window. Far cry from the kitchen cot, she thought.

Lying there, she pondered his letter. She wanted not to think about it, which had been easy enough during the last few days since they'd either been in the car with Deems or the druggist or stumbling into motel rooms stiff and sullen after sixteen hours in the back of the Dodge. Speeding east through hours and towns, her thoughts had rushed past as quick and unfocused as the roadside. We'll talk soon, he'd said in the letter. This seemed their first real chance, no druggist or Deems in the way. But instead of initiating the conversation he initiated instead the breaking in of the double bed.

They drifted off with the lights still on; mid-morning he woke her with his tongue. She had only a flicker of remembrance — *we are supposed to talk* — before she realized that she'd found a way to clear the clot from her mind. He was ready always and was damned good as far as she knew, which was not that far but she felt strongly, despite her lack of experience, that one knows these things, that knowledge rises up from blood, bone and flesh to signal fair, better, just plain bad.

Between kisses he spoke of the future. It was hard to pay attention with his hands sculpting the slope between rib and hip, but she caught snatches: where they'd settle when soon they left town again, somewhere swept sparse by frozen breezes, the opposite of this sunken green world where everything became tangled and where nothing — not people, not the unbearable sun, not the tendrils of plants — could stay put, leave you alone. He talked about her finishing school and going on to college if she wanted. He talked about a wedding, a small one with just one witness, Randall maybe.

She was glad when the plans trailed off and in a good-natured reenactment of that night in the cabin he mumbled something about metaphor and pushed her hand across his stomach, pleading with her in a hokey voice to grasp what he pronounced proof of our success. And she grasped willingly, surrendered willfully to what followed, which lasted for hours, three days finally in the double bed during which she had no worries, during which what she did with her body purged her thoughts until her mind felt empty, cleansed, cleaner than sleep or even death could be.

No one in the drugstore saw Roy enter through the back door. He stood unnoticed in the dark corridor by the basement, watching the sunlight settling on the diamond tiles and thinking of a time when he was young. Riding around Ypsilanti on a wintry Sunday with his mother: they'd driven three times past the house where they'd lived until six months before, when the bank had foreclosed and they'd been forced into a boxy two-room apartment above an appliance store. On the fourth pass his mother turned into the drive. She grabbed his hand and pulled him up to the door where they were greeted by the new owners, a snotty young loan officer and his bank teller wife who treated them as if they'd come to her barred window with no more business than a greasy bill to be broken. His mother spoke to the couple in a voice so thickly solicitous that even at his age Roy understood she was being patronizing. His name was mentioned but he paid no attention to things not eye-level, like the rungs of stools and the thatched speakers of a radio console. His mother held his hand and began to pull him through rooms which seemed to him all wrong, rooms remembered with the intense and visceral familiarity with which an eight-year-old remembers carpets, wallpaper designs, the bristly weave of a horsehair sofa.

But the carpets were gone and the walls were wainscoted and painted beige and the coat closet where he'd spent so many winter mornings wedged between a box emblazoned with a lion's head and the carpeted stomach of a vacuum cleaner bloated with dust, lint and pennies was part of a vestibule now. In this vestibule the expensive toys of another child were strewn.

At first he was traumatized: how dare they rearrange a space which held such significance, it was like knocking out a wall in a room in his mind where the most sacred memories were contained . . .

And then he realized that if anyone was at fault it was he and his mother, that they had no right to be there. From that point on it was he who led his mother through the house.

Going back had been a mistake. Remembering that day now, Roy decided to leave the drugstore but just as he was turning to go Ruby McClaurin spotted him on her way to the basement, and said in a voice loud enough to carry up the aisle to where Lehmann stood: "Well, will you look here?"

"Hi, Ruby."

"Back visiting?" As she drew closer he felt her nervousness — she avoided his eyes and stopped a few feet away. Ruby who used to hug him after a half-day off, whom he once knew well enough to ask about her sister's affair with a Rocky Mount doctor, her brother's bad drinking.

Roy smiled weakly, thinking it's too late now, I'm stuck, because at the top of the aisle Lehmann was making his way toward them with a grave look on his face.

"Just thought I'd stop by, say hey."

"Real nice to see you, Roy," said Ruby. She squeezed past, opened the door to the basement, descended into darkness. Halfway down the stairway he heard her jerk the string to the light switch and he remembered how much he loved that about trips to the basement, how instinctively he used to reach overhead above the fourth step, search out the string with a sweep of his hand. The way it danced above his head, the beaded cord jangling against the fixture, came back to him. Lehmann was almost upon him now; with a final summons of nerve he decided to do what he'd come to do, maybe.

"Green, how you getting along?"

Roy took the hand offered him but was embarrassed by Lehmann's arthritic grip and pulled away too soon, too roughly. Lehmann asked if he was on his way out of town.

"Haven't decided what I'm going to do yet." Why doesn't he take me up to his office? But he couldn't suggest it, and he realized he'd fallen back into his pattern, second-guessing everything Lehmann said or did, finding fault. Like visiting family, he thought, even after years away you take up where you left off, years of willful change rendered void when you walk back in that den, among them again.

"Plans not finalized yet?" asked Lehmann.

"I've got a little money saved." *No thanks to you, Keane paid me more a week to slurp Scotch and read box scores than I made here in a month.* "Don't want to do anything rash."

"No," said Lehmann. "Listen, about this thing you've done for that boy, taking him up to that hospital . . ."

I wonder if he knows about the girl, thought Roy, if the whole town knows, if they think we took her along like a party favor, took turns with her or what. He thought of what her life would be like if she stayed here, thought of how little he cared about Keane anymore, how she had become the one he had to save.

"I want to commend you . . . ," Lehmann was saying.

Even if Lehmann knew about the girl he'd say nothing, seeing as how it was connected with the desires of a Keane.

". . . chance to make something of himself again. I know he's got it in him, got plenty potential, they say he's just as damn smart's he can be."

Why should I give a damn what he knows, or what any of them think, *I could stay in this town until I die but I will never live here again.*

"I owe you an apology," said Lehmann. "It's a fine thing you done, and I'll admit I was wrong letting you go. I realized how wrong I'd been that night you came here and filled his prescription so I wouldn't get in trouble over it. Lots have asked after you, Roy.

Acted ill with me when they found out you were gone. You got yourself a following around here."

"I guess I listened to their problems."

"This new boy ain't much of a listener," said Lehmann, nodding toward the drug counter. Roy held back this rough mix he felt: of pride, a dull but palpable edge of competitiveness, boredom with this whole slow scene. It was going blandly well, as if he'd written the script then read over it too many times.

"I'd love to have you back with us, Roy."

"You've got enough business for two druggists?"

"Well, you know these boys coming out of pharmacy school nowadays all want to get on with one of these chains. I don't think he's going to be real happy here in Trent, tell the truth. Besides like I said, he's not so good with people and if you can't talk to a man it don't make a damn what line of business you're in, you're —"

"Wouldn't feel right taking his job. First job he's had, straight out of college, right?"

Lehmann leaned forward and said through an oily smile, "That's working for us instead of against, Roy. He's young, he'll bounce back, probably get on with Rexall or Mutual up in Raleigh and we'll be doing him a favor by letting him go."

"Something tells me that he wouldn't see it exactly that way."

"Way I see it's this: you've got both feet in this town. You know the people, you're established here. You're at an age where setting up all over and again someplace else is a tall order. That boy'll make do."

"As long as you think we're doing him a favor."

"Tomorrow morning then. Expect a raise. You're worth it."

"You mean the oil went right up inside of him?" asked Randall.

"Yes."

"And run through him like blood?"

"Yep."

"And that's how come he's so good at working on cars and driving them?"

Eureka nodded. She knew this story would delight him but couldn't be too distracted by Deems's wild fibs or Randall's enthusiasm for them. Earlier that afternoon she'd hidden in the alley and waited for him. She heard him before she saw him, heard the staccato click of the four of clubs he'd clothes-pinned against the spokes. He braked so hard when he saw her he skidded sideways across the pavement. He started to speak but she shushed him and said, "Episcopal church after work."

When he walked into the courtyard she hugged him, brushing back his cowlick, clamping his head against her breasts which she forgot were there but which he noticed; he tried to wriggle away but she held him tight, telling him he'd grown, that she missed him, bad.

Then she sat back down on the bench where she used to come in the late afternoons to do her lessons and he stood in front of her and talked. He took off his shirt to swat mosquitoes and she watched brown skin ripple over his ribs. He took big breaths and started stories that he was too excited to finish.

"Kentucky," he said. "Did anybody out there ask you about the ocean?"

"I made the sound of it for an old man who ran the grocery store where we went to buy stuff," she lied. She made up stories about the grocer she'd hardly spoken to, included details about his seven sons who worked in coal mines and who came to see him on Sundays, coughing and sputtering so much in the tiny apartment at the back of the house that the whole building shook. All seven had fingernails black as if they'd been painted, and one of them tried to date her, offering as enticement a look at his helmet with the flashlight mounted on top, the very thing he wore when he crawled around under the earth.

"He asked you about the ocean?"

She made the sound for him, a swirling crescendoed whistle. When he stepped forward out of the shadows to hear, she noticed the scar. She grabbed an arm, reined him in to the light.

"What happened?" she asked, tracing a circle around the bruise with her fingertip.

He told her that he'd fallen down the basement stairs.

"What were you doing down in the basement?"

When he didn't answer she said, "Did he tell you why he was going to beat you?"

"He won't going to beat me. He wanted me to help him bring up some kindling he had hid down there. Druggist got his old job back, today's his first day."

She knew he'd changed the subject to cover his lie but she was so stunned she fell silent. Though she rarely understood exactly why the druggist did what he did — she wasn't sure he understood it himself — this made the least sense of all.

Randall was talking. "Going away with him again?"

"You know the answer to that."

"Thought of a name for him yet?"

"He has a name."

"If you're going to live with him in that

house I'll paint it if he'll pay me."

Eureka burst out laughing, reached for his hands and pulled them taut, swung their arms back and forth. Lulled by the rhythm, both grew giddy. They had a history of such clumsy dance: during the farm days she used to put her hands on his shoulders and steer him through the fields, both heads bent low, Randall droning some wordless tune which mimicked their shuffle. Sometimes toward the end of their afternoon scouting trips they would trudge Siamese-twin-shouldered down the street, slanted into a roving triangle.

"What do you know about painting houses?"

"Hal'll help me. He quit the graveyard, he's painting houses now."

"I wouldn't want to be near a ladder Hal's on."

"Hal has to help Pa to bed nights now."

"Since when? Randall, how come?"

"Drunk."

"Worse than before?"

"Way worse," he said. He dug his heels into the dirt, threw his head back. Straining to support him, she leaned back on the bench and looked too. Clouds, shadows black against deepening blue, no stars. She imagined running into her father before they left town, pictured an awkward meeting on a deserted stretch of downtown sidewalk. Slight nods, averted eyes, no talk. Each quick sidestep a word, the scramble to avoid each other a dense, unintelligible sentence.

"What's he said about me leaving?" she asked.

"Martha told everybody you went up to Norfolk to work the shipyards. Said you ain't cut out to be a Rosy Rivet and that you'll be back soon and that you made a damn fool out of yourself running off with some sick rich boy and that down at the laundry your name's mud and the only one misses you is some colored girl named Rose."

"What else?" Not that she cared what Martha told anyone but it did distract her from the thought of Hal helping her father to bed.

"That no boy around here's going to touch you now with a ten-foot pole."

"Let's hope. I'm sure she had lots more to say which you can tell me later. Now tell me what Pa said about me leaving."

Randall wrenched his hands away and stepped back into shadows. "He hasn't said nothing."

"Does he know I'm back?"

Randall dropped to the ground, lay in the grass with his eyes shut, his body gone limber. For ten seconds he was still, then he shuddered once and contorted his limbs as if he'd fallen from the branches above.

"Randall?"

He didn't move. In the scant streetlight she saw his ribcage rise but he kept character even when she feigned a giggle, hoping her laugh would loosen one from him in turn.

When she prodded him with her foot he sat up and spat.

"Talk to me," she said.

"I don't know what it matters that he knows you're back if you're just going to go away again."

"It matters."

"Say his name," said Randall.

"Why?"

"Say it."

She shrugged. "Edwin."

He crossed his arms, half-satisfied.

"He's done bad things," she whispered.

"So?" said Randall.

"So don't you go telling it," she said, wondering why she'd mentioned it in the first place. She needed to tell *someone;* she'd thought of sneaking over to see Rose, but if she told Rose the truth, surely Rose would advise her to leave him. In the past she'd been scared to say too much to Randall, knew that her reserve was no match for his curiosity. Going away — even to Lexington — had changed that, made her both stubborn and secure.

"You mean like Hal's done bad things?"

"I mean worse."

"Did he do them to you?"

Her newfound resistance flagged. "No, he didn't do them to me."

"Well, did he say he's sorry?"

"I don't think it matters if he's sorry."

"It matters."

His certainty made her furious. "Don't act like such a brat," she said. "You don't know anything about this. There's lots you can't begin to understand."

He glared at her, then hunched over, grabbed his ankles and began to rock back and forth. He seemed sweaty and cross, the way she remembered feeling herself on summer nights in the country. During the last hours of light on those longest days their play had grown desperate and aggressive, as if they were trying to stave off both sundown and waves of a shared loneliness. Those nights had ended badly: Randall in tears when his intensity erupted finally in scratch or sprain, she sullen and jaded, angry at the coming dark.

She sensed a similar tension, only this was no game. No one was going to come out onto the porch and call them in for the night. Below her, Randall rocked, his eyes closed and his forehead resting on his kneecaps.

"Randall, talk."

To and fro he rocked, into, out of the light. *To* he was lit, *fro* shadowed; in the light his swollen cheekbone bulged and his bruise, sweat-glistened, shone purple. Silence from him now was maddening; it made her bones ache, made the shadows of the courtyard loom. She lowered herself from the bench and sat in front of him. A breeze sent down a shower of leaves which landed in the narrow space between them.

"Here, where's your shirt?" She found it balled up in the grass and handed it to him but he kept rocking, eyes open but thickly glazed. She draped his T-shirt across his back, then held his shoulders tight to still him. He shrugged her off and rocked even faster.

She began to cry. "Stop it," she said. "Talk to me."

When it came his voice seemed lower, older. "You left me here."

"I had to. You knew I would. We talked about it a hundred million times." She reached around to rub his face but in the dark she pressed hard in the center of the bruise which she realized, as he flinched, might as well have been raised by her own hand.

Randall bolted, throwing her to the ground. She looked up to see his heels scattering gravel, then lay back down in the grass to make promises: never to involve him again in what happened between herself and anyone else in the world, between herself and the world.

15

"You went with them, didn't you?"

His mouth stuffed with grilled cheese, Roy held up an index finger to Speight, signaling that he couldn't talk. Speight stood at the end of the aisle and stared while Roy chewed, swallowed, chased the slightly burnt and butter-drenched bread with a slug of cola.

"I went, but it wasn't like you think."

Speight had grown more haggard in the few weeks since he'd seen him. Skin stretched thin over his bones and veins, faint black goggles of fatigue circled his eyes.

"What are you doing back here?"

"They gave me a lift. I was planning on heading to Michigan but I decided while I was there that this is where I belong, at least for now." Roy dabbed his lips with a napkin. "Unfinished business."

"What does he want with her?"

"He told me he plans to marry her but you and I know it'll never happen. Not considering who he is."

"*How* he is."

"You know, then."

"I didn't wonder it was castor oil he used to call up here begging."

"I know of a way you can get her back."

Speight looked up the aisle toward the sunlit street. "I can't get her back now."

"Away from him, then."

Speight said nothing. His silence made Roy feel like an overeager salesman.

"Just by making a few deliveries."

"You must have me mixed up with my boy," said Speight. "He's the one delivers."

"Randall will have to help. But I need you to talk to him."

"Randall's smart," said Speight, and Roy paid close attention, it wasn't like Speight to digress. "Her and Randall are just as smart as any in this town. She don't talk half as much as he does but she's damn smart."

"I know. That's part of the reason why I'm back here trying to help."

"Because you want the same thing he wants? And you come to me to help?"

"I'm not interested in that." Roy had expected this response and felt relieved, as if he was on track.

"How come you want to help, then?"

Roy was quiet, thinking of all the times he'd heard Edwin or his mother on the phone, the tens of times Lehmann had acquiesced. *Be-*

cause I hear voices, he wanted to say. Why does anyone do anything? *Because low voices give tall orders.* But he knew how risky it was to talk about the voices one hears, and didn't want Speight to think he was anything less than lucid.

Besides, it had grown so much larger now, larger and more complicated than those earliest feelings of impotence and rage. There was a part of Edwin's letter that had stayed with him since he'd read it. A line about him not being able to finish his sentence, this sentence summing up everything he hated about his life but was afraid to admit. Roy realized that the way he felt about things — Keane, his job at the drugstore, life in Trent — sounded much like Edwin's disgust for his own life. When the letter ended up in his hands (he wasn't big on miracles, it wasn't luck which led him to intercept it) it became clear that he had inherited Edwin's sentence. Now it was his duty to finish it for both of them.

But Speight didn't need to know all this. Speight had his own reasons, simpler ones involving a stray daughter and a kind of honor that Roy could care less about, though he'd play up to it if it would help see things through.

"She's young," he said. "Smart, hell yes, she's smart, a lot smarter than she lets on.

But inexperienced. She's at a tough age, doesn't see things clearly always. Doesn't see him for what he is. I just want to save her time. I like your daughter a lot, Speight. I respect her. But I swear to you it doesn't go any further than that. It's just that I happen to be in the position where I can save her some time."

"How is it you think you can get her to leave him?"

"Just by making a few deliveries."

"I take it this ain't legal."

"As legal as three-quarters of the deliveries we ever made to him."

Speight said, "I don't think we ought to involve the boy."

"Impossible without him, I'm afraid."

"Why can't I deliver it?"

"You said it yourself: Randall delivers, you clean up. If all of a sudden I start sending you out on deliveries, Lehmann would notice."

"Seems like you could take care of Lehmann since he fired that boy to hire you back."

"He hired me back because I needed work." This was true, thought Roy, I needed work badly, not only to live off of but to justify living. Yet my work these days has nothing to do with answering the telephone or counting pills. "Lehmann won't give us any trouble.

365

Since I've been back, he's stayed out of the way. He's taking the whole day off today, which Ruby said he hasn't done since I left."

"It's not Randall's business. I don't believe in using him to do things he don't understand. Besides, those two are real close. He couldn't keep a thing from her for a minute."

"I find it hard to believe that he'd want her to throw her future away for a few months with a man who has no respect for himself, much less her. Sit the boy down and talk to him. Haven't you talked to him about her since she left?"

"It ain't my way to talk my problems over with eleven-year-olds."

"He's not your typical eleven," said Roy. "Look, we don't have a lot of time here. Keane claims they're leaving again, that he just came back here to drop me off and tie up some loose ends. They may be planning to leave today for all I know. Your daughter's not fond of Trent. She won't stay here any longer than she has to."

"What about him? He hates it, too?"

"He loves her, or claims to. He's promised to take her away, and she'll hold him to it."

"Or go without him."

"What's that?"

"If you got a way to keep him here, she'll leave on her own, without me having to get

366

messed up in it."

Roy smiled. He thought it was settled and was reaching for his sandwich when Speight spoke.

"If we use the boy you got to promise he can't get in any trouble."

"What trouble?"

"I know how people sometimes'll get a child to do something a court won't hold them responsible for. If that's what you're up to she's better off where she's at."

"I already told you, Speight. What I'm going to do is as legal as anything we've done here before."

"That don't sound like much of a promise."

"He won't get in any trouble," said Roy. "Think I'd sacrifice one of your children to free the other?"

"I think two things," said Speight. "One's that you talk a lot smoother than you did before you went off with them. Used to I could listen to what you said and not have to worry about what you didn't. Other thing is that I don't have a lot of choice here. Short of going over there and shooting him, which I don't even own a gun what works anymore, I don't have any other way of getting her back."

"Then you do want her back?"

Speight looked up the aisle again, as if gleaning answers from the daylight playing across the plateglass. "She'll be leaving anyway. I want her away from him."

"So you'll talk to Randall?"

Speight's black eyes found his and held them, and Roy remembered the time not long ago when Speight had stood in the same place and they'd talked about the boy coming to work. He'd hardly used his eyes then, had trained them on his shoes or let them rove in search of Lehmann.

"You ever talked to that boy?" he said.

Roy smiled, was about to say *of course I've talked to him, plenty of times and every time a pleasure. I'm sure Randall will want to help* when the bells above the back door rang and both men turned to watch Randall streak past them up the aisle. At the soda fountain he climbed atop a stool and spun himself around in wobbly circles, pushing off the counter while Ruby fixed him a cherry smash. Spinning wildly through the still-life drugstore afternoon, Randall seemed both younger than his age and vulnerable, an impression not lost on his father who said nothing but turned back with a look that drew a promise from the druggist.

To Randall only a few places left were any good. So many more ruined, like the courtyard where the last time he'd seen her they had quarreled. He had left there running, hot and itchy, a child. He couldn't go back there ever.

Nor to the warehouse, the abandoned one on the outskirts by the train tracks where they'd spent that afternoon in the storm. He'd returned once; someone had padlocked the doors. He found a broken window in the office and climbed in. He tried to think of that afternoon, for he had remembered it fondly always, even though Eureka seemed to lapse in and out of melancholy spells and the way she'd talked to him had made him feel uncomfortably adult. But there was no trace of that afternoon. As his eyes adjusted to the shadows, rustlings in the corners became rats. In the office he discovered a stack of musty green ledgers and after examining the tiny figures in the columns for mistakes he tore out pages by the handful, carpeted the floor and left.

He needed a place not ruined. Walking home from work his father had said: "Saturday we're taking off at lunch and me and you will go somewhere. To one of those places you used to tell me about."

"Where?" He'd not been anywhere with his father alone, besides work, since the farm.

"Your pick," his father said. "One of your special places."

"What are we going to do?"

"Just talk," his father said. "We'll carry something to eat."

He thought of the farm, but they could never make it out there and back on a half Saturday. And he'd promised himself he would not go back there until he was twenty. It had to do with memory: he knew, or thought so, each square yard and was easily able to call up, say, the first crook of the branch below the tobacco barn. He wanted to see how long he could remember, how much it might change.

Finally he thought of the river. He was always being sent there for reasons unknown to him, and while there was uncertain about what to do. Trips to the river were exiles into "free" time. Randall preferred work; he resented being ordered to "go play." The river became a blindspot in the minds of adults he knew, a place where they felt he would be free from their intrigue.

Nothing much changed there: the bank beneath a tupelo might wash away, leaving a ribcage of roots where captured trash would spin and bob. Or a breeze would loosen a strand of moss from a cypress branch, breaking up the line for the rope swing as the boys dived for it; whoever recovered it from the current would wear it on his next turn, a limp tress departing in midair. Otherwise stillness:

a rockless river, the scrub on its banks hunkered motionless in the heat, its flow checked by felled trees and frequent bends. Randall understood how they might see it as some kind of sanctuary, although he detested being banished. But it wasn't ruined, like the courtyard or the warehouse, nor was he saving it like the farm. And if it was one-half the sanctuary that the druggist seemed to think, it would be the perfect place to go on Saturday. With all its mystery, the river was the opposite of the basement, where they'd always gone for a reason.

Speight saved it while they walked through downtown and on through the crust of Johnsontown, saved it as they passed the first of the big houses, ones with pontoon docks and boathouses, gazebos and gates of varnished wrought iron. He was silent, saving it, when the river veered finally into sight, merging with the namesake road.

Another mile of quiet, the river invisible behind the high boxwoods of the estates. The boy was silent, too — had been all morning. He'd seemed anxious at work. There were no deliveries so he'd helped Speight with the sweeping up. The pushbroom was too big for him; he gripped it crosshanded, the handle high above his head, and leaned into the sweep, as if the faster he herded the green flank of dustdown up the aisles the quicker noon would come.

The path they took wound through thickets of sumac and blackberry. Midway to the river they stopped to pick berries. Noon sun reached them when the clouds shifted. Speight stripped his shirt off and laid it across a bush. When the sun disappeared he plucked up his shirt; the bush twitched and sprung skywards.

They ate, their fingers stained purple.

Speight said, "We got dinner, too. Ham biscuits so don't get full."

Randall wandered off. Speight followed, thinking it's time, now is the time. But he couldn't get started. It makes it harder when you've thought a lot about what you're going to say, he decided. They reached the river. Randall chose a low trail beaten clean by fishermen. Speight followed, struggling with those first words.

They came across a group of boys lined up for a ropeswing on the far bank, scrunched together in a tangle of elbows, ribs, kneecaps blackened by scabs and mud. Speight watched them shiver. The creak of the limb faded around the next bend and it was quiet. The trail thinned, then disappeared beneath damp ferns. In the middle of the river bars of ribbed sand funneled the current into a trickle.

They came to a clearing in the woods where the skeleton of a cabin loomed beneath honeysuckle.

"This it?" asked Speight.

Randall sat down on the ruined foundation and nodded yes. Speight pulled biscuits from the soiled bag. He'd asked for ham and Martha had packed sidemeat but even the thick fat tasted good after the long walk. Sometimes screams and clumsy curses drifted down from the ropeswing but mostly there was silence while they ate.

Speight, pointing, said, "There's a lizard."

Randall looked but said nothing, chewing hard.

Those first words still lodged tight. Speight wondered if he'd saved them for too long, gone over them too many times.

"Steamboats used to come up the river from Wilmington. But not this far."

Randall nodded.

Speight felt flushed. He imagined himself walking home at dusk, a sullen Randall following, an unpleasant afternoon of silence separating them. At home he would drink twice as much as usual.

"Man out west got struck by lightning three times," he said.

"Who said?" asked Randall.

"I heard about it."

"He's still alive?"

Speight chewed furiously and swallowed. "The first time was in the fields. The man had gone up on a rise after supper to check on his crops. They were a week or two from being ready. Wheat I believe they said it was. The sky got black but he was thinking about money and didn't pay no attention. But soon he noticed, whenever the rumbling started. He thought he saw a funnel but it won't anything but thunderheads gathering. Eyes playing tricks. Still he was scared. It looked black enough for hail and he had a lot to lose to a hailstorm. He climbed up on back of his wagon to see better. They say his wife was looking out the window and seen the lightning playing down him like he was a chimney. The hail started right after. She sent her oldest boy out after him and the boy found him stretched out in the back of the wagon with his arms folded across his chest like somebody had laid him out in his coffin. Still coming down hard when he drove up in the yard but the boy's grief was such that you could pick out the tears from rain on his cheeks. His tears were bigger and muddy-colored, like he was crying up blood. The mother came up slow but the daughters run out screaming, falling all down in the puddles, stepping 'cross each other. Just then the man started to shake. They carried

374

him inside. He shivered for two hours and then went to sleep. When he woke his right leg wouldn't work but other than that he was fine."

"And the wheat was okay?"

"Fine," said Speight.

"Sacrifice," said Randall. "But he got struck again?"

"Two more agains," said Speight. "This man was a good man overall but he had his streak, like us all. His particular streak won't all that special or odd: he liked young women. He would get to drinking and want to go out to places like they have over in Johnsontown that your brother's favoring now. After he'd drunk a good amount he'd go back in his head to an age where he was taking several women around and had several more interested. Or so he thought. And when he'd get to that point with his drinking he would forget that he was married to a good woman and had three boys and four girls and he'd think it won't fair how certain things seemed closed to him and he'd wonder how come he couldn't go back to having strange women wanting him."

Speight stopped suddenly and said, "Don't you tell your sisters this. This ain't meant for them."

"I won't."

"One night the man was out in the barn

drinking and he reached that point in his bottle and so he climbed in his truck to head to a joint in town where they had some dancing. His wife saw the lights of his truck as they swung by the kitchen window and she ran out in the yard and asked him please not to go nowhere. It was late and raining hard and he had work to do the next day and she knew him well when he was drunk, knew him even better on the day after. But he just laughed and to convince her things were fine he pushed open the door and tried to pull her up in the cab with him. She shook him loose and went inside, on to bed.

"At this juke joint he drunk some more and went even further back in time. In his head he was nineteen and beating the girls off with a hoe handle. Which never was the way it was with him but the liquor he was drinking didn't know that. Most of the girls had come with dates their own age but because he won't a bad looking fifty he managed to find one girl to dance with him. And after a while he got her to come on out to his truck for a drink."

Speight stopped again. "You're ten now, is that right?"

Randall nodded, remembering the last time his father had guessed at his age, the flattery he felt when he got it right, what had followed.

Ten was close enough.

"Then you know all about this mess?"

The nod again. He'd heard about it at school but the version offered was without charm or pleasure, something done in haste in a bed of pine needles.

"So he started up with this gal but she said she won't going to put out in no parking lot so he drove her to a spot he knew. It was still pouring and the road was muddy and when they got down in the woods good they got stuck. He tried again with this girl, but she said she won't about to put out in no marooned vehicle. She said that getting out in the driving rain to push his truck out the mud won't exactly her idea to wrap up a night of romantic love. So he started toward some lights he seen through the trees, cussing himself and laughing and stumbling and saying over and over and over, a night of romantic love, a night of romantic love."

"That was the number two time," said Speight.

"Got struck then and there?"

"Farmer found him the next morning."

"Get caught with the young girl?"

"She got tired of waiting and walked her wet ass home."

"Hurt bad this time?"

"Blinded in his left eye. Patch of hair above

377

his ear didn't never grow back. Claimed to have lost all memory of what he was doing back down in them woods."

"Punishment," Randall said. "Then what?"

But Speight didn't answer, he wasn't listening. Spoil the boy not with toys nor candy but with stories. And he was not bad at it — did it without even thinking. Of course he had heard a story like this before, but it had happened in Tidewater and the particulars were long forgotten. Still, he must have had it in him always, this trait which had bloomed so prodigiously in his son, and not even known it. As thrilling as it was it also terrified him, this sudden glibness; he must try harder, think better, because the boy had more experience than he did.

Then what? Speight thought of all the times he'd heard this phrase coming from the boy, how few times it had been asked of him. They were beautiful words, they made him feel powerful. Down here by the river nothing moved except waterbugs and the boy's blinking eyelids. He held his breath, withheld his words, teasing his audience which now included everything, animate and inanimate, in his field of vision.

Then what? He'd just start talking again, open his mouth and a third and final bolt of lightning would emerge. But would it strike in the right place? He remembered his purpose. These stories carry responsibility, and so far it's been idle chatter, yammering on in vain. I must make it fit, he thought, to make him see.

"Then number three. A long time passed. Years. There were storms summer and fall but our man weathered them without trouble. Sometimes he'd set out on purpose during a blow to see if he'd get struck for no reason — not that he thought he'd been hit those first two times for any one reason but being outside when he shouldn't and not having an extra supply of what they call luck."

"But there were reasons," said Randall. "The first time was sacrifice, the second was punishment."

"I don't know about any of that. Hush now and listen. People pointed him out on the street. He had some age on him now and his injuries had got worse with time: he limped from where the second bolt left out through his toes, his bald spot was sunburnt and scaly in the heat, he took to wearing a black patch over his bad eye.

"People called him freak.

"His wife was devoted to the Lord first and second to her children; what little she had left over he got, which was watered down. She saw to it that he kept working as much as he could but usually she didn't think much about him like I said, just checked after him like he was clothes hanging on a line out the kitchen window, touched him on occasion to see was he dry.

"But people stopped his children in the street to ask questions. His boys learned to fight or to make fun of him whichever mood they were in but his girls were ashamed. He had one girl who was his favorite. This happens even when you fight it, even if you kick and scream against it it'll happen. You think because you seen them all when they were six minutes into the world and you remember how they look, wrapped-tight red things that sleep all day — you think because they come to you the same sleepy wrinkled way there's no difference between them and no difference in you either, you think they're equal and that your thinking of them will continue to grow along the same lines. Then one'll come along that you want to look at more and at first it's just a watching out the corner of an eye, never a stare or a I-can't-take-my-eyes-off-of-it or a all-out smile. Just a fuzzy picture that stays with you when you close your eyes, a ghost you carry around with you because you spend so much time trying not to look at it or think about it.

"But whenever you go turning things into

shadows you're in trouble. He tried to deny that he cared more, he tried to figure just what was it about her, he told himself once it was because she looked like his mother, he told himself next time it was due to her not resembling anyone he'd ever seen. Finally he gave up giving a damn why.

"She reached that boy stage. He'd never thought much about it with the other girls, because they were both scared and ashamed they run off with the first thing that come halfway up the drive and he didn't think there was much he could do. But with her, she didn't bite the first hook, she let so many pass they started coming in from the next county. Finally one come by she asked back. He came back three times before our man got worried. He was from a town twenty miles west, his father owned a feed store and a movie house, there was rumored a lot of land and a lot of money and there was a attitude. The fourth time he showed up in a Model A car. He highstepped through the yard in his waxed oxfords and his slick hair shined in the sun. Our man watched him from the shed near the creek. This boy pounded on the door for five minutes until he saw old dad down there and he strutted over slow, hands in his back pockets.

" 'They tell me you been struck by lightning twice,' he said.

"Our man didn't say nothing.

" 'Reckon you'll get struck again?'

"Old dad made like he was working on something, kept quiet. When the girl came around the side of the house they went off together into the field holding hands, the boy still laughing his smart-aleck laugh, the girl giggling, both of them twisting back to see him before they disappeared into the corn.

"It got late in the day and they didn't come out.

"Soon blew up a good one, black all the way to the ground for miles and the corn rattling and bent over. Our man sat down under the shed and lit a cigarette."

"He didn't go in after her?"

"Shut up," said Speight. "The thunder started breaking and it was the long drawed-out kind like the sky had something caught in its throat and couldn't clear it. At first the lightning was far away and straight, not the kind our man knew as the worst but quick little lines sent down to burn a hole in the wheat fields or take off the top branch of a tree. But then the other kind started, the leggy kind that reminded our man of the veins up under his eyelids when he shut them loose and looked up at the sun. He jumped up then and started into the field, big drops soaking him, so much so quick the furrows flowed like creeks, him gumming up in the new mud, the lightning coming closer, branching all out. Finally he seen a flash of blue between rows: the boy's blazer. He pushed through to find them wrapped around each other scared to move, clothes so soaked they was see-through, drooping off them so slack their bodies looked stretched. Both of them so scared they stared at him five seconds before they moved or spoke.

"Then that boy said, 'Hallelujah, the human lightning rod!'

"Our man had words ready for this boy he hated but they were lost in the corn as he flew backwards through the field, landing in a flooded furrow. He raised his head to breathe and when he did he shook himself and saw he was just sore, nothing broken, no burns. He stood and started to run only he didn't know which way he'd come from, which way they were, he was lost and dizzy when he come up on a clearing that won't there before, a perfect circle with the dirt smoothed out around it like a place he'd been taken to in the woods called the devil's tromping ground. They were lying in the center and their clothes had been burned off but pieces of rag was plastered to their skin like bandages, along with mud and small pieces of cornstalk. It was like the lightning had soldered them together."

Speight breathed heavily, his lungs sucked dry. "That was number three," he said.

"But you said *he* got struck three times," said Randall.

"He did, boy. That was the one he never did recover from."

Randall was silent for a moment, then said, "What was that one about, do you think?"

Depleted, Speight craved quiet now. "I don't know anything about lightning. Don't know what causes it."

"No, I mean how come he got struck that time?"

"I don't know how come he got struck any of those times."

"But I said already. It's simple. First time he sacrificed himself so the hail wouldn't ruin his crop, so his family wouldn't starve. Second time he was being punished because he was out with that girl. Third time he won't even struck, but you told it anyway, so I guess I'd have to say it was both. Sacrifice and punishment."

Speight winced. He'd started talking to get the boy's attention, kept talking because he couldn't quit. He'd begun his story aimlessly without knowledge of the next word, much less the next tale. Halfway through he'd felt the need to make a point, to tie things together, and now it seemed his design had done nothing more than create the need for these two big words.

"How come both?"

"Sacrifice because he went out there after her. Punishment because he went out there after her."

He could be right, Speight thought. There was a falseness to his own intervention in this affair, something deeply disturbing about it that he struggled to deny. Families seemed to him like farms — you try to keep them going, growing, if not profitable then at least above bankruptcy. Yet ultimately it was out of your hands, up to whim and wind, whatever the breeze blew by like this sickly rich boy of Eureka's. To tamper seemed almost a sacrilege. He used to feel guilty when clearing land, not even for the first time — he felt a tinge of resistance when he readied a field which had lain fallow, clearing a year's growth of cocklespurs and weeds.

Now he felt shy in the face of such power that five minutes before had led him to create black skies above wheat and corn fields, skies severed by veiny lightning in a part of the world he'd never seen. He wondered if he wouldn't have been better off hurling the third bolt at the man as he was doing something simple and irrelevant, like burning trash behind the barn. Because of his compulsion to make a point he had fixed things so that what followed — the true reason for this wretched day trip — would be relegated to either of these two big words.

He wondered if they taught this kind of thing in school or if, like most things the boy said or did, it was a pure product of his strange mind. Speight knew he was no match for it. He felt the gift of speech recede, sentences dwindling to fragments and grunts again.

"I told you I don't know nothing about lightning or how come it struck this man. Unlucky, I guess. Wrong place, wrong time."

Randall smiled.

"We didn't take off work early to tell stories anyway."

"Why did we take off early then? Besides to picnic."

No picnic, thought Speight. "I had something I wanted to talk to you about. Still do. Something serious. Got sidetracked."

"That's all right. I liked hearing about that man. I'll probably tell Eureka about it when I see her again."

"Again? Where'd you see her before?"

"Courtyard of the church."

"You two talked?" Speight felt more comfortable now, nudging the conversation along.

"She made me mad."

"How's that?"

"She left without telling me. Without seeing us first."

"Hurt your feelings?"

"I'm not ashamed to say so."

"Don't be," said Speight. "It don't matter. Say what you feel, son."

"I will." Randall spoke loudly, his head down.

"Look at me," said Speight, but he wouldn't. He bent over and began to pull up handfuls of weeds. Maybe it's too late for me to start talking to him about his feelings, Speight thought. "What did ya'll talk about?"

"She told me about a man with motor oil for blood. His grandson's real good with cars. About a man who had a hat with a flashlight fastened to the top. He wore it under the ground. She said he tried to date her."

A wonder the boy even listens at all, Speight thought, everyone spinning stories to get his attention. Still, it seemed to work. Unless he'd only been pretending to be interested, humoring his old man through those three bolts of lightning.

"What else?"

"She asked about my face."

"She knows why I had to take you to the basement."

"I told her you wanted me to help carry up kindling."

"Randall . . ."

"Well, you won't there. How am I supposed to know what to tell her? You never said anything about her being gone. You acted like it didn't even ever happen."

"Wasn't much I could say." He watched Randall jump up and walk toward the river.

"Come back over here. I'm talking to you."

Randall stamped back, his head down.

"Wasn't anything to say then, Randall. I didn't think she'd run off like that. Not with him. Now that she's back we have to keep her here. You hear? I won't keep nothing from you, you don't keep nothing from me. Right?"

Speight held out his hand, and Randall took it, thinking it was offered to shake. His hand disappeared within his father's huge sandpaper grip. Hidden there, it started to sweat. His father didn't seem to notice. Randall grew embarrassed and tried to pull loose but his father didn't seem to notice this either.

"Tell me what else she said."

"Asked about you." At the other end of his arm, Randall squirmed.

"What about me?"

"Wanted to know what you said about her leaving."

"What else?"

"Said she was going away again maybe."

"With him?"

"Said he did bad things."

"To her?"

"Said not. But I believe she might of been lying."

This information, as he'd hoped, loosened his father's grip. He dropped to his knees, exhausted.

"We can't let her stay with him."

"I asked her if he was sorry for those bad things he'd done," said Randall.

"And?"

"She said it didn't matter."

"Bad sign," said Speight. "A bad place, where there's not forgiveness. He's not the one for her, son. You know that well as I do. If we let her stay with him we'll lose her forever."

"Why don't you go talk to her? Tell her to come on home."

He remembered the last time he'd seen her. A few frenzied seconds in that dark kitchen but the image was as clear as the sight of the river a few yards away. Porch door sliding open slowly, books and dishes covering the small table, her clothes crumpled on the floor beside the cot, toes of her shoes peeking from beneath the pile. The way their bodies fit, clash of her dark thigh against his pale skin.

What he would never forget was the way he moved in her forcefully once even after he looked up and saw Speight watching. She'd tried hard not to respond to his thrust but Speight had seen, noticed and remembered everything, there were undeniable twitches of response: a widening of the eyes, a tightening around the mouth.

"She don't want to see me. We've got to do it another way. The druggist knows how to get her back, but we both have to help. He's got this medicine to give the man what will make Eureka leave."

"What kind of medicine?"

"That's not our business. He's the druggist."

"A medicine that will make Edwin not want Eureka anymore?"

"Don't say his name to me," said Speight.

"Eureka doesn't like it either. I decided it fits him fine."

"Never mind about that. You needn't worry about what the medicine does or don't do. All you have to do is deliver it."

"How come we don't have Eureka come and get it? She can put it in his food. I've heard of that."

"Eureka doesn't know nothing about this. If you want to help you can't see her or talk to her. If she tries to meet with you tell her

390

I need you at home."

"But I'll see her when I deliver the medicine."

"You'll wait 'til she's not there. Either me or the druggist will tell you what to do."

"And this will bring her back?"

"It will get her away from him."

"Can she take me to the beach when she gets back?"

"I'll take you both to the beach," said Speight. "Now we got to go before it gets dark and we can't find our way out of here."

"I know my way out of here by heart," said Randall. And he led his father from this sanctuary, last and most sacred of his special places.

Randall kept watch from the camp closest to Edgecombe, the one abandoned by the DeVone Street gang. He spied from a shanty built head-high in a sycamore, a box of tin, plywood, tarpaper and the double doors from a wrecked panel truck. One of the truck doors faced Edgecombe; the window was grimy and flecked with dead bugs but he could see the front and back porches of the bungalow clearly.

Watch the front and back, his father had told him, and whenever they leave go in through the kitchen. So he went that morning to the treehouse. By the time Speight showed with his lunch he was bored, and told his father so. Remember what you're there for, his father told him. Remember it's to help your sister. Randall tried to keep this in mind, but it was hard. This was a place he was banished to, not a place he'd been allowed to discover. He spent most of the afternoon trying to decide whether this was sacrifice or punishment.

For three days the only sign of life came from sparrows nesting in the chimney and Eureka hanging out wash every other day. Then one morning there was movement. Eureka first, out of the front door in a long dress he'd never seen. And a hat — he'd never seen her wear a hat like this. The door swung open again and *he* came out, dressed in a blue striped suit. Eureka stood at the edge of the porch, staring out into the street. He straightened the dress on her shoulders, said something in her ear. She shook her head, scratched her arm, spoke. He looked heavier, and his patchy beard was gone. He still limped a bit, Randall noticed as they started off down the flagstones, but he moved quicker, as if his feet touched the ground now.

The cot was missing from the kitchen and so were the stacks of books and papers and the phonograph, the record albums, the shabby chair. The floor had been scrubbed, the counters scoured, placemats were laid out at the small table. The windows were open toward Edgecombe. He walked down the hall to a large bedroom with a double bed. This door had always been closed when he'd come before. He spotted a pair of Eureka's shoes near the closet. The room across the hall was set up as a study. All the books and papers were filed away in shelves, the cot was here, neatly made up and pushed under the windows. The old kitchen wingback sat in the corner. In the front parlor he discovered the phonograph, the records stacked neatly on the floor beneath it. He felt strange walking through this empty house; it seemed he'd changed as much in the few months since he'd been here as it had. He remembered the first time he'd come, stale breath seeping from the thrown-open window, the bony arm retreating into the darkness. I wonder if it still has the face of my pa, he thought, and he decided to see. He had the front door half-opened when he remembered why he was there.

In the bathroom he opened the medicine cabinet and stuffed the bag on the middle shelf. There had been a long discussion, an argument almost, between the druggist and his father about where to put it. He had stood helplessly behind the drug counter while they had it out. The druggist was worried that Eureka would find the bag first and throw it away. "I can't believe we never thought of this before now," he said. "What we have to do is get the boy to lure her out for a while, give Keane time to discover it." "I thought of it," said Speight, "and you can forget that plan. I've involved the boy in this enough already. He ain't going to do that."

"How else can we make sure he gets it?" the druggist asked. "Stash it in the medicine cabinet," his father said. "All due respect, Speight," said the druggist, "but I think you're being a little naive." Randall could tell from the way his father said "How's that?" that Speight had no idea what naive meant. He had no idea himself. "She's cohabitating with him," the druggist said. "That medicine cabinet is half hers now." "You trying to say I don't know my own daughter?" asked Speight. The druggist shrugged. "Even if she was married to him she wouldn't just go in his medicine cabinet," said Speight. "That's the way she was brought up." "You brought her up not to go in a medicine cabinet that is by all rights half hers?" asked the druggist. His father's long and sullen silence had forced the druggist to say, finally, "You know better than me."

He stuck it on a high shelf in the medicine cabinet. As far as he could tell there was nothing in here that was hers. This pleased him — he felt very close to his father since their trip to the river, and he couldn't wait to get back to the drugstore to tell him that he was right and the druggist was wrong.

16

When the maid brought a tray of iced teas to the screened-in gazebo Eureka stopped staring at the river below to watch the way his mother reached for her glass: without looking where her hand was going, where the tray hovered, where the maid stood. Her eyes never left her son, while with one hand she held her glass of tea in midair and with the other stubbed a cigarette out in a nearby ashtray. The filters that lay crumpled across the bed of ashes were red so that her lipstick would not show its stain.

Since Eureka had been there she had been asked three questions.

What in the world did you all walk for?

First words out of his mother's mouth and only partially addressed to her. Maybe not addressed to her at all — she said "you all" but she had looked to Edwin.

"I could have sent Tillett easy enough," she said. She was slender and tough-skinned, a freckled, handsome woman with horrible posture.

"You know I need the exercise," said Edwin.

Walking up the long drive Eureka had held his hand up to that point where she'd been before, the curve where Edwin had ordered Deems to back out on the morning they'd left for Lexington. As soon as she passed that point she let go and slowed, and the corner of the house she'd seen before spread into three three-storied wings.

The sight of it made her melancholy. She hadn't wanted to leave the bungalow; they'd barely been out since they'd returned. Deems bought food and what Edwin called his supplies, boxes of condoms kept in the medicine cabinet. Once she wondered if Deems bought them at Lehmann's in plain view of her father and the druggist, but she had too much on her mind to worry about where Deems shopped.

Edwin had insisted she come, said things would run smoother with his mother that way. And he had to see his mother since last time, on the morning they'd left for Kentucky, she had been away on one of her long weekends.

She asked about his father, whom he never mentioned.

He said he'd seen him before leaving for Lexington, that this time he'd call him, settle some business, tell him to pay off Deems and let him go. His father, he explained, was of the era when travel was the remedy for all infirmities.

"Did you tell him *why* you were going to Lexington?"

"Sort of," said Edwin. "I said I was going to see a specialist."

"And we met at church."

"Come here," he said, draping an arm around her. She looked up to check for silhouettes in the tall windows. "He just figured I was seeking further treatment, which in a way I was."

"Did you tell him who you were traveling with?"

"Deems," he said.

She waited for him to apologize or explain, but he was silent.

"Does your mother know the druggist and I went along?"

He explained that his mother disliked the druggist, that she thought him insolent and ill-mannered though she'd never spoken to him in person, knew him only from the telephone. Eureka was amused by the idea of this woman disliking someone she'd never laid eyes on. She looked up to the phone lines loping away from the house to the woods, imagined the residue of his mother's distaste clogging the black cord.

"So she doesn't know about me?"

He said he was sure she knew by now, and it was obvious from the way Mrs. Keane received them on the gazebo — graciously low-keyed, calm — that she did know.

The next question was addressed to her: *Now Eureka, what do you do?*

This new dress made her neck itch; it was summer wool and the way it held its shape made her feel as if she was wearing a cardboard box. "I plan to finish school," she told Edwin's mother. "I used to work at Miss Ilgenfritz's laundry over on Beamon."

Edwin's mother smiled back and thumped more ashes from her red filter.

Now tell me you two, what are your plans?

Partially addressed to her again but she made no attempt to answer. Her question had been answered already. What did she do? She planned to finish high school. She used to work in the laundry. Lame as it sounded, it worked. She sagged into her lawn chair, invisible. Edwin answered this time and she sensed that neither of them expected her to speak.

He talked of returning to college after they got married, of finishing his degree while she completed high school.

"The married student life," said his mother. "Your father and I went that route. Wasn't easy. What about your immediate plans?"

"We're leaving town," said Edwin.

"When?"

"This week. Tomorrow or the next day, as soon as I get everything in order with Dad."

"Where are you going?"

"Our itinerary's still a little sketchy."

"Then you're taking a trip?"

"Excuse me?"

"You said itinerary. I gather from that you plan to come back."

Eureka watched the river but listened carefully. "Of course we'll come back from time to time," Edwin said.

His mother changed the subject, bringing up a cousin who had announced his engagement while Edwin was away. She said *away* as if Edwin had gone to the store for a loaf of bread. It was obvious to Eureka that something crucial and private was going on between them, and she listened less and less to what they said, heard only the intermingling of their voices as she watched a man mow the grass in the field sloping to River Road and wished to be free of the dress. She longed for the moment when she would peel it off, push it back into the shadows of his closet. Here she was having tea with his mother, this woman who doled hate out over the telephone, who acted shocked at the thought of them walking

400

over here through the middle of town like two migrants who'd missed their crew bus, and all she could think about was stripping off her dress.

Edwin would probably call this a metaphor. She would say that it was not either, that her neck itched and she was hot as hell, that metaphors were worse for him than the medicine he used to take.

She wasn't interested in his metaphors, or any more of his methods to save time. She couldn't believe she had let herself be led back here, and she stood suddenly to leave.

"Eureka?" said Edwin.

"I'll let y'all talk," she said.

"Tillett will be happy to drop you off wherever," Mrs. Keane said.

Eureka turned and said, "Oh. It was nice to meet you and thank you so much for the tea."

"I'll see you at home," said Edwin, but Eureka kept walking across the freshly mown field. Both of them watched her pick across the lawnmower's swaths, furrows of clipped grass losing their color almost as she stepped over them.

"Well, she's beautiful," said Edwin's mother. "Luscious coloring. Just stunning."

"Thanks." He lit a cigarette, stared down

at its slow and even burn. He shouldn't have brought her, he should have somehow made her stay.

"Love her name. Is it family?"

Edwin smiled, shrugged.

"I've met her before. She tell you?"

"No, where?"

"Actually, not met — seen. At the church-yard. She was there collecting leaves."

"She didn't mention it," said Edwin.

"Of course she might not have recognized me. Or maybe she did but didn't want to say anything. You know."

"Yep."

"You don't want to talk about her?"

"Well . . . I mean, she just jumps up and runs off. Maybe I wasn't paying enough at-tention. I'm sure she was nervous as hell about being here and we're gabbing about some cousin's fiancée's father."

"She sensed we wanted to be alone, and she was right. I respected that. She scored some points with me on that one."

"I imagine we were both down a few."

"That's not a neighborhood where things go unnoticed. Despite your low profile the last year or so, people over there look out for you."

"Heavy biddy contingency."

"All of them with party lines."

Edwin looked up at her. "Had lots of calls?"

"Your father told Essie Gaddy last night if she called here again she'd have to find herself a new lawyer."

"Hate to make him lose his clients."

"Essie Gaddy? He'll manage. Besides, he works all the time anyway."

"Well. Won't have to worry after Friday."

She stabbed her cigarette into the clamshell, grinding until tobacco tinted the ashes. "This is all about Sarah, isn't it?"

"What do you mean?"

"I never have felt exactly right about you moving out, Edwin."

"I think it was your idea."

"It was. At the time I thought it would help. But now I know it was a mistake."

"Because I met her?"

She glanced across the lawn where Eureka had disappeared, then to him again. "Because while you were in the hospital, up at Duke, your uncle Arthur sent by a friend of his to talk to us, a psychiatrist who told us that the main thing we needed to provide for you was a supportive environment. And Thomas and I made jokes on the way home, pointing at old shacks and tobacco barns all the way down highway sixty-four and calling them supportive environments. We acted like we couldn't understand what the man was saying, he used so many forty-dollar words, even though we knew exactly what he was saying. It scared us so we pretended he wasn't saying anything at all. We were scared, see; we didn't know what we were going to do with you, so we acted like he was the one who was ignorant."

"Supportive environment? Sounds sort of egg-heady to me, too."

"Don't you start," she said. "Just listen. About that bungalow: I put you over there more for me than you. I wanted my own life to start again and figured the way to do that was get you out on your own."

"And now you're worried because I met Eureka, and you think I never would have met her if you'd kept me here."

"Not true," she said.

"Actually, the day I met her? I was coming to see you at the courtyard. But the Lobster Women had called it a day."

"Is that supposed to make me feel guilty?"

"No," he said, thinking that he should leave now and catch up with Eureka. Yet he didn't want to leave; he realized how much he'd missed talking to his mother, missed her honesty and the satisfying shortcut rhythms of their conversation.

"You haven't said a word about the medicine, by the way," he said. "About Lexington."

"I'm not sure what *to* say. I always thought

you needed it for your back."

"My back's okay. It's been healed. Long since."

"But you never told me. You just kept lying to get more. I had no idea that it had become such a problem."

"Mother," he said. The word hung in the late afternoon air. When he said it again she turned on him with eyes the flat brown of the river.

"Well, I didn't. I know I couldn't have stopped you, either. I wonder what Walter Lehmann must think of me. And you really let me make a fool of myself with that poor druggist."

"He forgives you. He went with me to Kentucky, by the way. He helped me out."

"And she went also?"

"Eureka."

"Well, I guess she really cares for you then. There when you needed someone. Supportive environment."

Her eyes had settled on the bend at the far border of their land, and it seemed she would not look at him again that day.

"I've got to go," he said.

"Be mad, Edwin, but I'm going to say this: I can't stop comparing her to Sarah. I won't ever be able to, and I'm not about to apologize either."

"I didn't love Sarah," he said.

"She just comes up out of nowhere and you run away with her."

"That's one of the things I like."

"You were unsure about loving her is what you mean. Nervous about marrying maybe. You weren't sure of the life you chose. Thought somebody else chose it for you. Well, I'm not always sure about mine either. But nobody was making you marry her. I certainly wasn't. I approved, but I'm allowed preferences, aren't I? Nobody was forcing you."

"I know that."

"You were acting like a coward."

"You're right."

"I know you're my son and I shouldn't . . . your father would absolutely die. I'll have to figure out something for supper because I can't face him tonight. If he knew I was saying these things to you?"

"He'd die."

She did look at him then. "A couple of days after the accident, your father got a visit from a detective. He came down to the office and told Thomas he was having trouble with the accident report. He said from all he could put together he couldn't figure out why you wrecked. You weren't going that fast, wasn't bad weather out, wasn't a thing in the road. They found a bottle of gin in the car, but

406

when they did the autopsy and took blood samples, turned out Sarah had more to drink than you.

"This detective was wondering what to do. Sarah's father had called him twice asking to see the report. Seems Skipper put him on to it, said Skipper had been telling folks you'd had a breakdown, that you hadn't been treating Sarah well, that you'd been avoiding her and that you had mentioned to several people you were going to break up with her."

"Why are you telling me this now?" asked Edwin.

"Well, I was horrified. That Byron Teague would let his son go around and say those things, that people would listen to it. And these policemen, these detectives — how did they think they could look at some marks in the road and tell exactly what happened? Couldn't there have been a dog in the road, your daddy asked them?"

She mimicked a deep-voiced deputy. " *'Well, we didn't find no dead dogs.'* 'Well, what if he swerved to miss the dog? Think the dog would hang around to testify?' your father asked. *'Well, uh, it won't really that type a swerve which don't matter much as that Mr. Teague keeps calling us up asking these questions,' "* she said in her deputy's growl. " 'I'll take care of Mr. Teague,' your father said, and he went right then over to Byron's office and when he came home I asked him what happened and he said that there had been a dog in the road and that while swerving to avoid him you overcorrected and that Byron Teague just wished to hell you'd taken your chances and run over the goddamn mutt but understands of course how people react in the face of things."

She stopped and reached for her cigarettes.

"Byron Teague understood that first impulses aren't always to be trusted."

She lit a cigarette and spoke to him through a cloud. "Now I don't know, Edwin. I wasn't there. How can I know what happened? I never really asked. At first we assumed you'd been drinking, because you were home from school and you were going to a party at somebody's river house. And when we learned that you weren't drunk, we all agreed to the presence of this dog in the road."

She blew out a thin, deliberate stream of smoke. "This dog that got away easy, considering."

He didn't say anything.

"It may have been that you were unhappy. That you were allowing yourself to judge people you didn't really even know and that you were holding them responsible for things they had nothing to do with. But these same people, when it came down to it, are the ones that helped put that dog in the road. You understand me, Edwin? Do you hear me? Do you hear?"

He spotted her marching up the slight grade past the mill shacks, almost to the "Welcome to Trent" sign. He asked Tillett to pull in behind her but Tillett ignored him and coasted beside, punching the gas, keeping up in spurts. She never once looked over to see who was trailing her, kept her eyes focused on the sign.

He rolled down the window and told her to get in.

At the sound of his voice she cut her eyes, staring first at the colored driver who stared back, his attention split disproportionally between her and the road, then to Edwin hanging half out of the window, a pale panic showing beneath blotches of red open air had brought to his cheeks.

"You get out," she said.

The door slammed. The Packard bucked away. "I won't ask why you left," he said, scrambling to match her pace. "Hated to ask Tillett for a ride but I had to get out of there. Never going back, either."

"What if you run out of money?"

He laughed. "You hated her, right? That's why you're mad?"

"At least she asked me questions." Walking along, she'd been thinking about her own mother, wondering if she would have found herself in this predicament if her mother had lived. Probably so, for what could her mother have done to change things? I still would have gone to the courtyard to collect leaves for that stupid science project, still would have met him, still would have gone to his house to return the letter, still have ended up in Kentucky. None of these actions seemed avoidable to her in retrospect, nor wrong. Only staying with him here and now in this place seemed false.

"I sent Deems for champagne," he said. "Figured we'd need it after our visit."

"I'm leaving," she said.

He grabbed her hand and stopped walking. They stood on the roadside in that dusky moment when drivers switch their lights on.

"I'm sorry. I shouldn't have taken you there. Shouldn't have gone myself."

A horn bleated two feet away. He put his arms around her and walked her to the edge of the ditch. "Tomorrow, I promise," he said.

Everyone promising everything, she thought. Why not? No one seems to hold you to it. "I don't believe it," she said. "Something here that you can't leave." She looked down the road at the line of cars, anxious to be moving again.

"There's nothing holding me here," he said. "I don't need a driver or goddamn laundry pickup." He spread his arms out in the gauzy twilight. "I'm well. I didn't even know I was sick, it took you to make me see. Let's say, for optimism's sake, that I would have eventually come out of it. You saved me years just by showing up and bringing me into the present."

Inches away, cars flashed by. Behind the darkened windows, she saw silhouettes and felt exposed: Hal could have hitched a ride home with one of his house-painting buddies, for all she knew her father could be out running an errand in Lehmann's car. Suddenly Edwin pulled her close again, too close; it hurt for a moment until she gave into it, and then she no longer felt the risk of exposure.

Entwined by the drainage ditch on the hill going out of town: Eureka smiled and let herself dissolve. A wall-eyed headlight passed through them like smoke and she saw them as chemicals blending to form a third. Edwin's avoidance of the past quarantined him there; her looking always ahead marooned her at a point beyond which it was worthwhile to do anything over. Yet together, the present they formed was entirely empty. His was a past crammed with odors, sounds, odd images: a

411

face pressed against a rusty screen, a grown man going to bed with his favorite book. Her future was equally cluttered, with the hairstyles of her sisters' husbands-to-be, olive skin of some girl falling — years from now — for Randall.

But this present of theirs was odorless, tasteless, eerily quiet.

"Just by your being there to receive those letters . . . ," he was saying.

She pulled away. "I thought we were going to talk about that letter."

"Seriously? Now? Here?" He grabbed both of her hands again. "Listen to me: I wrote that letter so we wouldn't have to waste time talking. If we start in on all that, we'll never get out of here."

That letter was tied to Trent, to his life before her. Surely it would seem worthless in some far northern Great Plains place or among the steep windy streets of a Rocky Mountain town.

"Take me home," she said.

While she roasted a chicken he drank champagne and brooded.

"Randall told me Green's back at the drugstore," she said.

"Figures," he said. "What else is there for him? Still, hard to believe he'd go groveling back to Lehmann."

After a long pause he said, "I feel bad about the druggist. Feel like I owe him for helping me out. But at the same time, I feel like I don't owe him a damn thing. That his self-righteousness keeps me from owing him anything."

He poured more champagne and leaned against the kitchen counter in her way. To force him to move she asked to taste his champagne and said, "Okay, you can fix me one of those." He smiled and poured a glass, watched closely as she sipped. She'd had only a taste of her father's rye years before, those few beers with Deems in Lexington.

"Sure does slow you down quick," she said after a half glass.

"It's the bubbles. They get inside your bloodstream and block traffic."

She had a second glass with dinner. The meal dissolved into fits of giggle and flushed self-consciousness, sloppy attempts at eating chicken now and again. Then a third glass for dessert, which she carried half empty to the bedroom, Edwin following with the bottle.

After all the elaborate fantasies she'd had about disrobing, the dress came off without ceremony: she sat on the bed with her arms pointing to the ceiling and laughed while he yanked it overhead, tossed it over his shoulder. In the process he popped a button, and she leaned over to see the rigid dress collapsed on the rug. Several times Edwin trampled it as he pulled his own clothes off, then the rest of hers. She fell across the bed, her feet dangling off the side; he knelt and started with his tongue between her toes and as he rose she imagined tomorrow, how she would rouse him from bed to bathe with her in the clawfoot tub, how the rising sun would spot them making waves near the bow. She'd pack a suitcase full of new clothes, he'd appear around a corner in a suit she'd never seen him in before, pulled from the recesses of his closet, a lightweight khaki thing which made him look like a Raleigh lawyer: rumpled and relaxed, elegantly frayed. She would brush her hair by the Johnsontown window while he fixed breakfast, tea and toast and fruit and eggs and bacon, Deems would toot twice when he pulled up in the sideyard. In the train they would have a double berth, a couch, a tiny closet, a stainless steel sink which could fold in the wall even when filled with water, a wide window which she would sit by as the train lunged away from the platform at seven in the morning, crawling past warehouses, feed and seed stores on the verge of opening, shadows of clerks behind the plateglass, lights winking on tentatively, cars coasting up to the sides of buildings from which sleepy men unfolded. She would stare outside while he curled sleeping beside her, as the train picked up speed and skirted Johnsontown she would watch for someone she knew but would see no one save a few men walking the track bed to work. She would see only men and she would wonder why the morning of her departure would belong only to men. Not until noon when they made their way down the aisle to the club car would she see another woman. She would join him in a glass of wine and they would both order the seafood platter and eat shrimp, flounder and oysters a dozen feet above the peanut fields of Tidewater, having passed the last outskirts of Trent and broken finally into open country, open air.

After lunch they would return to their compartment, pull out the overhead bed and spend the afternoon alternating shallow naps with a call and response timed to the tremulous rhythm of rail travel, speeding toward someplace she would not wonder about now. She would save it for later, she thought as he pulled his tongue from her ear and replaced it with whispered words — *I'll be right back, he said, you hurry, she said* — would save it for when she arrived.

Rummaging around in the medicine cabinet Edwin noticed the bag. To anyone else it would have appeared ordinary, white paper with black lettering, top folded twice, slightly creased. An ordinary bag tightly shelved between a can of Barbasol and a box of condoms. But the sight of it brought the dormant warmth upwards, caused his bones to tingle, then fade.

He pulled it out far enough to see the Lehmann's logo. Surely it was filled with toiletries. She ordered something without telling him, asked her little brother to drop it off outside. *She's sick and she's afraid to tell me. It's medicine for her.* The thought worried him, but he felt better. He set the bag on the back of the toilet, stared down at it for a moment, then snatched it up, pulled it open, turned it upside down and collapsed onto the lip of the tub as the contents — several vials of morphine, two new needles — clattered onto the porcelain.

It took several minutes before he could focus on how a bag of morphine could appear in his medicine cabinet.

The druggist topped his list, but it took only seconds to discount him. The man who did everything he could to clean me up? Whose tireless attempts to wean me cost him his job?

Speight? Since that day he'd walked in on them Edwin had anticipated his revenge. Yet he doubted Speight was desperate enough to risk his job, and the druggist would know if someone were pilfering his narcotics.

He leaned over to the window and lifted the blind slats, wondering if his house was being watched. The delivery must have been made while they were at his mother's, he realized, and as soon as he thought of her he understood. It would explain why she had not asked him about Lexington, why she'd taken up so much of the hour with small talk about cousins, skin color, names. Of course she had opened up a bit after Eureka left. He'd not let himself think about what she'd told him until now, and now he wondered what it changed, her knowing. If he had confessed the moment he awoke in the hospital, she would not have believed him. Yet either way — if he confessed or if she found out the way she had — nothing would come from it. Nothing had. He'd known this as his hand sweated on the steering wheel; it was partly why he'd given in.

He'd admitted nothing, though there were things he wanted to say. He'd wanted to tell her about Tremont, about how his sentence had hovered unfinished in the car. Of all the people he knew she was the only one who would not say *But you hardly knew this Camp Tremont fellow, how in the world could you pos-*

sibly hate him? She would understand how little it had to do with Camp Tremont.

He wanted to remind her of the time she'd told him a story about a woman who was rude, snobbish, intimidating, the bane of his mother's unhappiness until a brain tumor sweetened her up for a few weeks, then took her away. Originally she'd offered the story as a warning of sudden changes in people, but now Edwin realized that his mother had used this Helen Butler in the same way as he'd used Tremont, focusing her failings onto this woman she hardly knew.

Yet his mother had not driven the family Dodge into the swamp on the way to a party when his father had asked what in the world was it about Helen Butler that she so disliked. Helen Butler became the ideal friend — mysterious, inquisitive, engaging. And then she died.

Or did she? Even if Helen Butler was as pure an invention as the dog he'd swerved to avoid, it made little difference, since she served her purpose, imparting before she disappeared the strength his mother needed to survive. He couldn't say as much for Camp Tremont, he realized, and with this realization came the tug of the sentence again. Immediately he thought of ways to make it subside. Morphine first, its thick fade beginning in him physically and starting to erase the sentence before he understood what was happening.

Next Eureka: she was waiting, no doubt wondering what was taking so long. He reached over and locked the door. Staring down at the vials, he easily imagined his mother's intent: *so she can visit again, pull the wingback up to the cot and slump and bask in the attention I allow her for as long as the effects of the shot last. So that I will no longer be seen walking the streets with some girl who billowed out of nowhere, untraceable and traditionless.*

Nor was it hard to imagine how she'd engineered it. Call up Lehmann with some made-up injury, anything, a slight sprain, it didn't matter. Lehmann would be happy with the most meager of excuses and would fill the prescriptions himself — it wouldn't be the first time — and Green would have to ignore it again or leave. He had nowhere else to go — hadn't he proven that by tagging along to Lexington? He'd stay at that job until he rots, in a year's time he'll be just another drugstore fixture like catatonic Ruby McClaurin or the papier-mâché mortar and pestle that hangs above the drug counter, dissolving in flakes with each swipe of the ceiling fan.

Edwin stood and made his way slowly to the door. With each step he felt stronger. He would return later and flush the vials, would leave Trent tomorrow for good, forever.

In the hallway he held his breath and listened: no sound from the bedroom. The door was ajar and through the crack he saw Eureka stretched across the bed, her legs tangled in sheets. A slow breeze rippled the curtains over the bed, rustling dry December leaves in the air above the swamp bottom where he lay broken, bloody, mired. He started across the room but stopped when he came to Sarah lying facedown between himself and the safety of high ground.

Finding a vein could have easily annoyed him now, but instead of a roadblock to bliss, he treated the search as sport: the discovery of a blue wisp along white thigh like a fisherman spotting silver darts beneath swells.

Only seconds then before the warmth spread from that small lump in the center of his stomach, blotting outwards like water spilled on a tablecloth; seconds more before the swamp faded into the deep of early afternoon.

There were new instructions: don't worry about *him* now, just wait until *she* leaves to deliver. The druggist had told Randall this while his father was cleaning the windows one morning.

"What if she don't leave?" Randall asked. The druggist promised that she would. But three days had passed and he'd seen her outside only twice since — once to hang out wash, once to strip it off the line. Each time she dallied, as if in need of sun or fresh air, and once or twice her eyes had lingered on the treehouse, but Randall knew that from the backyard the treehouse was invisible.

He felt safe enough, but spying had lost its luster. The sight of his sister shielding her eyes from the sun, wicker basket hoisted onto her hip like a sleepy toddler, made him homesick. Made him want to call out *Hello down there.*

The third day the front door opened and she stepped onto the porch, wearing the same dress he'd seen her in before. She must be going somewhere serious dressed like that, he thought; must be going to try and get her job back. She didn't look around this time, just crossed the yard and started up the sidewalk toward town.

He beat his way through the scrub. Judging by the way she was dressed, he felt he could take his time, but when he pulled back the screen door and entered the dark kitchen it seemed he should hurry. The room looked exactly as it had when he'd first seen it: windows open to the wood, phonograph set up on a small bureau, table covered by papers and books. Glasses and ashtrays strewn across the floor among mounds of clothes, mateless shoes. Randall saw the cot in the corner beneath the windows, a body crumpled along its length. He moved closer, picking his way through the debris. While he was standing over the cot, the shade flapped open, sending sunlight across Edwin's face; his mouth was open, his hair wet and matted. A beard spread across his cheeks and chin in scraggly outbreaks, like an infection.

Randall hurried down the dark hallway to the bathroom before the wind could blow again. He'd just crammed the bag onto the highest shelf he could reach when he heard the door shut behind him. He turned to see a hand, spread wide and splotched red, and behind it Eureka, who looked huge, her face the same deep blush of her hand. Before he fell back into the tub he watched her fingers curl into tight fists. He swallowed sobs and hunkered, hoping she'd tire soon.

Exhausted, she fell back on the toilet, pulled strands of hair down to hide her face. A few seconds later she half-stood, lowered the lid and sat again. They passed minutes in private sobs, not looking at each other.

She said finally: "I know I never hit you before. But I didn't think you'd ever be part of something like this."

"Like what?" It made him feel worse to say this, something a child would say, an ignorant and reflexive response.

"You know what. But not even this really" — she nodded toward the medicine cabinet. "Anything to hurt me."

"To help," he said. "This is supposed to help."

"Who said?"

"Pa said we could go to the beach."

"You're not supposed to say? You promised, is that right?"

"He said he'd take me down there."

"I know you."

"Said he'd take you, too."

"What is it you're not supposed to tell me, Randall?"

"Swim all day long. Catch crabs with chicken livers on a piece of string. It's not about an hour's drive due east."

She sank against the porcelain tank as if it were plush upholstery. "You're not helping me," she said. "This isn't helping me." Between sniffles she said: "We were about to leave. And he was about to tell me about it, I could feel it."

"Tell you what?"

She stared at him for a long time. He dangled his feet over the edge of the tub, and suddenly she reached down, took a foot in each

423

hand and began to swing them together idly.

"I don't even know if I really cared about her, about what happened. If she was still alive I bet I wouldn't even like her."

"Who? You talking about somebody dead?" His legs were growing numb from the knee down.

"It's like he teased me with those letters."

"Who did? *He* did?"

"But see, I believed in it. I did, because I wanted to save time just like him. Back then I felt like I had less time than he did even. I felt like if I didn't make it out of here before noon one day I'd be stuck here forever. And that day came and there I was over at his house and we were alone and didn't even take time to move from the kitchen."

Randall tried to hold his legs still but she was stronger and kept swinging.

"I wanted to save time, too, to take his shortcuts, so I asked for those letters. I asked for them. Even though I didn't understand all of what he was saying, I felt like I could pick up things just by the way I felt when I read them. Like if my bones ached or if my blood ran. Read these and they'll save us years he told me, and I believed it. Should of just said, look, I don't want to hear any more. Save it. It's none of my business. We could of took our time like everybody else.

But too late now."

"I don't get any of this and my foot's killing me it's so asleep."

She was shocked: she'd thought he'd understand, at the least act curious, but here he was ignoring her after she'd opened up finally.

"Both feet," he said. "Let go."

He drew his feet back into the tub and began to massage them.

"Who sent you?"

He grabbed the towel rack above him, hoisted himself up and began to shake his legs out one at a time, as if they were wet.

"Pa," she said. "I knew he wasn't through." She watched him closely for a sign but noticed the patch of purple skin beneath the scar on his cheekbone and felt foolish for opening up to him about things he couldn't understand seconds after she'd slapped him. *Eleven years old and once again he's borne the brunt.*

"Nope." He spoke to his feet. "Not Pa."

"Who then?"

He slapped at one leg, then the other. "I'm paralyzed."

"The druggist? Randall, the druggist?"

Noises from the kitchen: a shuffling, then the sound of a glass rolling across the floor, rocking to a stop.

"He's up," she said, reaching over to turn the latch seconds before the knock came.

"I'm in here," she called as she pulled open the window, whispered *"Go"* to Randall. He patted his legs and shrugged.

"Eureka?"

"I said I'm in here." She helped Randall out of the tub, hugged him, whispered, "I'm sorry, I swear, now go."

When he was safely out of sight she flushed the commode, then opened the door to find Edwin leaning against the far wall. In the dark hallway he looked even worse.

"I need in here now," he said.

She pushed past him, and when the door closed she thought: I should have asked how his back is now. This was the excuse he'd given her when she'd awakened to find his side of the bed empty and had discovered him stretched along the cot in his study. "It just went out on me," he said. "While you were asleep. I was reaching for something up high and suddenly I couldn't move. I had some medicine left over from before. I'll only need it until the pain goes away." The next day he said he was in too much pain to travel. He moved the cot into the kitchen. The ventilation was better there, he claimed. Next he moved, in stages, his books and papers, his phonograph, his clothes. He asked her not to straighten up the kitchen and there was hardly room to cook, but he didn't eat much, only asked for pancakes and syrup for supper which he picked over, sitting at the table for an hour or more. He drank sodas and sucked on penny candy brought by Deems. Days and nights he smoked and stared out the window into the J-town woods.

The night before he'd said, "I'm almost out of medicine and the pain's still bad. You'll have to go to the druggist tomorrow."

She told him she wouldn't do it. "I don't ever want to see him again, besides you should go see a doctor about your back. This is wrong. We're headed the wrong way. We were supposed to leave here days ago."

"I'm in pain," he said.

"Well, anyway, the druggist said he would never —"

"You don't know the druggist. Besides, I thought you wanted to leave."

She lay awake most of the night, decided finally to see the druggist; he was the only one who knew the situation, the only one she could talk to. That morning she'd started out, but halfway up Edgecombe she realized she'd forgotten the empty vials Edwin had asked her to take. She had returned to discover things in the bathroom of the bungalow: Randall, the medicine, Edwin's lies.

★ ★ ★

427

"So where's your Scotch whiskey?" she asked, taking a seat across from the druggist at the card table in his kitchen.

"I had nothing else to do then." He seemed irritated at being reminded of Lexington, as if that were only a brief flirtation with a way which did not fit him.

"Got your job back."

"Randall told you, I guess. Seen much of him since you've been back?"

"Saw him today."

"I didn't see him at all today," said the druggist. "Matter of fact I haven't seen much of him these past two weeks. He must be sick."

"There's nothing wrong with him."

"Well, then, your father or Lehmann must have him busy doing something else."

"You haven't had many deliveries lately?"

He laughed. His back was toward the light, and as that light retreated he became increasingly dim and featureless.

"If you're interested in the business I'll tell Lehmann. Maybe you can help out at the lipstick counter. Then there will be a majority and we'll have to change the name to Speight's Drugs."

"I know," she said. "I caught Randall with the bag. Edwin told me he hurt his back and I halfway believed him. He asked me to come see you for more and I was on my way this morning to ask you to help me out of this. Because I thought you wanted to help him, too."

"It was your father's idea," the druggist said.

She focused on the fading light behind him and said, "Randall said my father didn't have nothing to do with it."

"Randall's your brother."

"But he doesn't lie."

The druggist leaned in close. "Why do you think he's delivering the medicine? He'll lie if he has to, to bring you back."

"Why are you helping, then? Even if it was Pa's idea he couldn't do it without you."

He reached behind him and switched on a lamp. There was a moment of silent adjustment while they both blinked. "I wasn't going to tell you this. I'm not proud of it. That letter he sent you in Lexington? While you were out, I read it."

Her anger was balanced by relief. That someone else had read the letter absolved her of responsibility.

"Against my better judgment. As much as I wanted to help I never thought I'd read his mail."

"Wasn't his, it was mine."

The druggist smirked. "Yes, well." With

a bony index finger he tapped his left temple. "I meant that which was not meant for these eyes."

Lots wasn't meant for those eyes that you haven't closed them to, she thought. For a second her outrage won out. *I'd rather be alone with this torment than accept what he's done.*

"Up until now I've managed to stay out of all that's happened between you two. Getting in the middle of someone else's love affair isn't exactly my idea of a good time."

She remembered her first visit to this apartment, his talk of a sordid rectangle. And those times around the kitchen table in Lexington when he'd tried to persuade her that she could "do better" than Edwin. Still, he'd read the letter. It was hard to stay angry at him even in the face of his lies.

"So you read it."

"With great reservation."

"Then you know about what he did?"

"I knew about the wreck, but only that there was one, that a girl was killed. I remember there being some question as to what caused him to run off the road, but anyone who's ever driven that stretch knows how it can hypnotize you."

He stared at her for a minute, then continued. "Heard rumors about the hunting trip. I'm not convinced his version is accurate. He's remembering it through a year of more grains of morphine per day than most people could handle in a week."

"I thought of that," she said. "That he might of remembered it wrong. He's hard on himself."

"On the other hand . . ." The druggist left his chair to stroll through the shadows. "On the other hand the details seem awfully convincing in places, if memory serves me. Especially the part about how the Teague boy and his lawyer crony looked after the gun went off. Of course Keane's silver-tongued, isn't he? You like that about him, don't you?"

"Who he shot at and missed don't concern me."

The druggist sat back down and let out a long whistle. "That could certainly be categorized as cruel and unfeeling."

"He missed. Those two are still walking around."

"In the case of Skipper Teague, still stumbling."

"You believe it about the girl?"

"That he did it on purpose?"

"That he ran them off the road because he couldn't tell her how come he hated some man he hardly knew."

"Why don't you ask him?"

"I have. He says he wrote it so he wouldn't

have to talk about it."

"I guess I'd say the same if I were him."

"You're taking his side?"

"I didn't say that. Look, why do you think he couldn't finish that sentence?"

"He said why in the letter. That he thought he'd be rejected if he did. But then he wanted to break up with her, right? It doesn't make sense."

"Makes sense to me. Haven't you ever started a sentence you couldn't finish? Haven't you ever realized halfway through that you're digging a deeper grave with each word?"

"Hasn't everybody?" she shot back. "Most people'd just change the subject."

"Which only puts it off. All I'm saying is that I give him credit for even starting it. I know well how hard it is to finish a sentence you know is going to make your life a thousand times more difficult."

"You sure don't sound like the man I knew in Kentucky. Taking up for him and all."

"Just trying to help."

"What you're doing now's not helping."

"I told you that was your father's idea. You shouldn't hate him, Eureka. He's only trying to salvage things."

"But how did he think he could keep it from me? If I wouldn't have walked in on Randall today it wouldn't have been long."

"I don't think he cared to keep it from you. Once Keane starts up again, there's not much you or anybody can do to stop him. You'd have to go to your father for help or put up with it."

She said, "I hate him for using Randall. For mixing him up in all this again."

The druggist slumped in his seat, sighed and said, "Your father was trying to help, just like I was. I agreed to do it because I saw no other way to wean you away from him. You wouldn't listen to me in Lexington. And of course I read the letter. I knew what he was capable of."

"But you said before you thought he could have remembered wrong."

"I'm used to thinking of him as a victim. But it's time for us to recognize the true victims."

She was silent. He leaned over and said, "Seems to me there's one way to get at the truth. To get him to talk. See, what your father's up to, it's the right move, but for the wrong reasons," he said.

"What does that mean?"

"He's making those deliveries so you'll stay put. But the truth is, Keane's never going to leave here until he finishes that sentence. Seems to me he talked to you a lot more, a lot more honestly before he went to Lexington."

She considered it: he had avoided her since he'd taken to the cot again but when she found herself in the kitchen with him she noticed that he did talk more. His style had changed, too, from the threadbare statements of the past few weeks back to his former torrents. A few nights ago he had launched into a tirade about the proper way to massage tired muscles and even though she thought the subject irksome, she'd been carried away by it.

"You want him to talk," the druggist said. "You need him to finish that sentence or you'll never get out of here."

"Unless I leave without him," she said.

The druggist's smug laughter spilled from the shadows and she thought of Lexington, how he'd acted there, how she preferred him sarcastic rather than resigned as he seemed tonight.

"If you were going to leave, you'd have left."

She was quiet for a long time. "One thing," she said finally.

"What's that?"

"You can't use Randall anymore."

"Impossible. Randall's the delivery boy. Besides, he doesn't really understand what's happening."

"One day he'll understand. And he might blame me for allowing it, and hate me, and

I can't have that."

"I don't think you understand how much his innocence could work to our advantage here. If anything were to happen with Lehmann . . ."

"But I do understand. Things like this, they may not seem like nothing to you, but they ruin people. Forever. I won't leave here 'til you promise," she said, and she sat quietly until the promise came.

She kept watch from the front bedroom, her room now. Speight appeared at dusk, hugging the long shadows cast by the sycamores, stepping carefully over the root-ruptured sidewalk. She waited until she made out his slight movement, an imperfection against the still settling-down of dark.

He left the bag on the back stoop. If Edwin ever saw Speight passing beneath the window, he never mentioned it. He never mentioned anything that had to do with the medicine. They spoke as if nothing had changed.

And she waited for him to talk. She was running out of patience. In a matter of days his body had paled and shed pounds. It would be better to pretend things were normal until he talked, so that soon enough things could be normal again. Until then she would assume an air of imperviousness which she

435

would model on the most impervious person she knew: her father.

She watched Speight disappear around the corner, listened for him on the back porch but heard nothing.

Suddenly she bolted from her perch by the bedroom window, hurried down the hall to the kitchen, past the cot where Edwin lay twisted.

Behind the screen her father was bent over, placing the bag on the threshold. Sweat dappled his grey workshirt. She smelled the soured fabric and his other scents: breast-pocket bag of Bull Durham, his whiskered skin. The last time she'd seen him he'd been standing in the same spot. She mumbled an awkward hello. He said her name and nodded. They watched each other through the screen until he lowered his eyes and started to back away.

"Wait," she said. She held the door open. "Come in."

He hesitated.

"He's asleep. I want to talk to you. We'll go in the front room."

He entered the kitchen but stopped when he spotted Edwin in the cot. She eased the screen door shut and peered around her father at Edwin twitching in sleep. In the parlor she wrenched open the drapes and motioned for him to sit on the couch as she searched for the switch on a floor lamp. The lamp diced harsh light from the dark, an oval of dust thick as drizzle. He sat to the left of the light, half his face in shadow. *Why am I doing this?* She wondered.

"I want you to know I'm sorry you had to see me like that," she said.

His face did not change, but his focus shifted from some point above the curtains to a place just above her forehead.

"I mean I didn't know. If I had of known . . ."

"That I was coming?"

"I guess," she said.

"Then what? You wouldn't of done it?"

"Well, no. I would have anyway."

"Yes," he said.

They fell silent.

"Thing is" — he lowered his gaze and looked at her directly for the first time — "thing is I expected it from one of the others. But not you."

"Listen," she said, leaning forward. "And I need an answer, all right?"

His focus seemed to slip away, as if to say, maybe you'll get an answer, maybe not.

"Just what is it you need me for? There's Martha to run things, Ellen to take care of you. Hal to worry over, Randall to listen to, the other ones to keep up with. I would like to know just what is it you think you need me for?"

He said, "I wish I knew."

"You don't." She slumped back in her chair. "You don't even know."

"I let you go your own way too much. You and Randall both. Thought that was a way to show favor. Now it don't seem so right. Maybe it's time I quit this" — he held up the bag — "and let you alone for good."

She realized that she sat waiting for the men in her life, sequestered in opposite corners of this bungalow, to open up to her. Provoking her father with questions that fell flat, plying Edwin with the druggist's truth serum. I give up, she thought, and she decided to force her father out with quiet. But as soon as he spoke again (*It's this town, he said, this goddamn town I never did like it shouldn't of ever come back here*) she forgot her plan.

"Think things would have been different back down in the country? You think staying down there would have saved us?"

"Yes."

He really believes it. Had they stayed there she would have left even sooner, yet there would have been no Edwin, and to him that was the difference.

The claim he had made seemed so debatable

that hundreds of possible arguments overwhelmed her, forced her into silence again.

"You can come on home," her father said.

"Don't think so."

"Then you better find someplace better than this," he said, looking around the room. "Somewhere a long way from this town." He set the bag on the floor and stood. "I'll leave out the front here."

On the porch she leaned against a pillar to watch him away. A few steps into the yard he turned and stared up at her. He fished a bent cigarette out of his pocket and lit it. Blowing smoke, he said: "It about killed me to have to come back to this town. But I was too tired to try something new. Didn't think at the time about what it'd do to y'all, living here."

He reached out with his cigarette and knocked it against the pillar. She watched ashes rain into the high grass.

"It is not either this town," she said. She couldn't believe the sound of her voice — high and unfamiliar, as if it broadcast over the radio. Yet she believed the words themselves even though for years she'd based dreams of escape on the idea that life here was life buried alive. Now, listening to him confess, she saw how alike they were, how wrongly both had laid blame.

He shifted his weight, stared down the street. "I won't ask what you think that means."

"Don't. Too late now."

"You really are leaving me. I can tell it's for good this time."

"Tomorrow."

It was dark now, humid and moonless. She could just make out his face.

"I have to get back in," she said.

"Since you're already gone I suppose I should ask you this instead of tell you." He paused while more words gathered. "But that ain't the way it's going to be. You're mine, Eureka. I'm telling you now once: don't you try to take Randall away from here."

She said she wouldn't think of it, and she watched the fiery tip of his cigarette swinging in the black until there was nothing left of him to see.

"It's here," she said, sitting beside him on the cot. She put a hand on his collarbone and shook. "Okay? It's here now."

"Who were you talking to?"

She pointed to the open window above him. "You should shut that when you want to sleep."

He leaned into her as his feet danced around the cot, feeling for slippers. "You'd better eat something," she said, crossing to the sink to run water in a jar. She heard him rise, heard the crunch of paper as he snatched the bag off the table, listened to his feet slap the floorboards.

Five minutes of quiet. She stood at the sink, staring out the window into blackness. The bathroom door creaked open, then more silence. She stepped into the middle of the room, spotted him leaning against the wall a few feet away from the bathroom door. His lips were moving as she walked him back to the cot, helped him out of his robe.

"All right now?"

"Never better," he said.

He plucked an open book from the floor but instead of reading it he flattened it across his chest and lit a cigarette.

"I'll be in here," she said.

He stared at his slippers. She'd never seen him like this. In the bedroom she stripped, settled into bed and tried to clear her mind. She lay loose and still, seeking that airtight calm that preceded sleep, but thoughts seeped in like spring breezes, through corners, beneath doors, between chinks. Squalls of vague worry followed by sudden gusts of guilt so intense that when they died down she felt ravaged, a shred of opaque plastic flapping across a farmhouse window.

This is what we need, she told herself, *what we all need to set us straight again. It all boils down to a few minutes, people's lives together, comes down finally to a frank and naked quarter hour of words that most people manage happily to avoid.* As Edwin had said, this would be the end of most people, no one in their right mind would volunteer, knowing it would ruin them. So the necessary adjustments were made and people forged ahead, maintaining trust like a minimum bank balance, enough to cover debts carefully incurred.

She thought of the druggist and the life he detested, the feeble campaigns he waged against it. She thought of her father, acting not so much out of wounded paternal pride, or vengeance against a place he claimed to have always hated, as guilt for loving her more than the others. She held him responsible for that more than anything else, as if his feelings had made it all so much worse. Perhaps he held her responsible also. He had to know that this scheme had as much chance of driving her away as keeping her here. Surely her leaving was preferable than having her around, broken and miserable, to remind him of his favoritism and what it had done to all of them.

It was the only way out, the only way to release them from this allegiance of confusion and denial. It would redeem them all. The

442

druggist was right; he had to finish his sentence. *Even if they stayed here and nothing changed he had to finish it, even if she left him now and never came back he had to finish it.*

Sleep belonged to another life. She rose and pulled on her clothes, felt along the dark wall toward the kitchen.

Switching on the overhead light she saw that he was sitting up in the cot. The book had slid down to his waist, but was still open.

"Edwin?"

He turned to her and smiled.

"We need to talk," she said. "You need to talk to me."

He crushed his cigarette in an ashtray balanced in his lap. "You used to talk to me after your medicine. Why don't you talk now?"

"You want me to tell you now?"

"Yes."

"Sure you want to know what really happened?"

"Yes," she said, starting to cry. "And why."

"I'll need more," he said.

She shook her head no.

"To tell you I'll need more. To show you."

"You're fine until morning."

"You'll have to go get it."

"Just talk. Start talking. It'll get easier as you go along."

"In the bathroom."

"It gets better," she said. "Easier."

"The medicine cabinet. Hurry, okay?"

She stood. He sat up straight to watch her away, wispy down the long hall, disappearing into the bathroom. *To get color I need a shot because there it's not the black and white of this bland kitchen but leaves rust-colored as blood dried down my legs purple water blue dawn breeze.* He said aloud, "Are you crying? I can't take you if." He stared down the hallway to where dark pooled against the double-bolted door. When she didn't come and didn't come he went ahead alone, crawling through the swamp, as the chorus of tree frogs rose, cicada song faded. Far across on higher ground a rooster crowed. People were waking, passing logging trucks let off the gas, backfire and muffler-cough as their drivers settled down to coast through the long straightaway. He saw his hands beneath the inch of water, brown and curling, decomposing leaves. As he rested his cheek on a barkless trunk slick as innertube, light gathered on his back. Fading in and out, a skeleton found by Thanksgiving deer hunters, then crawling again to the determined pulse of remaining blood, not stopping to retch, spit, cuss, moan, make words that made no difference. The lights of the car pointed into treetops, grew fainter with brightening sunlight and weakened battery.

Little brother in those trees hovering a branch above the reach of headlight, below the cast of weak sun. Calling down hello in that mad wavy way he had, quivering trees sending down leaf storm. Once — he'd faded to bottomless black — a rubbery tongue swiped cold across his neck, panting in his ear. He opened his eyes to see the dog he'd swerved to save wagtail away. Clutching root and log and vine he followed, a paste of mud and leaves and blood crusting his arms and face, legs dragged behind like a bride's train draping altar steps. He came to Sarah and Sarah was dead. He touched the part in her hair running bone white across her scalp, pushed on, past the tree she'd been thrown against, scarless save a lock of hair lodged in bark as if a bear had backscratched against it. An hour to reach the bottom of the bank, hours to pull himself almost to the crest when she nudged him, handed him the bag.

"You have to," he said.

She shook her head no.

"I can't concentrate, you'll have to do it for me."

"No, Edwin."

"We can't go then," he said. "I can't take you."

"We got to." She kneeled beside him. "All your talk about us moving forward. This

445

is our shortcut."

"Don't cry," he said. "Can't do it if you're crying."

"I'm not," she said, drying her eyes with the back of her hand.

"I'll show you how much."

"I'm shaking bad as you now."

"I'll tell you how."

She weighed the bag in her hand. Once away he won't need this any longer, he'd proved that already in Kentucky. Time now to leave for that someplace far away and frozen he'd promised, crisp blue plain where she would see her breath always, where her words, too, would leave trails.

She tried to pay attention to his instructions, but the vision of that new world would not be dislodged; it was like fighting for sleep had been, but harder. Measurements and procedures performed themselves. She thought of everything but what she was doing, yet as she touched needle to skin and squeezed, she felt as if she was injecting him with words.

When it hit and spread his face flushed like always, but more intensely this time. *Here, now, finally,* she thought. During the few seconds before Edwin collapsed, Eureka leaned in close to hear his sentence find its period.